MURDER
BRITANNICA

*Just when you thought it was safe to go for
a nice bath.*

PAULA HARMON

January
Press

1

Dedication

This book is dedicated to my lovely mother-in-law Patricia with lots of love and immense gratitude for all your help and support.

Dramatis Personae

Resident at the villa

Lucretia	A rich Briton
Porcius	Lucretia's husband
Marcellus	Lucretia's son
Poppaea	Marcellus's wife
Julia	Marcellus's daughter

Family members visiting the villa

Prisca	Lucretia's daughter
Tullia	Lucretia's sister
Fabio	Tullia's son
Camilla	Tullia's daughter
Pomponius	Prisca's husband
Urbanicus	Porcius's brother

Slaves (in addition to the farm slaves)

Lollia	Lucretia's body slave
Lucco	Gardener
Briccio	Cook
Blod	Kitchen-slave
Ondi	Groom
Taric	Under gardener
Iris	Nursemaid

People from Pecunia

Anguis Superbus	Roman Decurion
Vulpo	Street Vendor
Tryssa	Wise-woman
Ritonix	Druid
Budic	Scribe
Dondras	Prominent Townsman
Olivarius	Secretary to Anguis

People from elsewhere

Gwil	Traveller
Gaius Contractes	Showman
Hastorix	Gladiator
Aurelia	Dancer
Slab & Gravel	Minders
Septimus & Novus	Thugs

Chapter One - The Forest Edge
June 1st (Kalendis Juniis)

AD 190
West Britain, somewhere a little west of Isca Silurum, a fair bit east of Nidum and quite a long way from everywhere else.

It should have been peaceful in the forest.

Hidden by trees, the young man looked southwards into the sparkling light towards the valley below. To the left was Lucretia's villa. People were wandering around it. The ones with purpose were presumably the slaves, but it was too far to see properly. To the right in the distance, barely visible down a lane, was the town Pecunia, a confused hotchpotch of roundhouses and bad copies of Roman buildings. He wondered which way she would arrive and whether she would surprise him somehow. He waited, impatient, listening and whispering her name under his breath and imagining her embrace.

At first he heard nothing but his own heartbeat, bird song, a tiny trickle of water. Then low urgent masculine voices interrupted his thoughts. They grew louder, then stopped.

'What are you doing here?'

He turned and blinked, his eyes struggling to adjust from staring into sunlight to the shade under the trees. He couldn't see who was talking. The voice was familiar but the tone was wrong. Completely wrong. He tensed.

'I'm waiting for...'

'Were you listening?'

'Of course.'

'What did you hear?'

7

'Nothing. She hasn't arrived.'

'What are you talking about?'

'I'm listening for her, but she either she isn't coming or she is hiding from me.'

'So you weren't eavesdropping on us.'

'I heard you, but I wasn't paying attention.' He turned back to the sunlight before his vision cleared, wishing they'd go away, peering out for her.

There was a pause. His heart thudded, the birds kept singing, the water dislodged a tiny stone and then trickled in a different key.

'She's deeper within the forest,' said another voice, authoritative.

'Is she?' said the young man. 'I thought she'd be here, by the spring.'

'Ah, no, that's where you're mistaken. She's in a grove, waiting for you. We'll show you.'

The young man rose and stepped into the dark green under the branches, following a pointing hand.

'Are you sure?' he said.

'Completely. Hurry now. She's waiting for you.'

Arms helped him forward. He was still a little blinded from the sun. The young man's legs were numb from kneeling and he stumbled a little but they urged him on, following, showing him which way to go.

Chapter Two - The Spring
June 2nd (ante diem iv Nonas Junias)

From the villa, the view was expansive. Below, the valley was a soft green under a trembling magical haze. Lucretia's son Marcellus had poured his thoughts about the vista into a poem and was declaiming it to mark the start of their family gathering:

'*Oh beauteous vale wherein lies verdant fecundity*
Thy billowing breasts nurture the crop and game
Whereon we feast and yet we pause
Our bows drop in our hand to watch
As shimmering above thy secret furzy verdancy
Our dreams sparkle like myriad spirits...'

'Is he blind or stupid?' muttered his sister Prisca to their cousin Camilla. 'They're not dreams or spirits. They're mosquitoes. We're looking down on a bog. You couldn't grow anything there but midge-larvae or marsh-gas for love nor money and the only thing you're likely to sparkle with is fever. It's why I hate coming home. We don't get mosquitoes in Isca. Bet you don't get them in Glevum either.'

Marcellus glared over the top of his scroll at the muttering but his face softened when he gazed at his wife Poppaea. As usual when he proclaimed his verse, she was staring into space, clearly carried into other realms by his skill.

Seventeen year old Camilla wasn't entirely sure about the way the evening was unfolding. There was never anything good about having to listen to Marcellus drivel on but at least it stopped everyone from planning another wedding for her. And really, she was glad no-one in Glevum could see her. It was a little common, a

9

little heathen to be sitting outside the villa in the garden, watching the sun set over the marshes rather than in the inner courtyard as if they were actual Romans. Admittedly, the courtyard wasn't very pleasant. When Uncle Porcius had insisted on building it to impress any passing Romans, he hadn't really anticipated the capacity for a west British summer to be quite so damp. Uncle Porcius' brother Urbanicus said that in Italia the world was sun-filled from dawn to dusk and the shade of the courtyard was essential to avoid heat exhaustion. It sounded highly unlikely to Camilla, but she wasn't going to get close enough to prod Urbanicus for details. He had already been put forward as a suitable husband despite the fact that he was at least sixty-six. To Camilla, not only did he seem so old he ought to be dead, but she also didn't like the way he leered when he thought she wasn't watching. It made her skin crawl.

If Urbanicus were rich, marriage might be worth considering, provided he wrote the right kind of will and assuming he'd do the decent thing.

Two years ago, her paternal grandparents had married her off to a husband so decrepit, he dropped dead immediately after carrying her over the threshold. From Camilla's point of view, at least this meant there had been no time for anything unspeakable to happen. Unfortunately he had left her neither money nor property and she had been returned home in disgrace as if the slavering old fool's death was all her fault.

She suspected Urbanicus was no better bet. Despite his boasts of city extravagance he spent most of his time living with his brother and sister-in-law, which suggested a shortage of funds. Camilla felt it was simply not worth being dribbled on if you weren't going to get rich out of it.

'I've run out of wine,' burbled Porcius. He wondered how long his wife would make them all stand out in the open air.

Marcellus was still declaiming: '*Thin trickling moistness oozing from thy...*'

'Oh really,' said Prisca, 'does he have to?'

'Marcellus, enough!' ordered Lucretia. 'I want to show everyone something wonderful and then we can go inside and dine.'

Lucretia pulled her wrap a little tighter and snapped her fingers. Two slaves brought a carrying chair over and bore her off in state, with the others following across the lumpy slopes east of the house.

'I shouldn't be expected to walk,' muttered Prisca. 'Why isn't anyone carrying me?'

At least you've got ugly sandals, thought Camilla. *Mine are too stylish for all this clod-hopping. They are going to be ruined. I'm so glad there's no-one to see me. Gods it would be so humiliating. I hate the countryside.*

She closed her eyes, imagining herself carried in state above the heads of burnished slaves, simpering behind her veil at fine equestrians... She caught her foot in a rabbit hole and tripped. She might have fallen but Urbanicus clasped her round the waist.

'Mother!' she snapped, worming her way out of his grasp.

'Yes dear?' said Tullia. She walked as if in a dream, her bosom heaving as she breathed in the cooling evening air.

'Mother,' Camilla repeated, catching her up, 'I nearly broke my ankle.' She added in a lower voice, 'and that old pig tried to pinch me.'

'Oh dear,' said Tullia, opening her eyes and blinking. 'I am so disappointed you didn't inherit the

11

second sight from me, darling. It would make such a difference, you know. You wouldn't have married someone who dropped dead before he could -'

'Mother,' snapped Camilla, 'you're the one who let them arrange it. Why didn't you foresee what was going to happen?'

'Don't argue with the stars, dear. Sometimes the sky is cloudy and yet they are still there,' answered Tullia.

'In the name of Minerva, what on earth does that mean?'

'Observe me walk without tripping, dear,' said Tullia, 'even though my eyes are shut.' She increased her pace and caught up with Marcellus. 'Marcellus dear, why did you stop? I was so enjoying your poem.'

Marcellus turned, his face eager. 'Why Aunt Tullia, thank you. I was just trying to convince Fabio to compose a tune to accompany it.'

Camilla's brother Fabio took this opportunity to drop back. Little Julia was dragging on Poppaea's hand and whining. Fabio picked her up and put her on his shoulders.

'If you really had second sight, Mother,' continued Camilla, 'you'd know why Aunt Lucretia's dragged us all the way to this swampy back-water.'

It was a short distance from the villa, but Lucretia was, for a small woman, solid. The slaves' muscles bulged under their tunics and sweat glistened on their faces. They lowered the litter and helped her off, then staggered away to sit under the trees out of earshot.

Lucretia waited until the whole family was assembled. Fabio, with Julia on his shoulders, had galloped up pretending to be a horse. Camilla rolled her eyes, but with a wistful glance which suggested that it was all she could do to stop herself from galloping too. Her daughter Prisca and son-in-law Pomponius, who

12

had been bickering, were some way in the rear. Presumably the arc of their argument had reached the not-speaking stage, although it was possible even at a distance to see that Prisca was coming to the boil for the last word.

'This,' said Lucretia, her bracelets clanking as she waved her arm towards a pile of bricks and a half-built wall, 'this is the sacred spring of Diffis.'

There was a pause. The summer breeze ruffled hair and veils, a song-bird punctured the evening with a burst of pre-roost trilling. Rooks argued overhead as they flapped towards their nests.

'Um,' said Fabio, 'what is?'

Everyone leaned forward. The edges of the bricks were damp as a thin trickle of water seeped up through the turf. Fabio prodded it with his toe. Mud smeared his sandals and an odour of rotten vegetation seeped up. The stench was almost visible, making the women cover their faces and turned away.

'Sacred or not, Diffis could do with a bath,' muttered Camilla to her brother.

Poppaea leaned over and whispered into Marcellus's ear, 'I don't remember anyone mentioning Diffis before. Is she some sort of wood nymph?'

'I was born and brought up here and this is the first I've heard of Diffis,' her husband whispered back. 'Or at least, I don't recall her. But then Mother never really encouraged my learning about local gods she was so very keen that I was a proper Roman citizen. On the other hand, I like the sound of the name. Diffis ... I can feel another poem coming on...'

'Oh good,' said Poppaea. Marcellus liked the way she was so unruffled, her voice so calm, so ladylike. He was sure his poems always thrilled her, but she reacted as if the prospect was as dull as ditchwater.

13

'Who's Diffis anyway?' said Urbanicus out loud. 'Local sprite or something?'

Lucretia drew herself up to her full height of four foot six and fixed him with a stare.

'Diffis is the Goddess of this spring,' she said, 'and we are descended from her, aren't we Tullia?'

Tullia jumped. Her eyes, now open, had been staring up into the trees or possibly the sky. It was very hard to tell.

'Diffis,' continued Lucretia 'is, as Tullia will testify, a goddess who bestows not only longevity to those who worship at her spring but also the second sight. Her sacred blood in our veins has enabled Tullia to prophesy - is that not so, sister? Don't you remember our father telling us about our sacred ancestry: the goddess who so many years ago, lay with the chieftain who was our forefather and bore him a golden daughter and left her with him to be brought up as a mortal and...'

'If you turned that into blank verse, she could compete with Marcellus don't you think?' whispered Camilla to Fabio. He grinned.

'Mmm?' said Tullia, chewing her top lip, 'well I don't recall, but of course I was very young when our father died. I just know that I am special... as are you of course.'

'I can't say I remember you telling me any of this before, Mother,' said Prisca, 'and what happened to the longevity? Grandfather had five children and only two of them, Mother and Aunt Tullia, still survive. Grandfather lived past sixty, which is nothing to be sniffed at, but even Uncle Rhys died before he was thirty.'

'That was a hunting accident, dear,' said Tullia. 'Longevity doesn't apply to being gored to death by a wild boar.'

'Sadly the other brothers inherited too much of the leaden blood of our mother,' said Lucretia. 'But then she was half Roman and half descended from the Durotriges tribe. And you know what they are like.'

Everyone nodded, trying to recall what they were like.

'Where do the Durotriges come from again?' said Prisca.

'Never mind that now,' said Lucretia. 'The point is that this spring has been lost for generations and it has now been found. More importantly, I think it would be a fine sight for some baths.'

'We have a bath-house, dear,' said Porcius. He had brought a wine-skin and was trying to see if there were any last dribbles to pour into his goblet. Finding it empty, he upended it into his mouth and suckled on it. Lucretia shuddered.

'It would not be a family bath-house, dearest... it would be for the discerning visitor.'

'What?' exclaimed Porcius, removing the wine-skin from his mouth with a pop. Trickles of wine trailed down his chin and soaked into his tunic. 'Strangers gallumphing over my land?'

'My land,' said Lucretia.

'My land,' argued Porcius. 'You have no existence in law, woman. What's yours is not yours, it is mine. What's mine is not yours it's mine. What's mine is...' He sputtered to a halt, frowning.

'If it can work for the goddess Sulis, it can work for Diffis.'

'But no-one has ever heard of Duffis,' argued Pomponius.

15

'Diffis. There's nothing to stop us letting the news of her attributes "seep out", shall we say.' Lucretia smirked at her own pun. 'By the time we've built up her image, the workmen will have built the bath-house. And before we know it, discerning citizens and even right discerning non-citizens will fall over themselves to pay what's reasonable to honour Diffis and keep her happy.'

There was a pause.

'Ah,' said Prisca. 'You mean... if we do this right, as her guardians, we can make a killing.'

'Exactly,' said Lucretia.

Chapter Three - Breakfast at the Villa
June 3rd (Pridie Nonas Junias)

Mid-morning the following day, Poppaea and Julia walked into the atrium to discover Lucretia having her moustache plucked by her slave Lollia. Poppaea settled down to wait. There was little point in conversation as the exercise was a noisy one. Whenever Lollia hurt Lucretia, which was with almost every tweak, Lucretia lashed out and invariably knocked something over.

There was something about the way in which Lollia managed to dodge every blow, combined with the frequency of the assault (despite having undertaken this revolting activity regularly for at least ten years), that made Poppaea suspect that Lollia was injuring her mistress on purpose out of sheer malice.

Poppaea perused Lollia. The slave had been in Lucretia's service for over forty years. She and Lucco, the kind old slave who managed the garden, should have been freed with a pension years ago. Poppaea had heard that Lollia and Lucco's children had been auctioned off as early as possible to the highest bidder, with no consideration of what future awaited them. Poppaea would not have blamed Lollia for pinching Lucretia's withered upper lip at every opportunity. In fact, if Poppaea had had as many stomach upsets as Lucretia, she would have thought very hard about hiring a food taster.

Poppaea supposed some might say that she should have warned her mother-in-law about her suspicions. But ten years of living under Lucretia's roof had hardened her heart. As she watched, disgusted at old women with moustaches, she simply hoped idly that Lollia would get on with poisoning Lucretia and save

17

her the bother of being tempted to knock the old bird off herself.

'I'm bored, Mummy,' said Julia, kicking at the statue of a goddess carrying a bow and an owl. No-one was sure if the sculptor had wanted to hedge his bets by covering wise Minerva and huntress Diana with the same sculpture, or whether it was supposed to be one of them holding the other's belongings for a bit.

'Go and find nanny, darling,' said Poppaea.

'I don't know where she is, Mummy,' said Julia, 'I *thought* she was in the orchard playing with someone. I could hear giggling, but I couldn't find her.'

'Oh dear,' said Poppaea.

'Will she squash the flowers?'

'Very probably.'

'Anyway, why's Grandma got a moustache? Grandpa hasn't. Does it mean she's a barbarian?'

'No darling, barbarians have beards.'

The slave twisted Lucretia's head and started poking at her chin with the tweezers.

'It's Gauls who have moustaches. Like Briccio the cook.'

'Is Grandma a Gaul then?'

Lucretia flapped out with her hands and pushed the slave towards Julia.

'Poppaea, there's a place for children and it's not with their parents. Lollia - take it off somewhere.'

'I'm not an "it", Grandma!' howled Julia. 'You're a horrible old woman with a big hairy moustache and I hate you!'

'Lollia, do as you're bid and remove it from my presence,' ordered Lucretia. 'Perhaps you could take it to cook to see if he wants its tongue. Maybe he hasn't enough larks' tongues for lunch.'

18

The slave lugged Julia, wailing, in the direction of the kitchen.

'Well?' said Lucretia, readjusting her dress and standing. 'What is it you want, Poppaea?'

'I was wondering how you were this morning, Lucretia. You were not at breakfast, and you seemed rather bilious at dinner last night.'

'I am perfectly well, Poppaea. It was rather an exciting day yesterday and I was wearied. I did note that you were rather quiet yourself and said nothing at the spring. Do you disapprove of my plans?'

'Certainly not Lucretia, they are masterful. It will make us very rich.'

Lucretia straightened her back and narrowed her eyes. 'It will make *me* very rich, but more importantly, it will honour my ancestor-goddess.'

'Whom everyone had forgotten.'

'Save Tullia and me, perhaps.' Lucretia scowled through the impluvium at the grey skies above them.

'Well of course,' said Poppaea, 'you and Tullia would remember the *old* days so well.'

'We are going to the dining room,' said Lucretia to a waiting slave, 'bring me something to eat.'

'Madam.' The slave sidled off.

In the dining room, Lucretia and Poppaea reclined. They eyed each other sideways waiting for the other to speak first. On the walls was a fresco of dancing nymphs and satyrs bringing wreaths to lay on a laughing young couple of great beauty. Poppaea knew, because it had been drummed into her from the moment she was carried over the threshold by Marcellus, that the young couple represented Lucretia and Porcius in their youth. It was staggeringly hard to imagine that Lucretia had ever appeared as innocent and simpering, with doe eyes peeping up from under a curled fringe, or

19

that Porcius had ever been so focussed. But Poppaea had never been brave enough to say so.

As if summoned by her thoughts, Porcius staggered into the dining room and dropped onto a bench.

'We seem to have run out of wine, dear,' he said. He looked with sorrow into a goblet and tipped it onto the floor to prove his point.

'Dearest Porcius,' said Lucretia in tones of honey laced with hemlock, 'it is not yet noon. Surely you don't need wine when there is mead and beer.'

Porcius sighed, then squinted at Poppaea and smiled.

'And who's this delightful young filly?'

'It's our daughter-in-law, Porcius,' snapped Lucretia. 'You've known her for ten years, since she was a blushing bride of fifteen, full of a promise which she has signally failed to live up to.'

'Oh yes, of course,' said Porcius. 'Sorry my dear, I'm off to the kitchen. Maybe the key to the wine store has turned up. It's been missing for years... Yet we always have wine ... eventually.'

He dragged himself off the bench and lurched out of the room.

'So,' said Lucretia, 'Poppaea, *dearest* daughter-in-law. I'm still so very disappointed you didn't name your daughter after me. It could make all the difference to my views on sharing any wealth the baths may bring.'

'We named our *first* daughter after you, Lucretia. But she died.'

'I really cannot help it you're not competent enough to keep a child alive, dear. But you did at least produce another, albeit another girl. Could you not have named her after me?'

'Her sister was still alive at the time, if you recall.'

'Yes well, when the sister died…'

'Then Julia would have found it rather confusing to find herself renamed after the sibling whose loss she mourned.'

'Does that matter?'

A slave appeared with honey cakes and mead. Poppaea hoped beyond hope that the honey cakes would choke her mother-in-law before she had to do it herself with her bare hands.

'Anyway,' mumbled Lucretia through her food, picking crumbs from her withered cleavage and flicking them to the floor. 'However nice it is that you would like me to think you care about my health, I'm concerned about yours.'

'Mine, Lucretia?' said Poppaea, frowning.

'Yes. In particular, you look rather pale and tired and a little bird told me you keep vomiting in the latrina even on an empty stomach.'

'I…er…'

'My point being, are we to expect a happy event in a few months?'

'Well, er…'

'Only, if you recall my plans to honour the Goddess Diffis, you will realise that the land and any … shall we say … benefits to be gained from the shrine belong to me, regardless of what your fool of a father-in-law says. Consequently, they are Marcellus's inheritance and thereafter the inheritance of his *son*. Naturally, if you finally produce a boy, I will be delighted, and will know that everything is as it should be. If you don't, there is a risk that everything goes to my nephew Fabio and that would never do. The boy's a fool.'

'He's hardly a boy, Lucretia,' argued Poppaea. 'He's nineteen.'

'And you are twenty-five. It is about time you produced a son before you get too old. Divorce is always an option I might put to Marcellus.'

'Marcellus would never...'

'I am his mother, dear. Never underestimate the influence a mother can have. When you ... *if* you have a son of your own, you will understand.'

'But Aunt Lucretia,' Camilla's voice made them jump, 'it's not fair.'

'No, it isn't,' agreed Poppaea.

Camilla flopped down on a bench, 'I mean, it's not fair you'd leave it to Fabio. He's only interested in music. You said it didn't matter that *you're* a girl, I mean a woman. You said the land is yours even though the law says it's Uncle Porcius's.'

'I'd prefer it to go to Marcellus's line. The alternative is that it goes to Prisca's son, whatever his name is.'

'He's your grandson, Lucretia.' said Poppaea. 'He's called Querius. Surely it can't be that hard to remember.'

'As far as I can recall from the last time I had to suffer the presence of him and Prisca's other incontinent, undisciplined horde...'

'There are only three of them.'

'It seemed like more. In my mind they are called Whinge, Whine and Puddle. They are far too much like their idiot father. Why I allowed Prisca to marry him I can't imagine.'

'His parents had money.'

'Well therefore, presumably, they have no need of mine,' said Lucretia, breaking off a piece of cake and dipping it in her mead. 'The point is, you should have produced a son by now and it will go ill for you if you don't.'

22

'It's not fair,' said Camilla. 'Why can't the land be inherited by me or Julia or Prisca? Preferably me. Because it's very fashionable nowadays to have a country villa as well as a town one. And after all, I'm the one who needs to get married. Well, Julia will, but not for ages. There's no point leaving it to Prisca and Pomponius. They'd just sell it for readies.'

'And what about your brother?'

'Oh him. Can't we just marry him off to some rich widow who likes music?'

'It's so heart-warming to know that you are all so keen to inherit that you're competing for my money while I'm still alive,' said Lucretia. 'Isn't one person going to say "Darling Lucretia, I can't even think about your dying, I'd rather stay poor if it meant you would live forever"?'

The only answer was the small squeak of a mouse running across the mosaic to pick up crumbs.

'Hmmph. Well in answer to your question, *dearest* niece, this land was my father's and as you know, your mother and I are his only surviving children. Now in Roman law of course, what is mine is regrettably your idiotic grandfather's. However in tribal law, it is mine, as one of royal and indeed divine blood, going back to the days of the mighty chieftains and warrior queens of.... do stop yawning Camilla. You need to learn that there are times to be Roman and there are times to be British, and the key thing is knowing the difference. Naturally, I anticipate outliving your grandfather who should have been dead long since, and when I die, the land will go to my son and his heirs, although...'

'Shouldn't it go to Mother?' interrupted Camilla, picking at a honey cake and crumbling it for the mouse. 'I mean, she's your sister. If you were dead, then *she* would be the only surviving child of your father.'

23

'Your mother is a fool as well, but in point of fact I intend to ensure that the proceeds of the spring benefit all of you, provided the land remains Marcellus's. However, that will only happen where you have been supportive of the endeavours to develop, I mean, bring honour to the goddess. Naturally, I assume you are far too keen to return to Glevum for a life of metropolitan excess if the alternative is the risk of stepping in a cow-pat while worshipping at your ancestress's shrine....'

Camilla popped a piece of honey cake in her mouth and offered one to Poppaea. 'Lunch smells nice,' she said, as if her grandmother's words had been of no interest.

Cooking odours wafted from the distant kitchen: hot fat, strong herbs and garum, the ubiquitous anchovy sauce. Poppaea felt the bile rise and swallowed, closing her eyes and trying to think of anything but food.

'I'm going to go for a walk in the fresh air,' she said, when she felt safe enough to open her mouth.

'I'll come with you,' said Camilla, 'if you wait for me to change my shoes. I'd really like to see the spring again. I know Aquae Sulis well and I think we could improve on what it provides. I just don't trust any of you old people to do it properly. You couldn't possibly think I wasn't interested Aunt Lucretia. If my name is going to be linked to this, it has to be modern. And I'm the only one young enough to know how to achieve that.'

Poppaea, swallowing and turning towards the front door, noticed Lucretia smile her secret smile, and ran off to be sick in the urn in the atrium.

Chapter Four - The Delights and Dignitaries of Pecunia
June 3rd (Pridie Nonas Junias)

The forum at Pecunia was third-rate to the extent that it was barely more than a few bored farmers with trays.

Tullia had forgotten how bad it was. Her bosom heaved in a sigh as she compared it with Glevum forum's colour and variety, where was always someone to talk with, always some scandal to discuss.

'Not that I ever listen to gossip,' said Tullia to Prisca, continuing aloud the conversation she'd been having in her head as if her niece knew what she'd been thinking. 'My mind is tuned to more spiritual matters. Perhaps my soul wearies to hear that someone has been spurned. Maybe I grieve that yet another husband has been found in the arms...'

'Aunt Tullia,' said Prisca, 'whatever are you talking about?'

'Oh my dear,' Tullia sighed again, 'I fear that the second sight has not been inherited by you either. How sad your grandmother would be.'

Prisca slowed, causing Ondi, the slave following them, to crash into her back and drop their purchases. She peered more closely at her aunt, who was, as usual, ambling with her eyes glazed and a smile which seemed to imply that either she knew a secret or she had trapped wind.

'What... (I really can't believe I'm asking this)...what is your second sight seeing?'

'Nothing at present. Why do you ask?'

'You were talking about spurned women and husbands who'd been caught in the act.'

Tullia frowned and sniffed the air.

25

They stopped by a street vendor. His stall oozed heat and spicy aromas. Ondi, stomach gurgling, shifted the parcels in his arms and tried not to dribble.

'Flat-breads with wild garlic and rosemary!' called the street vendor as if they were on the other side of the forum. 'Have a sip of Vulpo's sweet, spiced hot Iberian wine, ladies!'

'Oh do look at that graffiti over there, dear,' said Tullia. 'Hastorix the gladiator must be touring hereabouts. How curious, I wonder why they've compared him with ...'

'Beefcake!' yelled Vulpo. 'Genuine Pictish beefcake!'

'Have you heard of Hastorix? He fights in the arena at Isca, where you live, and I hear he's very popular. I don't care for muscly men myself, I prefer the intellectual type. I hope you do too, since Pomponius is rather -'

'Soft dough balls dipped in honey!'

'Do you think we could move away, Aunt Tullia?' said Prisca. 'I don't want my clothes stinking of grease and he's making me hungry, and I'm trying to watch my figure.'

'What nonsense, dear,' said Tullia. 'Men like women to be'

'Plump and juicy hens!' shouted Vulpo.

'Precisely,' said Tullia, nodding. She bought some flatbreads and motioned to the street-vendor to pop a broken fragment into Ondi's mouth. 'Hastorix, for example, or so I've heard, pursues women who are plump and over thirty - in the prime of life. Doesn't he?'

Prisca stopped scanning the forum and pulled her veil more closely round her head. 'I can't imagine how

26

you'd think I'd know, Aunt Tullia. I only go to the arena to see the horses.'

'Of course you do, dear.'

'Aunt Tullia, you did say something about deserted wives? Was that something your second sight foretold?'

'Deserted spouses and lovers are always to be foretold.'

'What else do you see?'

Tullia came to a halt and closed her eyes. Ondi crashed into her back again and choked on his piece of flatbread. Or possibly he swore. It was hard to tell. He came from a province somewhere in the north.

Tullia began to sway and wave her arms, her bangles clattering and her linen dress floating about her. On the pavement, her sandalled feet tapped a rhythm and she spun in a circle, twisting in a way which was highly inappropriate for a lady of nearly fifty. Someone whistled.

'Stop it Aunt Tullia, everyone is looking at us.'

Tullia paused in mid gyration and opened her eyes, which she fixed on her niece.

'Whatever were you doing?' hissed Prisca.

'Enacting the vibrations that came through my soul.'

'You might have been a common dancing girl... Oh my goodness, it's true. You do know everything.'

'Well, as I say, dear, it's a shame you haven't inherited the Sight. Julia may come into it when she reaches womanhood. And I have hopes for Camilla if only she would stop thinking about shoes and clothes.'

'Madam,' said Ondi, his arms straining under the parcels, 'I believe it is nearly noon and we should go back to the villa.'

'You're quite right. Remind me, where is the wagon again?'

27

'Can't you see it with your inner eye?' said Prisca.

'Don't be facetious dear,' murmured Tullia, 'the Sight is not to be used for trivialities. However, I believe the wagon is in the shade by the colonnade, or what they'd like to pretend was a colonnade. I really had forgotten how dreadful this place was. Dear Glevum. How I miss it.'

'We've only been here two days, Aunt Tullia.'

'Yes, but I have a feeling my sister has plans for us all to stay for quite some time. Come along. I believe it's larks' tongues for lunch.'

***

Shortly before the evening meal, the local Decurion arrived.

'He's on the look-out for a wife,' whispered Prisca to Camilla, as they watched his approach churn the dust in the distance. 'His first one died, so they say, of lethargy and homesickness for Tuscany. The rumour is that he thinks a British wife might be a better bet, since she wouldn't complain about the rain.'

'How old is he?' Camilla murmured. As the visitors came closer, she could make out three figures in a chariot. One tall and slender, one of medium build and one, holding the reins, with biceps thicker than his own head.

'Not too ancient, I don't think,' said Prisca. 'I hear he's almost patrician.'

As the chariot came closer to the villa Camilla and Prisca bit their lips, pinched their cheeks and attempted to appear simultaneously coy and alluring. Lucretia rolled her eyes, Tullia patted her daughter's hand and Pomponius pulled his wife behind him.

Claudius Anguis Superbus, however, was a disappointment. He was perhaps not as old as Camilla's last husband, being a more reasonable forty or so. He

28

was the tall one. But also very thin. Camilla could have wrapped her arms round him twice, which frankly didn't appeal. He looked down his nose at the welcome party, his mouth curling and his eyebrows raised, as if he had been forced to watch a display of country dance performed by the village inbreeding society. He bowed to Lucretia, hailed Porcius in the half-hearted way ex-Roman soldiers did to ex-Auxiliary soldiers and frowned at Urbanicus, who grinned and saluted but stepped back inside the villa out of sight.

'Will you take wine before we show you the site of the sacred spring, Decurion?' said Lucretia.

'Thank you but no, I would like to see the spring first and then relax over dinner. I am neither a wine-bibber nor a glutton,' he added, his eyes running from Porcius's red nose to his bulbous stomach. 'I am an abstemious man with a dislike for ostentation.'

He clicked his fingers and the secretary rearranged his toga, which had become dishevelled during the drive, to ensure that the gold trim was displayed to catch the sun.

'I hope then, that our feast is not too rich.'

'I'm sure that is unlikely,' said Anguis, staring at the villa.

The groom unhitched the horse and helped Anguis into the saddle. Lucretia summoned her litter but the Decurion held up his hand. 'I really don't think the women need accompany us on man's business.'

Even Tullia stared and drew in her breath.

Lucretia smiled and bowed.

'Oh no, no,' said Porcius, 'no, no. I … we need Lucretia to, er, explain matters.'

'She is the one with the vision?'

'Well now,' Porcius burbled, 'my sister-in-law Tullia is the one who has the visions.'

'I mean,' Anguis slowed his words as if speaking to a child, 'is your wife the one who she believes she knows what could be achieved to er...'

'Honour the goddess,' interposed Porcius.

'Indeed. Well, if you need your wife to explain, she may come.'

Lucretia waved the slaves away. 'No indeed, Decurion, I will not interfere with your observation of the spring. You can stand by it and make yourself at one with the goddess who is, naturally, one and the same as the goddess whom you worship. You may look down on the valley and consider how the weary may come and pay tribute to her. They will be staying in our humble town, in the tavern from which you take rent, and perhaps bring glory to us all.'

She clapped her hands at the other women and stepped inside the villa. After a moment's pause, the younger men followed.

An hour later, Porcius and Anguis returned and were ushered through to the dining room. Porcius, his feet muddy, cast himself on a couch and found himself handed a goblet before he had to call for wine.

Anguis lay himself down with elegance, and the secretary rearranged his toga. Then he reclined himself, lying carved and perfect as a marble statue.

'Decurion,' said Lucretia, 'welcome to our humble home. How did you find Diffis's spring?'

Anguis sipped and ran the wine round his mouth. 'A delightful drop, Lucretia. I am pleasantly surprised.'

'We would not give you anything but the best, Decurion. And in answer?'

'I did indeed look down on the town, on your husband's land - sorry Lucretia, have you something in your throat? What was I saying? Oh yes, when I considered your husband's land and the buildings I rent

30

out in Pecunia, I had a vision. Truly, Olivarius,' he said to the secretary, 'I felt the yearnings of Diffis to be honoured, and received a vision of a new sparkling town fit for the wisest goddess...'

'Minerva,' said Olivarius.

'Well, no,' said Anguis. 'Minerva is busy at Aquae Sulis, that is to say, she is Sulis, Sulis is her. Sulis-Minerva. Perhaps you didn't realise, dear boy, being foreign. Anyway, under the forest (which might have to be cleared a little to allow for building), a great huntress would shoot arrows in moonlight like cascading streams of...'

'Ah!' breathed Marcellus, 'poetry!'

'I wanted to call her Doris,' mumbled Porcius. 'Since Diffis is a water goddess.'

'Your husband seems a little confused by theology,' said Anguis, 'and suggested Diffis is an oceanid.'

'Well water's water, isn't it?' slurred Porcius. Lucretia stabbed a foot at her husband but his bench was too far away for her to make contact.

'This is river-water not sea-water, Porcius, and a goddess not an oceanid. Therefore, we can't name her for Doris. Besides, Diffis-Doris sounds a little odd. No, the forest is fine hunting ground, so I hear and so -'

'Diffis-Diana?' said Fabio.

'Indeed.'

'Well, Decurion,' said Lucretia, 'I am glad you are ... supportive. I think we understand each other. Now perhaps we should start on dinner.'

Dish after dish was brought in: jellyfish omelette, peppered sea-urchin, dormice the size of kittens stuffed with spiced sausage and basted in honey, roast boar with mushrooms. These were served with a leek salad and a nut tart made piquant with the anchovy savour of garum.

31

'Are there plans for an arena in Pecunia, Decurion?' asked Fabio, 'Only Mother mentioned there are gladiators visiting. Or at least *a* gladiator.'

'Really, which one?' said Pomponius, pausing with half a dormouse in his hand to glance sideways at Prisca. Prisca continued to prod about with a small toothpick and turned to Camilla to talk about sandals.

'Hastorix, I believe.'

'Really,' repeated Pomponius.

'I'm considering it,' said Anguis. 'It would need to be worthwhile. I'm certainly asking experts about feasibility. A theatre also. I've arranged for a small troupe of actors and dancers to be brought so their manager can pick a site. Naturally, I am keeping all those dubious types away from the townsfolk. I would not want them corrupted and you know how easily swayed a Celt - I mean an uneducated bumpkin can be.'

'Dance troupe?' said Prisca, turning away from her perusal of a plate of grapes. 'Any particular one?' She squinted at Pomponius through the edges of her veil.

'Surely they are all much of a muchness,' said Anguis. 'I do not care for the gyrations of loose women.'

'No *decent* man would,' snapped Prisca.

'As no decent woman would care for a brainless lump of muscle,' snarled Pomponius.

'I really hope this meal is not too extravagant for you, Decurion,' said Lucretia, ushering the wine away from Porcius towards their guest.

'Well, I must say that I wasn't expecting jellyfish and sea-urchin. I presume either your husband has an arrangement with Doris - ha ha ha - or your cook has a good supplier or is an expert at substituting local ingredients. He's certainly an excellent cook.'

'He's from Gaul. He says he'd like to put Gaul on the map.'

'Isn't Gaul already on the map?' whispered Camilla to Fabio.

'The *culinary* map,' said Lucretia.

'Really?' said Pomponius, 'Gaul?'

'Mmm,' said Anguis, motioning to Olivarius to help him from the bench and reorganise his toga, 'well I must leave you. Olivarius, could you check the chariot is ready, and perhaps send a message to Lucretia's cook to see if he could come and speak to ours.'

He stood and stretched. 'Farewell, I will return shortly with my architect to discuss plans for the spring. You needn't see me out. It seems Porcius may struggle.'

But Lucretia stood and motioned to the others to follow suit. The family, except for Porcius followed Anguis as he left the villa. As they left the dining room, Porcius raised his goblet and hiccupped.

'Old fool,' hissed Lucretia under her breath.

They watched the Decurion and his party rattle away in the dusk.

'Do you think he'd teach me to drive a chariot?' murmured Camilla.

'Who, the Decurion?' said Fabio.

'Snooticus? Don't be stupid. I was thinking of Olivarius.'

A crash and a shout came from the house. 'Madam! Madam! Come quickly!'

The family hurried back inside. Fabio, rushing through the atrium, knocked an unspecified nymph from her pedestal. In the dining room Porcius retched and choked, his face turning blue, and small sea-urchin spines fell from his mouth as his eyes rolled. His hand stretched out as the slaves held him, reaching towards Lucretia.

'Here sir, here,' said Lollia, putting a goblet to Porcius's lips. 'Take a sip, sir, just a sip, it'll soothe you. Calm down sir, calm down.'

For the first time in forty years Porcius pushed wine away as he writhed in the slaves' arms. His blackened, swollen tongue stumbled and slurred 'uh ... uh...'

He breathed once more and then slumped, his eyes glazed.

'He's dead, Madam,' said Lollia.

'Shall I get Ondi to bring the Decurion back, mother?' asked Marcellus.

'Don't do that!' begged Prisca.

'Why would the Decurion want to see this?' said Lucretia. 'Your father is ... was a pig and has finally choked on his own gluttony.'

'No Mother,' urged Prisca, 'I don't think so. I'm sure it's poison. Look at his tongue, Mother, look!'

'Poison?' said Lucretia, staring harder at her husband's body. 'Well you needn't all stare at me.' She paused. 'Get me Briccio the cook!' she shouted. 'Bring him here now! He could have poisoned us all.'

'I sent Ondi to do that already,' said Lollia, gesturing at one of the other slaves for a cloth to put over her master's face. A smash from the hall as another statue hit the tiles was followed by Ondi as he burst into the dining room.

'Briccio's gone, Madam, Briccio's gone!' he shouted. 'He's run away!'

Chapter Five - After the Funeral
June 13th (Idibus Junias)

Nine days after the funeral, Camilla threw off her black veil and wandered out of the villa to catch the sun. The haze of mosquitoes over the marshland twinkled. She slapped her arm.

In the distance the town also shimmered. It took a while for Camilla to realise this was caused by dust, kicked up by something approaching the villa. She had been inside too long. She rubbed her eyes and stared again.

A small but valiant pony was staggering up the lane despite the weight of two people on its back. One was waving something in his arms, the other was gripping the pony's mane while yelling. Not far behind them, a rather sleeker horse pulling a familiar chariot was gaining ground.

Camilla turned to shout for a slave, but Lucco the gardener was already at her side, armed with a hoe and a summer cabbage.

'Who is it, Miss?' he said.

'Well, I think one is Decurion Anguis Superbus and ...' she squinted, 'isn't that Ritonix the druid about to fall off the pony? I'm not sure who that is on the back or what he's waving.'

'Seems to be a scythe, Miss.'

'Have we hired another gardener?'

'I don't think so, Miss.'

The pony arrived first, sweat trickling down its neck and its knees trembling. Ritonix let go of the mane and slid off the pony's back. His knees were also trembling and he leaned against the pony to regain his composure. There was a risk both would collapse. Ritonix wore a long rough brown tunic and his long white hair and beard were braided, the latter knotted under his chin. From the back of the pony a young man swung himself to the ground and marched up to Camilla. She took a step back. Lucco waved his cabbage and as an afterthought, the hoe. Other slaves and the family were arriving.

Camilla stared at the young man. His hair and beard were dark and also braided. His eyes, under scowling brows, were ringed with long thick lashes and sparkled with the depths of mysterious pools. His tunic was short, exposing tanned, muscled legs. Handing the scythe to the older man, he crossed his arms and glared.

'Hello,' said Camilla, twiddling her hair.

'Ooh,' said Prisca.

'I saw him first,' whispered Camilla, 'and you're married.'

'Greetings Ritonix,' said Lucretia, 'and this is…'

'Budic, Lady Lucretia,' gasped the old man.

'Your apprentice perhaps?'

'No. Just a man of passion.'

'Ooh,' whispered Prisca. Camilla kicked her.

The chariot pulled up. The driver, and indeed his horse, stared down at the pony with their lips curled. If an animal could shrug, the pony did. His eyes glanced up at the fine stallion, then he sighed, ambled off to the grass and lay down.

Olivarius gave Camilla a small wink. He stood, still in the chariot, shining in the sun, his reddish hair glinting like gold, his green eyes warm as a glade in summer.

Camilla heaved a deep sigh, glancing between the two young men, and her heart pounded.

'Olivarius!' snapped Anguis. 'What are you waiting for? Brush this dust off my clothes.'

'Brush it off yourself, Roman!' snapped Budic.

36

'Calm now, calm,' said Ritonix, putting his hand on Budic's shoulder. 'We must not come to a house of mourning in aggression, but in comfort.'

Budic glared at Camilla again, who lowered her eyes and lifted her dress to cover her face in an effort to appear bereaved.

'You are the one bearing a weapon, barbarian!' said Anguis, allowing himself to be handed down from the chariot. He towered over the druid and straightened his back to emphasise the fact, speaking over the older man's head rather than acknowledge his face.

'It is not a weapon, Decurion,' said Ritonix. 'It's a symbol of death. For death has visited this house and yet, I was not summoned.'

'These people are Roman ... subjects.' said Anguis. 'In fact, some of them...' He scowled at Urbanicus, still lurking in the shadows. 'Some of them are even citizens. They have cast off the pagan superstitions of their ancestors...'

'Apart from Diffis,' said Pomponius. 'We haven't cast her off. Obviously. We've only just discovered her... I mean, re-discovered her, but we don't forget her ... again.'

'Oh, do be quiet,' hissed Lucretia.

'This family has cast off the pagan superstitions of their - your ancestors and have embraced the pantheon of Rome,' continued Anguis. 'They recognise that British gods are actually ours seen through a haze of barbarian ignorance. Only I have to say, Lucretia Siluriensis, I am rather surprised that I was not invited to your husband's cremation, and I gather the temple's priest was not summoned either.'

'That's because we didn't cremate him,' said Lucretia. 'It's rather unpleasant. We preferred to bury Porcius in the old manner. It's more dignified.'

Ritonix smirked. Anguis rolled his eyes.

'Well, I suppose some customs are harder than others to change. Where is he buried then? I would like to pay my respects.'

'Over there,' Marcellus pointed to a distant oak tree. Anguis nodded and pulled a solemn face.

'And over there,' Marcellus pointed to a willow in the opposite direction.

Anguis blinked. Ritonix smiled.

'I'm sorry,' said Anguis, 'I'm struggling to follow you.'

'We buried his body under the oak and his head under the willow.'

'But why? Surely choking on a surfeit of dormice doesn't make one's head fall off? Forgive me, Lucretia. I apologise for my crassness, I am just perplexed.'

Ritonix puffed out his chest and waved the scythe in the air. 'It is no wonder you don't understand. You Romans are so afraid of spirits that you grind your dead into powder and weigh them down with slabs of rock! (Apologies, Lucretia.) We want the spirit to be free, to escape, to roam, to be able to return and companion the living.'

'Oh gods, I hope not,' murmured Lucretia. 'We'll never keep the wine stocks up if his spirit can get where his mortal being couldn't.'

'The head and body have to be separate to release the spirit,' said Ritonix. 'You Romans know nothing. After a year or so, they can dig up the head and put it back with the body. It's all quite logical. But Lucretia, I still don't know how you managed without a spiritual adviser.'

'Indeed,' said Anguis.

'Unless they've tagged onto that cult what come over from Judea,' said the slave in the chariot. Everyone turned to stare at him.

'Silence,' said Anguis, 'these are law-abiding citi - I mean subjects.'

'They would never do anything so *heathen*,' snapped Ritonix.

Lucretia hid behind her veil and lowered her head, shoulders hunched. 'Gentlemen, stop, stop. We did indeed follow old customs, Decurion. I have no taste for cremation and, grief stricken, I implored my family to bury my...' she coughed, 'my beloved in privacy. My dear sister Tullia is, as you know, on another plane entirely, and she was able to speak the words to any listening deities which would assist him through to another existence. Lucco here, our gardener, performed the necessary sacrifice. Forgive us if we have offended either of you.'

'But who er, who removed the er... well, er, Lucretia.' Anguis shook his head and straightened up again. 'Dear lady, I came to offer my sincere condolences. When I think that I was privileged to sit alongside your beloved husband on his last evening, regaled by his wit and charm, it brings a tear to my eye.'

He wiped his dry face.

'And now,' he turned to Marcellus, 'I must address you sir, since you are heir to this wonderful opportunity, I mean this sacred spring.'

Lucretia dropped her veil and glared. Before she could say anything, Marcellus interrupted.

'I wrote a eulogy for him, you know, would you like to hear it?

Oh noble father, rosy with wisdom
how I will miss your hand to guide my adult path

as once you helped me stagger on the nursery floor
and wiped my little childish…'

'Marcellus!' snapped Lucretia. 'No-one wants to hear that again. There was only one thing your father was rosy with and it wasn't wisdom.'

'Lucretia, I must speak with your son about our plans.'

'It is my land. As long as I live, you will speak through me.'

'But in Roman law you have no entity, no existence.'

'It is, nevertheless, my land by our laws. More to the point, I am descended from the goddess Diffis, and I wonder if you want to tell a goddess she has no entity? Would you, for example, say that to Minerva or your beloved Diana?'

The Decurion blanched. 'Well no, of course not. I -'

'And that's the other reason we're here,' said Ritonix. 'I've been a druid man and boy for fifty years and I've …'

'Secretly longed to know where the lost spring of Diffis was,' interrupted Lucretia, 'as have we all, and now it's been found. Naturally, after fifty years, *some* people's mind starts to weaken, or so I've heard.'

'In which case,' Ritonix went on, 'that spring should be honoured, not exploited.'

'No exploitation! Equal rights for equal gods!' shouted Budic making everyone jump. He pulled a piece of parchment from his tunic and waved it under Prisca's nose.

'What does this say?'

'Er… I can't read runes.'

He pointed at another row of writing.

'Or Latin.'

40

'I won't pollute my pen with the language of the invader. It's Greek.'

'Oh. Or that.'

'It says that if there's a sacred water source it should be left alone and failing that, there should be nothing but worship there. I am going to pin it next to the spring as a warning. No goddess from round here is going to put up with Romans' filthy practices.'

'We plan to build a bath-house,' said Lucretia. 'You can hardly call that filthy.'

'It will be when it's full of Romans and their dirt.'

'You won't be saying that when those Romans are buying things from our people!'

'Now, now, gentlemen, let's go inside for something to drink,' said Tullia.

'And some of your cook's delicious food,' said Anguis, forcing a smile.

'Well, that may be difficult,' sighed Prisca, 'Briccio's run away. We've been living on bread, cheese and garam for nine days.'

Chapter Six - Unexpected Guests
June 13th (Idibus Junias)

Lucretia ordered the slaves to arrange the new arrivals around low tables in the garden. She commanded that they place her between Anguis and Marcellus. Ritonix sat awkward and upright on a bench between Fabio and Pomponius. Olivarius and Budic reclined on the warm grass on either side of Camilla's bench. She smirked at Prisca who poked out her tongue under pretence of licking her lips.

Despite Prisca's announcement, there was a little more than bread, cheese and garam. Briccio might have gone, but the remaining slaves had made honey cakes broken out the precious olives and served baked salt-preserved shrimps purchased from the market in Pecunia which had been intended for supper.

'It breaks my heart to see a people swept up in Roman ideas,' said Budic, staring up at Camilla then waving his tanned, muscly arms towards the countryside. 'The old ways will be lost. Look around you.'

Camilla dragged her eyes away from his chiselled cheekbones and her mind from imagining what he'd be like with his hair loose. She surveyed the scenery as commanded. The land fell away into the valley as it always had. The river, a ribbon of silver which twisted towards the sea, was, she knew, not very silver when you got closer. This far up, its waters were drinkable because the tanneries were further downstream, but it was muddy at the bottom and full of water weed. Scattered about them were ornamental trees in summer splendour. An orchard struggled with the soil to produce small, disappointing apples, and up beyond was the forest. The forest loomed, making her feel

42

simultaneously safe and nervous. On the one hand it was somewhere to hide, and on the other, somewhere where a stranger might be concealed. Tullia had told her and Fabio about childhood in these hills. She and Lucretia, hard as it was to imagine, had played on the edges of the trees, and in the autumn, gathered wild mushrooms and brambles. Meanwhile, the wild boar and deer hunted by the men folk were roasted over huge pits of fire. The villa was barely more than a Celtic roundhouse then. Camilla's grandfather had not always been fond of Romans.

Tullia managed to make it sound romantic but, to Camilla, countryside was all a bit open and very, very boring.

'It's green,' she conceded. 'But there aren't any shops or arenas or anything.'

'Oh my pretty, they've brainwashed you.' Budic sighed and closed his eyes. His jaw clenched.

He called me his pretty! thought Camilla, and sighed too.

'I think she just wants something more than trees, don't you, my lady? She is used to the bright lights and excitements of Glevum,' said Olivarius. His eyes pleaded with her and he brushed reddish hair from his brow with a hand so soft and smooth, yet strong. She could see the muscles in his arm and imagined him playing her a song with a harp and then stroking her face. *He called me my lady...*

'What would you know?' snapped Budic. 'Where are you from anyway?'

'Londinium. My parents were from Tarsus.'

'And you are enslaved.'

'No. My father was freed before I was born. I can speak, read and write in Latin, Greek and Aramaic. I

43

regret that I have not learnt runes. I am training to take part in government.'

'Still enslaved then and willing to enslave others. See... I apologise my lady, I don't know your name.'

'Camilla,' said Camilla.

'No Celtic name?'

'Oh er, well. Of course, my father insisted I was named for him and er, Mother ...'

'I will call you Rosyn because your blush is like the petals of a briar rose.'

'Camilla is a beautiful name,' said Olivarius, 'but if I had to choose another, I would call you Ruby, as your lips are like a jewel.'

'You should reclaim your heritage, Camilla,' urged Budic. 'I could teach you what your city upbringing has lost you. Walk with me in the hills: feel the very air speak in your ear and bejewel your hair with dreams.'

'Rain,' said Olivarius, 'I think you mean rain. It's what your hair generally gets bejewelled with around here.'

'You could cast off your Roman gown and wrap yourself in fine scarlet and talk to the spirits in the water and the watchers under the trees, you could -'

'Catch your death,' said Olivarius. 'Do you like poetry, my lady?'

Camilla glanced at Marcellus. 'It sort of depends.'

'Music?'

'Yes.'

'Perhaps I could arrange for your family, or rather the principal members of it, to dine at the Decurion's house and I could play for you. Perhaps I could teach you how to -'

'Drive a chariot?'

'Well, er...'

'You don't want a chariot and a foreign horse!' said Budic. ' You want a sturdy mountain pony and your arms clasped round the man who is one with it! Now what you should do is let me teach you everything you have missed so far -'

'What are you three whispering about?' called Lucretia. 'Camilla. Behave. It is not modest to talk to men so brazenly. Leave that sort of behaviour to Prisca. Go and get Julia from the nurse-maid.'

'Why?' said Poppaea. 'What has Julia to do with anything?'

'Be quiet dear, you look as if you need a rest. Or is it just the mourning clothes making you appear sallow?'

'Lucretia, I -'

'Camilla! Do as you're bid.'

Camilla, rolling her eyes, got up from the bench and went inside.

Ondi walked up and bowed.

'Madam, Tryssa the wise woman from Pecunia is here with one of the gentry, Dondras. I don't know what they want precisely, but they'd like to see you.'

'Yokels?' said Anguis.

Budic bristled.

'Bring them to us,' said Lucretia.

By the time Camilla returned with Julia, a middle-aged Briton with fine clothes and shining braided hair was standing in front of the family together with a neat grey-haired woman of around Lucretia's age. The man nodded to Anguis and Marcellus, glanced at Ritonix and Budic, then stood silent.

'Well?' said Lucretia.

'Lucretia,' said the man. He was clean shaven, like a Roman, and the trim on his tunic was imported.

'Dondras,' said Lucretia. 'I imagine you have come to pay your respects. Tryssa,' she glanced sideways at Poppaea, 'are you here on a professional visit? I thought we were all quite well. Although of course, mourning.'

'Do you recall when we were all children?' said Dondras. 'When I played with your brothers and my cousin Tryssa here played with you?'

'My brothers are long dead.'

Dondras stroked his chin and nodded. 'I recall your brother Rhys very well. I remember when he died by the goring of a wild boar in the forest. He was a mighty hunter and it was tragic but somehow right that he should go that way. Now he will be hunting with our fathers and our fathers' fathers and our fathers' fathers' fathers and our -'

'Yes, yes,' interrupted Lucretia.

'And now your husband has gone to join them,' said Dondras.

'Porcius wasn't especially interested in hunting,' said Lucretia. 'I imagine when his soul settles, he'll be waiting for the after-hunt feast to start and quaffing while he waits.'

Pomponius coughed and Anguis, with a groan, snapped his fingers for more wine.

'Lucretia,' said Dondras, 'this land would have been Rhys's and now it is yours. Your father gave you Roman names and took on Roman ways.'

'As did your father, although you did not change your name. A wise man moves with the times.'

Budic started to rise. Dondras held up a hand.

'Budic, do not think you can turn everyone's head with talk of rebellion. We have a saying,' he said. 'Do not throw out the cheese with the whey. It is possible to have the benefit of both worlds.'

46

Anguis said, 'Very wise. Think of what Rome has brought you.'

'Taxes, capital punishment, outside rule, slavery,' snarled Budic.

'You already had capital punishment and slavery,' said Anguis, 'and I daresay you paid tribute to your chieftain, which at the end of the day is no different to tax. And now you have roads to take you round the world, a standing army and a civil service.'

'Who wants the civil service?'

'Where would you be without it?'

'Free! Like we were in the good old days! Worshipping our own gods in our own ways -'

'Dondras, Tryssa,' said Lucretia, 'what is it you want? I am, as you can see, meeting with the Decurion despite my grief, to discuss matters of great importance.'

'We want two things,' said Dondras. 'Firstly, we want to speak with your cook. My son Enrys stole money and ran away two weeks ago. You must have heard. He was in love with a local girl, I don't know who. No-one of any importance, I understand. Not only that, but you know how boys can get...' He glanced at Fabio. ...'a little obsessed.'

'Dondras is speaking of the new spring on your land,' said Tryssa. 'His son wanted to be an acolyte of your goddess Diffis.'

Lucretia locked eyes with Tryssa. The other woman's face was unreadable. It seemed to hide more, bare of cosmetics as it was, than Lucretia's painted and frowning visage.

'Not *my* goddess, *our* goddess,' she retorted. Tryssa remained silent.

Oblivious, Dondras continued, his chin stuck out and his fists clenched. 'Not only that but Enrys said he wanted to marry this nobody. I told him it was time I arranged a marriage to someone suitable. He had the nerve to argue with me, and threaten violence. I would have had him thrashed, but he stormed off to take his temper out on someone else. I thought he'd be back after a few days of trying to care for himself. Clearly not. He is a waste of time. I have a better son worthy of my attention, but then my daughter went to Tryssa for advice.' He glared at the wisewoman as if it was her own fault she had been consulted.

'Ah yes,' said Lucretia. 'Tryssa has a reputation for sticking her nose into other people's affairs.'

Tryssa ignored the taunt. 'I discovered that the boy had taken to drinking with your slave Briccio and someone else,' she said. 'They were filling the lad's head with talk of rebellion.'

Dondras fixed his glare on Budic. 'I've been looking for you.'

'I don't even know your son.'

'So you say. At any rate, as I said, I would have washed my hands of him, but then I found he had stolen from me. And now that Tryssa has found out who he kept company with, I'm here to see if Briccio knows where my son has gone, and ask you to keep your slaves under better control.'

'Briccio, I'm afraid to say, has also run away,' said Lucretia.

'Ah,' said Tryssa. 'That was a rumour in the market, since he hasn't been seen buying his usual foodstuffs. I wondered if it were true. Perhaps your other slaves can help us work out where he's gone, since it seems that Dondras's son has helped him get away.'

'I have already asked them and they know nothing,' snapped Lucretia. 'I have several reasons to want him back. And now it appears he was coerced by a rich

48

man's boy. Dondras, it should be you apologising to me. Your son helped make Briccio's escape possible with your money. When they are found, we will have to decide who is in debt to whom. Now, I really have other things to do. What was the second thing you wanted to know?'

'My son is a violent thief and a sentimental fool,' said Dondras. 'He is no loss. I'm more interested in knowing what's in it for Pecunia.'

'What's in what?'

'This spring. I hunted in these lands with your brother, Lucretia. Perhaps we were influenced by the Romans. Perhaps they wanted to keep us away from the groves where our ancestors made sacrifices. I do not recall Diffis. But if she was lost and has been re-discovered, then she is part of my heritage, and also the heritage of the people of Pecunia, and she should bless us. My grandfathers and your grandfathers were leaders in this place in the days before the Romans. Your father was rich enough to leave you land and gold. My father left me land and property. But our town is small and no-one leaves the main road to detour here, nor do they deviate from the road between Isca and Moridumum. We want to know what you plan to do, and I want to know how I may help you.'

'Exploitation of a sacred spring is a travesty!' exclaimed Budic.

'Be quiet, boy,' snarled Dondras. 'I've had enough of young men with no common sense. It's not exploitation if the right people benefit.'

'We will consult with all the important townspeople,' said Anguis. 'Rest assured that nothing will be done to the detriment to anyone who can help make the spring a success. I mean bring honour to the deity. However, we are in the middle of discussions, and if you could both go away that would be appreciated. Now, Lucretia, where is this granddaughter of yours?'

Ondi ushered Dondras away, still muttering. Tryssa, after giving Lucretia another long stare and followed. They saw her tap the slave on the shoulder and say, 'tell me, Ondi, when did you last see Briccio?'

As their voices faded, Camilla stepped forward with her hands on Julia's shoulders.

'Oh here you are at last,' said Lucretia. 'I sent you for her ages ago. And don't pull that face, granddaughter. It may become stuck that way.' Julia's scowl could have competed with Budic's.

'Who's that man?' Julia whispered, pointing at Anguis. 'He's got a big nose and his fingers are like twigs.'

'What's all this about, Lucretia?' asked Poppaea, rising to stand by her daughter.

Anguis put down his goblet and frowned at Julia.

'She's rather small,' he said. 'How old did you say she was?'

'Ten or eleven,' said Lucretia.

'She's six,' said Poppaea. 'Her sister would have been twelve.'

'Of course, how silly of me to forget you managed to lose a child. Try not to lose any more. Unless it's a third girl, in which case it doesn't matter.' Lucretia sipped her wine and nibbled her olives.

'Well,' said Anguis, 'it's rather a long term plan. How can I be sure she'll live long enough to marry?'

'You can't marry her!' exclaimed Poppaea, hauling Julia behind her. 'She's just a child.'

'My dear woman,' said Anguis, 'I have no particular desire to marry anyone. Women are, I have found, at best wearying and at worst as irritating as a mosquito bite on sunburn. I am merely considering whether to become betrothed until such time as she's old enough to be a bride. Naturally, during that time she would have to be trained up, as she seems to be rather too rebellious at the moment. The women in your family, Lucretia, do seem to struggle with knowing their place. I suppose an alternative would be to marry your niece.' He looked at Camilla, who took a step back and trod on Budic's fingers.

'A discussion for another time, perhaps,' said Anguis.

'Over my dead body,' muttered Budic and Olivarius together.

Camilla's heart flipped.

Chapter Seven - A Hunting Trip
June 14th (ante diem xv111 Kalendas Julias)

There was a limit to the skills of the kitchen slaves. Breakfast the next day was dull: the baked goods were dry and, though supplemented by some fresh herbs and beans from the garden, all the fresh produce bought from the forum the day before was now limp.

'I can't believe it's so hard to find a new cook,' complained Pomponius, picking at his crumbling honey cake.

But at least the meal was not dull in any other respect. It was interrupted by a visit from an angry father from the village, who forced his way past Lollia and dragged a young woman, bundled up in a loose dress with her head cast down, to stand before Lucretia.

'Where's your slave Briccio?' he demanded.

'Inasmuch as it has to do with you, he's run away,' said Lucretia, barely raising her eyes from her plate. 'Why?'

'See what he's done to our Lys!' The man pointed at his daughter's stomach, over which she crossed her arms as if to shrink it. 'We're a respectable family, and your slave's been luring her out with pastries and letting her stroke his dormice. Now look at her!'

'Well, it's hardly my fault,' said Lucretia. 'Her mother should have kept her too busy to go off with strange men, especially slaves.'

'Don't I know it. Lys could have had that son of Dondras if she'd played her cards right. He mooned after her like she was made of star-dust, and she used to lap it up. Forever sneaking off with him. We didn't mind that. It would've been a step up, marrying him. Then she started complaining. "He's too boring," she said. "Too ordinary," she said. "Not exotic enough," she said. Said he'd got a temper, or got maudlin, or got religion, or - something. We couldn't think what was going on, but you know what girls are like.' He glared at Camilla. 'Heads turned by foreigners every single time.'

'What foreigner?' said Marcellus.

'Briccio. He was a Gaul, wasn't he? Tempting her with his moustache and wild talk of a land with sunshine every day all summer. Like anyone would believe that. What are we going to do with Lys now? One moment of madness and now she's up the duff. And I can't even marry her off to that son of Dondras, because it turns out he's a thief and he's run off too. I don't know what we're going to do -'

'Can she cook?' interposed Prisca. 'If she can, we could buy her.'

'I'm not selling my girl!' spluttered the man. 'I just want compensation to use as a dowry so someone will take her off my hands and bring up your slave's brat.'

'I'm not responsible for his misdemeanours,' said Lucretia. 'Naturally, when Briccio is caught, he will be executed. Any savings he might have had will be forfeit, and I will ensure you have them. It seems,' she said as an aside to Marcellus, 'that we are allowing our slaves too much spare time, if they're able to wander off and cavort with the locals.'

'She only cavorted just the once!' said the father. The girl didn't move her head, her feet drawing circles in the dust on the mosaic.

'Mmm,' said Lucretia.

'Don't you have that Briccio slaughtered till he's told Lys what he was thinking of, running away like that without even a last goodbye. I mean it's not as if he knew what he'd done, is it? She's only just figured it out, despite being brought up with cows. Though I

53

suppose, since he was a slave, he can't marry her. And now I can't even palm her off on Dondras's son. She told him before she told anyone else and she thinks he went to sort out your slave. But I'm not so sure. I think those feckless lads just both legged it.'

Lucretia whispered to Marcellus. He rummaged in his money pouch and handed over a denarius.

The father squinted at it.

'You'd get a better price if you sold her as a cook,' said Lucretia. 'Or were you really hoping to marry her to some stranger who'd only take her if she had a pot of cash as well as a bun in the oven?'

The girl nudged her father and gave a small sob.

The father drew in a breath and handed back the denarius.

'Forget it,' he said, 'we'll manage somehow. Come on Lys, let's go home. I don't know what we're going to tell your mum. Perhaps you could go and stay with your granny out in the hills for a few months.'

They turned and trudged out of the villa back towards town.

Prisca unpeeled herself from the bench. 'I wish you'd tried harder to buy her, Mother. I'm really bored with the food. I think we should send down into town to get that food trader to come and work here. I'm about to faint with hunger. My ribs are nearly poking through my skin.'

'I hadn't noticed,' said Pomponius.

'As if you come near me anymore!'

'As if you'd let me!'

'Stop it!' shouted Lucretia. 'I have an idea. What about a hunting party? It's been a few years since we had one. We could invite the Decurion. He seems fond of hunting, or at least the idea of it. Marcellus, it's time to put down your pen and take up the spear.' She sat up and clapped her hands. 'Come along. You!' She pointed at Ondi. 'Take a message to Anguis Superbus. And you!' She pointed at the men. 'Get ready to bring in wild boar and deer.'

'I would love to join them, but I think we have things to discuss, dear Lucretia...' said Urbanicus.

'Well of course you needn't go. As you say, we need to plan ... organise ... talk. The other men can go and bring in the dinner. Ah, it brings back memories: seeing my menfolk run in the wilds to bring back food, their limbs smeared with mud and blood, pride in their eyes. When I think of my brother, that big strong man, sweaty and weary from the chase, I feel like a girl again.'

'Me too,' muttered Pomponius. 'Lucretia, shouldn't I stay home and help draft plans for the baths? In fact, I think we should *all* stay behind, and for once my darling wife has a good idea. The slaves can go down into town and get that street vendor. Surely you don't want to send your heirs into the forest where your brother was so tragically lost.'

Lucretia shrugged. 'It was a long time ago, and he was rather irritating. Besides, risk is good for you. You men have got too soft with your writing and composing. It's time for you all to live up to your ancestry. Think how it would please that whipper-snapper Bendic.'

'Budic, Aunt Lucretia,' said Camilla.

'You shouldn't be paying attention to strange young men, Camilla. Now on with all of you.' Lucretia wafted the men away as if they were chickens.

***

It was over an hour before the men, including Anguis and Olivarius, entered under the canopy of leaves at the edge of the forest. It had started raining

55

when they were half way up the slopes, and their clothes were muddy. Even Anguis had deigned to wear leggings like the Britons. His lip had curled as he put them on, but now, when he saw the smears and snags made by the undergrowth, he simply hoped no-one important would see him.

The rain pattered onto a roof of leaves so dense that it was hard for any water to penetrate, but from time to time a drop trickled down their necks and onto their bare arms. Now and again little puddles pooled on leaves which then collapsed, dumping cold water on the hunters' heads.

They walked on quiet feet, communicating with small nods and gestures. Even Pomponius, tripping over roots and scraping his hands on bark as he steadied himself, felt his city-bred heart beat faster, shaking his head to replace the pounding with the steady breaths of the forest.

Their eyes slowly grew accustomed to the green light and as they spread out, bows, daggers and spears at the ready, they glanced from side to side, looking for that tiny movement or that sparkle which meant something was watching them. Pomponius hoped that if there really were things observing them, they were simply watching and not planning an attack. He was startled to see how Marcellus, his poetic brother-in-law, walked alert and focussed. Marcellus had changed, breathing with the trees, smelling for the musk of any animals. Pomponius opened his mouth to speak, but Marcellus shook his head. They had lost sight of the others, and Pomponius hoped that what he could hear was twigs being snapped by friendly humans rather than bones being crunched.

Fabio crept forward alone. He memorised each tiny sound and the way constrained, restricted light made sharp angles of colour through the leaves onto the trees and bushes. A song started to form in one part of his mind, but the other was alert for prey and watchers in the undergrowth.

Anguis felt dampness seep through his shoes. He must be on some part of the forest which linked with the spring. The skin rose on his neck as he recalled military service. Only Parthia had been dry and hot rather than wet and warm. Back then, the enemy had lurked behind bridge and wall. In west Britain there appeared to be nothing but hills, boulders and curving paths: the enemy long vanquished. Perhaps. He glanced at Olivarius. Who knew what a freedman's son thought of the man who could make or break him?

A little way off he could make out Marcellus, no longer a day-dreamer but a huntsman at one with his surroundings. He wondered if the veneer of civilisation was thin, if these men still carried in their blood the resentment of their forefathers. They moved silent as wolves among trees where their ancestors had hunted and died. Could they therefore be trusted? Anguis breathed calm and slow. He recalled his army training and looked from side to side. His eyes perceived a face in the shadows, and then nothing, and then a face again. He must be getting to the point when one's eyesight started to fail. Olivarius made a tiny sound, a catch in his throat and stepped sideways into the undergrowth. Anguis felt his blood pump faster, his mouth dry, his bladder prepare to empty. He stepped into a shadow and watched Olivarius from behind a tree. Olivarius was not alone. He had come across that young Briton. The trouble-maker was like a furious cat, so much so that Anguis imagined his tail swishing in fury. Budic was even growling.

'You must follow me,' he snarled.

'Why should I?' snapped Olivarius. 'Haven't you got a job in town? What were you doing in the forest?'

'Hunting. What are you doing in here?'

'Hunting.'

'All of you? No wonder there's nothing to be had with you all thumping about.'

'No-one's thumping.'

'Not even your pet Roman? Or are you his pet Tarsan?'

'No-one is anyone's pet and I'm a Briton.'

'Huh.'

'And he may be a fool in many ways, but not when it comes to moving about stealthily. He could be right behind you and you wouldn't know till it was too late.'

'I am afraid of no Roman, and there is nothing to be found here but what I've found. Come.'

Budic gestured and started to step deeper into the forest. Olivarius hesitated, and Anguis stepped out from behind the tree.

'Do you trust him?'

'I don't know.'

'Should we summon the others?'

Olivarius breathed deeply. 'Yes, I believe we should.' He let out the low hoot they'd agreed as a signal.

After a moment, two hoots from different directions answered and with half-heard footsteps, the other men tip-toed towards them.

Budic, waiting on the other side of the glade, beckoned with more urgency and they stepped towards him.

'What is it?' said Fabio.

'I don't know,' said Olivarius. 'He wants us to see something.'

As they followed step by step, the musk of the forest was overwhelmed by a smell which grew stronger and stronger, from sweet odour to stench.

Above them the rain had stopped and sun sparkled through the leaves, painting in gold the torn and shredded corpse of a man in slave's livery. A torn scrap of a richer man's cloak was clasped in what was left of gnawed and rigid fingers.

'Briccio,' said Marcellus, covering his mouth and nose.

'Oh gods,' said Pomponius, 'then there's *no* chance of a decent meal tonight.'

Chapter Eight - Questions
June 14th (ante diem xv111 Kalendas Julias)

Anguis pulled a face at what Lucretia's family called a bath-house. His Roman upbringing felt that an outside building with a warmish hot pool and a tepid cold pool was in no way adequate. He doubted it could remove either the mud on his body or the sense of pollution in his soul. No-one had expected the bath-house to be required until much later. The hypocaust, therefore (which Anguis imagined as damp and full of spiders), had only been lit an hour before the men staggered out of the forest with the wrong kind of corpse.

Really, thought Anguis, shivering as he dried off, *in this climate, there is no real need for a cold pool. Simply standing about naked could give you hypothermia within minutes. Even in summer.* He tried to recall Italia, tried to remember the feeling of being hot and dry. He sighed, wondering if Lucretia's wine was strong enough to take the taste of death from his olfactory system.

Anguis came out of the bath-house dressed in his normal tunic. The rain had started again, and lashed against him. All of a sudden he missed the leggings. In some respects the Britons were more sensible than he'd ever publicly admit.

Some distance away he could see the compost heap where the slaves had put Briccio's body. They had covered it with old sacking but nevertheless Ondi was green, throwing up over the discarded turnip tops. The rain soaked into the sack-cloth, moulding it round the shredded remains beneath. A gnawed foot stuck out at the end of the stretcher, half a second-rate sandal still attached. Anguis could see Lucco poking it with a hoe and hoped there was enough tissue to hold it all together. Swallowing hard, he redirected his mind to the villa. In the kitchen doorway, Lollia was chivvying the kitchen slave. The girl's wails carried through the pattering rain.

'He said he loved me!' sobbed Blod. 'And you won't let me see him! And he's all chewed up!'

Lollia was looking nauseous too. As he stepped towards the shelter of the villa, Anguis heard her say 'well, maybe it's best this way. If he'd been caught he'd have been executed anyway. I think being killed by a wolf is quicker and cleaner.'

Blod howled louder. 'He was led astray! He was training me up! He looooved me!'

Lollia was clearly biting back words which would break the bubble of the girl's illusion. 'He would want you to be brave, Blod, wouldn't he? Come on, let's put his training to the test.'

'I can't cook without him!'

'You only have to make a simple meal. They're sending down to town for dinner. Start by making some bread - take your feelings out on that.'

Their voices faded as Blod was dragged into the kitchen, and Anguis made his way towards Lucretia's voice at the front of the villa. As if things couldn't get more annoying, it appeared that Ritonix and that wisewoman had already heard about the discovery of Briccio's corpse, and had arrived to discuss arrangements for its disposal.

'Are you still going to remove the dead cook's head, Lucretia?' said Anguis as he reached her side. 'I'd have thought, given that he's been "open" to the elements for nearly two weeks, his spirit will have escaped.'

'I will leave that up to the druid, Anguis,' said Lucretia. 'I am not concerned about a slave, and have no idea about Gaulish customs. Ritonix, why have you brought Tryssa?'

'I have brought her to inspect the body,' said Ritonix. 'She has brought pungent herbs, in case you have insufficient.'

'It will take more than herbs,' said Pomponius, joining them from within the villa. He was clean now, but still retched from time to time.

'Surely there's no need to subject Tryssa to an inspection of the body,' said Marcellus. 'It's clear how he died. When he ran away the night of Father's death he must have -'

'He ran away when Porcius died?' interrupted Anguis. 'I hadn't realised that. Why that night, do you think? Was there anything -'

'Co-incidence,' cut in Olivarius. 'I've found out it's true that he used to drink with Dondras's son. I imagine when the lad absconded with his father's cash, Briccio thought he'd follow. Besides, they were both involved with a local girl who'd been playing fast and loose. It was only a matter of time before her father found out anyway. Pretty much everyone else knew.'

'Nobody tells me anything,' complained Anguis. 'I'm supposed to be informed of all criminal activity so that I can summon someone else to deal with it. What do people think they're paying their taxes for?'

'Nobody tells me anything either,' said Lucretia. 'And from our point of view, to make matters worse, it turns out Briccio had been seducing our kitchen slave Blod at the same time as the trollop in town. I have no idea where he found the time or energy. I assume he hoped to accompany Dondras's son through the forest to the main road and then, presumably, find his way back to Gaul.'

'Someone should have told him about the wolves,' said Fabio.

'At least the wolves won't be bothering anyone else for a while. Unless they're waiting to see if anyone else fancies being a snack.' Pomponius sniggered then belched.

'I'd like to see the body,' said Tryssa. 'It's unusual for wolves to kill at this time of year.'

'Nonsense, woman,' Urbanicus's voice came from the doorway of the villa. 'If food is put before you, do you not eat, even when you are full?'

'No.'

Nodding to Lucretia, Tryssa followed a slave up to the compost heap. She covered her nose with the edge of her veil and indicated for the body to be uncovered.

After a few moments she returned.

'He is so severely mauled that it is impossible to tell how he died. He could have been killed by boar or wolf. His ankle is broken and -'

'The jaws of a wolf,' interrupted Marcellus.

'No, it is not broken from pulling. His skull also looks broken, as if from a blow, not the bite of a large animal. Perhaps he tripped and fell, cracking his head against a tree, and then either died from exposure or was attacked by animals where he lay. It's a shame no-one can take me to see the spot.'

'Poor young man,' said Ritonix.

'A slave,' said Lucretia, 'and a disobedient one who ran away and left us in chaos. It served him right. Ritonix, if you wish to take his remains to dispose of them with the dignity you think he deserves - which in my view, is very little - please do so immediately. Otherwise the body will be taken back to the woods for the animals to finish. Tryssa, thank you for your observations but trouble yourself no further. I don't wish to think of this unpleasantness anymore. Please dispose of it beyond the borders of my land.'

She glanced at Tryssa, who had not moved. 'Why do I always look at you and wonder what you're thinking?'

'We ran together as children, Lucretia. I was close to your brother Rhys.'

'Yes. I remember. But what you have forgotten is that the only riddle you could not solve was how to get him to marry you.'

The two women weighed each other up in silence.

'Well, Tryssa,' said Lucretia. 'For the sake of old times, you need not go with Ritonix and the ... remains. The wagon is about to go to town and it can take you home, where I hope you will stay. Should I have a puzzle, I will certainly send for you. Otherwise, as you can see, I am rather busy.'

Chapter Nine - Entertainers
June 14th (ante diem xv111 Kalendas Julias)

Tryssa was finally off the premises. Ritonix and his grisly cargo were out of sight beyond a clump of wizened rowan. The drizzle had stopped and the sun was muscling its way through grey clouds, making everything steam.

Lucretia gazed down the lane, digesting the leaden lunch which Blod had provided. She had sent Ondi down to town for proper food, but what was coming up the lane was neither familiar nor welcome. She folded her arms.

'What in the name of Gaia is happening now?

A wagon bearing five strangers, rattled up, its wheels wobbling. Two large men clambered down, causing it to overbalance. The pony skittered.

'Grnsn,' said one of them.

'Drnghn,' agreed the other.

They lifted their noses as if trying to locate a smell, and stood with arms crossed as if turned to stone. Lucretia twitched. Remaining in the wagon were a buxom red-headed woman, and two men so different in size that one looked like a figurine and the other like a pillar of Hercules. The smaller man, wrapped in a cloak, alighted and approached Anguis, Marcellus and Lucretia.

'All right?' he said. He was chewing on a stick, moving it about his mouth as he spoke. The remaining man clambered down and swung the woman to the ground. They disappeared towards the garden.

'Who are all these people?' said Lucretia.

'Gaius Contractes,' said Anguis, 'this is Marcellus Siluriensis, legal owner of this land, and this is his mother Lucretia, who has been visited by a vision.'

'Have you, Mother?' said Marcellus. 'That doesn't sound like you.'

'Marcellus, leave these conversations to me. Go and write a poem. Anguis Superbus, please could you set aside your assumptions and speak with me. It will save a considerable amount of time in the long run.'

'She's right Guv, I could see that straight off,' said Contractes. 'The key thing in my business is to get to instinctively know who the top dog is and in this case I can already tell the top dog's a b - a beautiful lady.' He bowed and kissed her hand.

Lucretia raised her eyebrows. 'And you, Gaius Contractes, you are?'

'Ring-master, herdsman, facilitator, magician.'

'Sorry?'

'Contractes runs shows,' said Anguis.

'Don't make it sound so flat, guv,' said Contractes in hurt tones, pulling the stick out of his mouth to wave it around. 'See, Anguis and me, we go back a long way.'

Lucretia blinked and recovered herself. 'Well, let us go inside where it's dry.'

***

Further along the veranda, Prisca was gazing round the edge of her veil at Hastorix.

'So, are you moving ... I mean are you being moved from Isca to here, Hastorix?'

'Think so,' said Hastorix. The rain had dried on his arms and now the feeble sun picked out his tattoos. Ropes and knots and tail-swallowing serpents twined around his arms, and across his chest a dragon reared. There was barely a scrap of un-inked flesh even on his face. Every tattoo, however, was kinked and crossed with scars. His eyes flickered first at Prisca, then at Pomponius who was deep in conversation with Aurelia.

66

Or possibly he gazed at Aurelia herself as she batted her eyelashes at Pomponius. Prisca couldn't tell. Then Hastorix shifted his gaze to the forest and heaved a sigh. Finally, he looked back at Prisca. In all this time, his expression of blank politeness did not change.

'What will the ladies of Isca do without you? The arena will be very dull. I will be very sad.'

Hastorix frowned. 'There's not just me.'

'No, but you are the star. I - I mean we ladies admire you so much. When you fight it makes some of us weak at the knees. Not me of course,' she tittered. 'After all, I am a respectable matron and happily married.' She cast a venomous glance at Pomponius, then recovered herself. 'I simply appreciate your skills and prowess.' She ran her eyes over Hastorix from dark braids to sandalled feet and sighed.

'Mmm,' said Hastorix.

'Will you be in combat if you move here? Who will be your opponents?'

'I think I will just act. The band will play. I will act.'

'Oh, a show! How thrilling! And you don't run the risk of being slaughtered.'

'I will die an old man.' said Hastorix.

'You don't sound very happy about it.'

Hastorix said nothing, his gaze returning to the forest.

'It's possible that I - I mean we will be moving here,' said Prisca. 'Or to the town at any rate, to be near my aged mother. And perhaps you could call and tell me, I mean us, all about your fights, and how you earned every scar. I might have a salve for some of them. I have a knack for making and applying salves.' She licked her lips.

'I do not talk of my fights. I was bought then trained up to kill. It is a job. One day it would have been me who was killed. Now I'll be a slave till I die. No chance of quick death. Just a slow one.'

'Oh dear, this is getting rather depressing,' said Prisca. 'Tell me about life as a Pict. Are Picts very wild? I imagine them as slightly rough and needing a good wash.' Her eyes sparkled.

Hastorix's left eye bore a scar across it. A sword had once caught his brow and cheekbone to leave a jagged white line through the tan. His frown deepened and Prisca thrilled. Was he angry with her? She imagined a row with him; not the squeaking, patronising bickering of Pomponius, but a deep anger expressed in heavy silence and the coiled strength restrained until with honeyed words she talked him round and the strength became passion, hot kisses burning her lips, those muscled arms pressing her to his firm body.

'I don't know,' he said. 'I was just a boy when they took me. One day I had hoped...'

He stared back up to the forest.

'Come now,' she said, the thud of her heart slowing. She was aware of her own flushed cheeks and reddened lips, but he was not observing her. 'Hastorix, don't dwell on what can't be changed. Just think. You needn't die in the arena now. That's good. It would have been such a waste. And you needn't think you must now live out your days playacting. You are in your prime and would make a fine father. I am sure you could be freed with the right ... er ... influence, and then perhaps if someone else was free, a woman of influence and anticipated wealth, perhaps... these things may take a little time, but don't despair.'

Her slippered foot stretched out and touched his.

'Oh dear, I'm so sorry,' she said, but didn't move her foot.

She turned to see Urbanicus pass by. He gave her a large wink.

***

'I'm Contractes' patron,' explained Anguis, under cover of the atrium. 'He approached me with plans to start shows in Isca. His bona fides were good and his ideas, or so I was advised (displays of excess not being to my taste), his ideas seemed sound. I invested money in his first venture and he has returned that investment a hundredfold.'

'Well that's all very wonderful for you, Decurion, but it does not explain what he, two trolls, a sulky-looking lump of a man and a sly-looking woman with hennaed hair are doing wandering on my property when we're trying to maintain order and...' she thought of Briccio and hoped the lingering smell was in her imagination, 'tidying up.'

She spotted Camilla leaning against the wall under the thatch, twiddling her hair and flicking her gaze between Budic and Olivarius, who were interrupting each other and jostling. 'Not to mention I have sufficient of my own family to herd.'

'Don't be like that, Lady,' said Contractes. 'Sorry if we've turned up at a bad time, but it's like this. Anguis Superbus here had already been discussing plans for some kind of theatre-arena here in Pecunia. It's just, you know, no offence and everything, but I wondered, "what's in it for Gaius? What's in it for the Decurion?" Never let it be said that Gaius Contractes would take a man's money if there's no hope of a good return. I was about to break it to him gently. But then he told me about Aquae Diffis. Now there's a plan. You've got a sacred site where you can offer the chance of the punter

69

dipping his toes in and hopefully coming out with the goddess granting him the chance of living past fifty. If not, at least he's getting a nice soak. So what does this mean? It means you've got an audience. Now an audience gets bored quick. There's only so much worshipping or even bathing a person can do. That's where I come in. I got dancing girls, I got performing animals, I got a gladiator who can put on a display of swordsmanship so fast you'd think he was fighting himself! If we can get this thing off the ground, we'll all be rolling in denarii.'

'Naturally, I'm only interested in honouring the goddess.'

'Naturally. We all are,' said Contractes. 'But I've yet to come across a god or goddess who doesn't come with money-making potential. Anyone who doesn't make the most of that is missing a trick.'

'Therefore,' put in Anguis, 'knowing we'd be back from hunting, I asked Contractes to view the site and discuss ideas.'

'Here?' exclaimed Lucretia. 'You want to put an arena here? Have you seen the slope?'

'Never say never,' said Contractes. 'Although you could be right. Nearer the town, nearer the forum - not that it's much of a forum at the moment, more like a camp with people selling off the back of wagons. Anyway, the nearer the town, the greater the potential investment. Someone who owns or is patron of a local business can make a packet.'

***

Aurelia stepped out into the sunshine. The grass was wet but the light was soft, and warmed her painted face. Her cheeks were rosy with circles of rouge and she bit her lips to redden them, before turning her smile on Pomponius who had followed her out from the veranda.

70

He glanced back at his wife. *Ridiculous woman,* he thought, *flirting with that gladiator at her age. Grounds for divorce really. If not worse. Has she forgotten our children? Her sacred role is mother, not temptress. And that brainless gladiator is encouraging her by feigning indifference. It's nauseating. Well, things could change couldn't they? If she continues to make a fool of herself...*

'Pomponius Iscatoris...' murmured Aurelia, 'am I boring you?'

She pouted and her large kohl-lined eyes filled with tears.

'No no, of course not, my dear. I was just thinking how young and fresh you are.'

'Perhaps I'm just a silly uneducated girl with no noble blood, simply a reviled slave...'

'Not reviled, Aurelia, never reviled. Your voice is like a skylark's, like starlight, you dance like a butterfly, like...' For once, he wished Marcellus was about. 'I wondered if you might sing for me, for us. It would make this rather trying day seem happy and bright!'

'I am not sure.' Aurelia glanced up at him, her eyes still wet. 'I feel all alone and soon I will leave Isca and no one will visit me...'

'Well I will try; I am thinking of moving to Pecunia.'

'It's no good,' sobbed Aurelia. 'You are free and married and I am... I am nothing. I must seek comfort from the other slaves. Maybe...' She shuddered. 'I must answer the summons of that other man who says he yearns for me. But I do not love him, whereas you... Oh I must not say it.'

'No no, don't think like that! My wife, as you can see, is false...'

71

'I would never be false.'

'No Kitten, you wouldn't. If you will just give me time, I must make arrangements to transfer her potential wealth to my children. It would be under my control of course. And then, you know it takes time to organise a divorce, your purchase, your emancipation... our wedding.'

Aurelia's eyes narrowed as she dried them with the tip of her gown. 'How long?'

'Maybe, oh I don't know, a few months. I need to speak to my parents, Lucretia, and make suitable arrangements for Prisca.'

'You said you'd never loved her the way you love me.'

'Well no, how could I? But she *is* the mother of my children.'

'Well, there is another gentleman waiting.'

'Don't be like that, Kitten, be patient.'

He reached for her hand.

***

'Well this is all fascinating, Contractes,' said Lucretia. 'But I am hungry and I don't want your creatures, I mean your people eating all the food which is arriving shortly. Why did you bring half your troupe with you?'

'I tell you, Lady,' sighed Contractes, 'the tigers are easier to manage than that Aurelia. It's better to keep her where you can see her. And as for Hastorix, he doesn't get much fresh air. If he's not training, he's being invited to wine bib with ladies. I thought it would do him good to get out for a bit and besides, he might have thoughts about the suitability of the land. I live in hope he's got some thoughts about something. I'm afraid he may have been knocked on the head a bit too much before I bought him. You know what,' he said, loosening his cloak and putting the stick back in his mouth, 'it's almost hot. All right, we'll be off. I'll get Lump and Slab rounded up... Oh sorry Lady, I mean the minders. It's not their real names, but it seems to suit.'

He took a deep breath.'Hastorix, Aurelia, get back here pronto!' he yelled.' It's time to go. Slab and Lump never got any dinner and we don't like them when they're cross do we?'

Aurelia moved away from Pomponius. Hastorix padded across the grass, clasped her arm in silence, and steered her towards the wagon.

'Goodbye, Kitten,' whispered Pomponius in her ear, 'be patient. Remember who your Puppy-Fluff is. Not long. I promise.'

Aurelia sniffed.

Hastorix turned to stare at Prisca. He frowned and her heart thudded. He appeared indifferent, but she knew it was just show. He was sorry to leave her. She knew it.

The wagon, carrying Contractes and his staff, slowly rumbled down the drive.

Chapter Ten - Dinnertime
June 14th (ante diem xv111 Kalendas Julias)

The household wagon came up with the solution for dinner just as the drizzle started to roll down from the slopes again.

The wagon was moving more slowly than usual, the horse rolling its lips and whinnying in the equine equivalent of a monotone grumble. When it stopped the first person to jump down was Vulpo, demanding help with his brazier and stand. Hot coals sizzled in the rain and a tirade of abuse mingled with his instructions.

'What do you think you're doing? Are you as stupid as a lump of yeast? Keep the covers on, move it over here, over there, are you a fool? It took me hours to prepare those chickens, my marinade is fit for gods, even Roman gods. Yes, yes take the flatbreads under cover, as long as the brazier hasn't gone out from your incompetence I can crisp them up again. Where's the lea of this awful house? Who designed it? What were they trying to do? It looks like the bastard of a mating between a roundhouse and a villa. There must be somewhere dry under the thatch! That'll do, move move move.'

'It all smells marvellous,' sighed Pomponius.

'Vendor!' exclaimed Lucretia, 'you can take it all into the kitchen.'

'Missus,' said Vulpo, pausing in his gesticulations, 'I've seen Roman kitchens. They're not big enough to boil an egg. How anyone can refeather a roast peacock when asked is anyone's guess. Vulpo needs space.' He swung his arms in circles, narrowly missing a slave passing with a platter of sausages. 'Big flavours need room to grow! I will finish my cooking and I will serve you outside where the fresh air will enhance the taste.'

74

He rushed off after his brazier to the shelter of the thatch.

'This is ridiculous,' said Fabio. 'What kind of fool stands outside in the rain just because it's summer, waiting for food to be cooked outdoors?'

An hour later Vulpo flipped the last of the fritters and sausages. Poppaea, picking at a piece of flatbread, shielded her nose from the smell of animal fat, but it didn't help. Hopefully everyone would put her nausea down to the earlier discovery of Briccio. She wondered what Ritonix would do with the corpse, and shuddered. Beside her Tullia sat in silence, her eyes half-closed, apparently mesmerised by raindrops dripping from the thatch. They sat upright to eat. It reminded her of when she and Marcellus had been newly married and he took her to the meadow. They would sit silent in the sun to eat wormy apples, bread and cheese. She had been so young, missing her nurse, resenting the mother who had married her off, and there had been nothing to talk about. They barely knew each other. The only thing they had in common was the knowledge that Lucretia was waiting for a grandchild. At least Marcellus was kind if a little vague; willing to divert his thoughts into verse rather than force her into making an heir before she was ready. He would recite his terrible poems and she would close her eyes imagining that one day Lucretia and Porcius would be dead, the odd villa in its lumpy land would be Marcellus's, and she could live in peace.

Fabio, on her other side, ate a third plateful with his eyes on the brazier, presumably trying to gauge whether he had room for more.

The rain paused again. A sickly sun parted the clouds.

A sensation of discomfort made Poppaea shiver and turn.

Urbanicus, standing in the doorway a little way off, was watching her as he licked his fingers clean. He neither smiled, blushed nor averted his gaze. In fact, his eyes ran from her head to her feet and back, pausing where her dress was bundled around her waist, until he was staring into her eyes again. Then he looked away.

Marcellus rushed past him and ran to Poppaea, 'I'm off after Ritonix,' he said. 'He left before I could finish my elegy.'

'An elegy for a slave?' said Urbanicus. 'It's hardly as if he was an old family retainer, or you knew him well.'

'Every man deserves some dignity, Uncle,' said Marcellus, 'particularly one who met his end in such a gruesome way.'

'Which would not have happened had he stuck to his duties.'

'Nevertheless. And besides, the Muse spoke.'

'Marcellus, I need to talk to you,' whispered Poppaea.

'In a while, my love, I need to catch up with the Druid. Or do you want to hear some verse first?

Oh Briccio, once we tasted your dishes
Yet now the wolves have tasted you -'

'Oh, really!' said Poppaea, rushing off with her veil over her mouth.

'What did I say?' said Marcellus.

'Does your poem mention chewing?' said Fabio, glancing at the chicken leg he'd been eating and blenching.

'It may do,' said Marcellus. 'Anyway, I'll be back soon. I could recite it later, during dinner. I'm especially proud of the bit about crunching.'

He ran off to the stables. The sun had made it back through the clouds in time to set.

Vulpo packed his things away, muttering. It was too late to search for anything which might be missing. Still, at least he'd been asked to return the next evening, perhaps with a more specific menu. The money was good, that was certain.

Night fell. Anguis departed, dragging Olivarius away from Camilla. Budic smirked until Camilla was dragged away by Lucretia.

'Go home,' Lucretia told him. 'You have no business here.'

Under the stars, the villa twinkled. Little oil lamps shone around the dining room and now that the visitors had gone, Lucretia sent slaves to summons the family. As they lounged on the benches picking at olives, she surveyed them, from her idealistic sister to her secretive daughter-in-law.

'Poppaea, where's Marcellus?' she barked.

Poppaea, reclining on her side, jumped and looked about her. 'Oh. I don't know. I thought he must be with you and Urbanicus, planning.'

Lucretia tutted and gestured to a slave to go and find her son.

There was silence.

'I wish we had Aurelia here to sing,' said Pomponius. 'That's what I call music.'

'Huh,' said Fabio, 'popular music. Simplistic melody, no core progression, three chords. And she sounds like a crow, I'll bet.'

'You have no taste, boy. Typical of the younger generation. Don't know a good tune when they hear it. Call what you play music, do you?'

'Yup.'

An awkward silence..

'Well, at least there's less chance we'll have to hear Marcellus's poem,' said Pomponius. 'I wasn't looking forward to the bit about crunching. Or any of it, really.'

Silence.

After a while they heard the discordant sound of a lame horse, and muttering. The voices grew louder. Lucretia frowned. It was unlike Marcellus to raise his voice.

Lollia entered. 'There is no sign of Master Marcellus, Madam, but a gentleman has arrived,' she announced. 'He says he would have been here earlier but his horse threw a shoe. He says he is a relation, and seeks welcome. I thought perhaps he could have the Master's room. I'm sure Master Porcius is not "walking" quite yet.'

She ushered in a tall man in his thirties, dressed and coiffed like a Roman but, as far as could be made out in the lamplight, with the colouring of a Briton.

'How delightful,' said Lucretia. 'More guests. Just when I thought I hadn't enough relations. Perhaps you could introduce yourself and explain why, however implausible it will be, you think you are related to me.'

'I am Gwil Lucretiensis,' said the stranger.

'Indeed?' said Lucretia, sitting up and peering harder.

'Yes,' said Gwil, 'I am your nephew. Your dead brother Rhys's son. I am, in fact, the rightful owner of this land.'

Chapter Eleven - Nighttime
June 14th (ante diem xv111 Kalendas Julias)

'That can't be!'

Poppaea had never seen her mother-in-law startled.

'I mean, you must be mistaken,' said Lucretia, settling her robes around her and reclining once more. 'My brother did not marry, and if he had children before his untimely demise, then he did not speak of it. That suggests either he did not know or - and I apologise for any hurt feelings - he did not care.'

'Perhaps he simply did not care to speak of it,' continued the stranger. 'I have proof that my birth is legitimate, but nevertheless, it is late and I throw myself on your mercy, for the sake of your brother. Or I can pay for my stay here, since my only other choices are what passes for lodgings in the town or a damp night under mosquitoes.'

'Are you really Rhys's son?' Tullia rose and stared up into his face. 'You have the look of him but if it is true, your mother was not from our people.'

'Iceni, from east of Londinium.'

'Don't let him too close to any flames,' said Urbanicus, 'in case he's inherited their tendency to burn things down.'

'The Iceni only burnt Roman things,' said Gwil, 'and not for over a hundred years.' He bowed to Lucretia again. 'May I?'

'Very well,' Lucretia waved her hand towards a bench. 'You may stay until morning, when we can see you better and discuss matters. I hope you're not very hungry. We are having something of a culinary crisis.'

'The forest must be teeming with wild game.'

'They are particularly wild at present. You can sleep in my late husband's room. He is recently deceased and we have absolutely no idea what his spirit is doing, although I wouldn't put it past him to be causing all the trouble through sheer incompetence. He's probably bumbling about searching for the entrance to the Otherworld. I hope you will not sleep too uneasily with a ghost.'

'I have been a soldier, Aunt. If I were to be troubled by ghosts, I would have stopped sleeping many years ago.'

Lucretia, bridling at the word aunt, summoned a slave. 'Still no sign of Master Marcellus?'

'No, Madam.'

'Then send Ondi out with the cart and see if *his* horse has been lamed. It seems to be that kind of day. Tell him to go all the way to the druid if necessary. It's quite possible that Marcellus is still declaiming his eulogy. Although what there was to eulogise about Briccio I have no idea.'

'His dormice stuffed with raisins and pine nuts were superlative!' said Pomponius.

'Hmm. Would you like to remembered for what you did, rather than who you were?'

'I wouldn't mind,' said Pomponius. 'Speaking of which, I know what will cheer us all up!'

Lollia and red-eyed Blod came in, bearing trays of cheeses, savoury biscuits, small cakes and jugs of wine. Poppaea wrinkled her nose at the cheese and nibbled at a cake.

'Ginger cake again,' noted Lucretia. 'Our supply will run low if you keep ordering it, Poppaea. Spices are not to be sneezed at.'

'Apart from pepper,' sniggered Pomponius.

The others stared at him.

'Enthral us, Pomponius,' said Urbanicus. 'What do you plan?'

Pomponius waved his arms at the fresco. 'This is old and tired, you have to agree. It must have been painted when you married, Lucretia. In that painting Porcius must be barely thirty, and you a mere slip of fifteen. And now you are -'

'A little older.' said Lucretia.

'Well given that Tullia is forty-seven, you must now be -'

'A little older,' repeated Lucretia. 'And with age came wisdom. It happens to some of us. You should try it.'

'Well, anyway, I thought that as a fitting tribute to my esteemed father-in-law and to your still vibrant beauty, I would paint a matching mural on the other wall, portraying you both as you are now, in all your mature grandeur.'

'Porcius? As he is now?'

'Not as he is now, naturally. Unless of course I depict you embracing his dead body or clasping his severed head looking woebegone.'

'I often pictured myself holding his severed head,' said Lucretia. 'Although not looking woebegone at the same time. Very well, if you can find someone with the skill and it will keep you quiet. What is it, Camilla?'

'Shouldn't Marcellus, Poppaea and Julia be on that wall?'

'Not until an heir is born. A male one.'

She glared sideways at Gwil, who lay sipping wine, watching her. He raised his goblet and winked.

'The stranger's talking nonsense,' whispered Urbanicus to her. 'I knew your brother, remember. It was through meeting him that I was able to introduce you to my brother and thereby lead to your marriage.'

'Oh, happy day,' said Lucretia.

'Rhys never had a formal wife. He might have planned to marry, but if so, I was unaware of anyone special. I know your father was pressing him to choose a local girl and settle down. Perhaps he might have had someone in mind before that hunting accident, but honestly, I think this young man is at best deluded and at worst a trickster.'

Poppaea rose. 'I am going to see if Julia has settled properly,' she said. 'Then I am going to my room to await Marcellus's return. Goodnight.' She rested her eyes on Gwil and frowned. He seemed so familiar. His face shape was so like her husband's, but his hair colouring was different. Where Marcellus was dark, Gwil was reddish-blond like Olivarius. Gwil stared back. The contrast of his copper hair with those dark brown eyes was striking. But his claim to be related was coincidence, surely? Lots of people look similar to other people. There must be only so many faces.

'You make entirely too much fuss of that child, Poppaea,' said Lucretia.

'Nonsense,' said Tullia, 'it's natural for a mother to worry about her children. Prisca, you must be missing your three terribly. Such a shame you didn't bring them here with you. It would have been lovely to have them all running about.'

Lucretia shuddered.

'Give Julia a kiss from me,' said Tullia.

'I think I'll go to bed too,' said Camilla, rising. Poppaea took her arm and they left the room.

In the atrium, however, instead of turning towards the bedrooms, Poppaea opened the front door and stepped outside. She could make out the diminishing dot of light which was Ondi and the wagon, searching for her husband. The night air was warm, stuffy, damp. Moths and mosquitoes danced in the torchlight.

'Poppaea,' said Camilla, 'can I ask you something?'

'About that Gwil? Do I think he's who he says he is?'

'No, not that, although ... no I don't think so. I could see Uncle Urb pulling faces throughout that speech. Can't think why Aunt Lucretia let him stay.'

'Probably prefers him inside where she can get someone to keep an eye on him, to outside sizing up the property or getting his story straight. The one thing she isn't is a fool.'

'Mmm. Well, anyway, what is Marcellus, fifteen years older than you?'

'Twelve. I was fifteen, he was twenty-six. My parents were impressed by the family descended from chieftains who hobnobbed with the Decurion and had a villa with its own bath-house. Of course they'd never seen a proper villa, and didn't know the bathhouse was just a shell. Lucretia was impressed that I was the only child of rich parents. My dowry paid for the bath-house completion, I think.'

'At least Marcellus wasn't sixty.'

'True. I can't imagine what your mother was thinking to allow that marriage.'

'It wasn't her choice. It was my grandmother's. At least the decrepit old goat died before - Anyway, what I wanted to ask was, did you want to marry Marcellus? Or would you have preferred someone your own age?'

Poppaea glanced sideways. In the shadow of the doorway Camilla was biting her lip and peering out into the night as if it was *her* husband who was missing.

'I didn't really know anyone,' said Poppaea after a pause, 'not properly. There were lads who flirted of course, some who were more serious perhaps, but my parents were holding out for a bigger fish.'

'What if you'd had a choice?'

'Women aren't given choices. They have to make them with what they've got.'

'Yes, but if you had had one.'

'Marcellus is good and kind,' said Poppaea.

'It's a wonder, given his mother. Sorry, I shouldn't have said that.'

Poppaea laughed. 'Fortunately she had nothing to do with his upbringing. There was a very good, kind nurse who did that.'

'But I bet there was an exciting boy you could have married instead.'

'It doesn't matter what could have been. Perhaps the exciting boy - if there had been one - would have strayed. Perhaps Marcellus had another girl in mind. We've never discussed it.'

'But you have to listen to his poems.'

'Could be worse. Come on inside. Olivarius won't be back this evening and if Budic is lurking about then he must have made friends with the dogs. I think we're going to have a storm tonight. I do hope Marcellus comes home soon, he's the only one who can settle Julia when there's thunder. He recites his poems and it makes her laugh.'

***

Camilla woke as the first flash of lightning lit the sky and the roll of distant thunder echoed around the hills. The night was still stifling. She wondered if Marcellus had returned by now and was making up poems for Julia. She thought about her conversation with Poppaea. What would she herself prefer? Wild boy or poet? Not that Olivarius was a poet, nor was Budic exactly wild. She sighed and imagined telling them how afraid she was of thunder so that they could comfort her, but in truth, she found storms exhilarating.

She rose and left the room so she could step outside to watch the lightning. Passing Julia's room, she could hear whimpering and Poppaea's soft comforting murmurs. Outside the door of what had been Porcius's room, a slave slept on the stone floor. Lucretia was taking no chances with Gwil. The front door was closed, and the house was mainly in darkness but for one lamp shining in the atrium. Quiet voices muttered. She moved on her bare feet as quietly as she could and listened.

'Nowhere?' it was Lucretia's voice.

'No, Madam,' Ondi sounded fraught. 'I looked all along the path and went into town.'

'Did you go to the druid's place?' Urbanicus's voice was low and hard to catch.

'Yes Sir, Ritonix is in a high fever and -'

'Not expected to live?'

'I don't know, Sir. His wife was hysterical and someone had gone for the wise woman.'

'And you found no sign of Master Marcellus?'

'Not precisely. Well, that is to say, Madam, I found the horse and have brought her home. She was frightened and sweaty, wandering back towards home and -'

'And? Speak up!' Urbanicus commanded.

'And I found his poem, Sir. At any rate, this piece of parchment with writing on it.'

There was another flash of lightning and the roll of thunder was closer.

'Hand it over.' Urbanicus's voice was harsh. 'Where was it?'

'In a ditch, Sir. I only just saw it, the torch lit up something lighter than the dirt and I thought maybe the Master had been thrown. But -'

'It lit up a tiny fragment like that?' Lucretia mocked. 'I can't believe you saw it.'

'No Madam, not this, it lit up sacking. It was -'

'Sacking? What are you talking about?'

'It was Briccio, Madam. Or at least, it looked like Briccio's body, all wrapped up in sacking like it was on the back of Ritonix's horse, but just chucked in the ditch. This scrap of paper was tucked half under it. Is it the Master's poem?'

Camilla heard some muttering before Urbanicus spoke. 'Yes, it seems so. And you didn't think to lift the body to see if the Master was underneath, or indeed open the sacking to make sure he was not inside?' A slap coincided with the lightning. The thunder was now nearly overhead.

'But Sir, Briccio had been mauled, he had been dead two weeks, there were maggots! A stench!'

'Go back!'

'But Sir! The storm!'

'Is the storm more frightening than the wrath of your mistress?'

'N-n-no Sir.'

Another slap.

'Go back. Go and check to see that body is really Briccio and your Master is not there too.'

The door swung open to a world which flooded with light, then plunged into darkness, and a crash of thunder made the household gods rattle on their shelf.

Camilla's heart thudded. She pulled her wrap more closely round her and kept in the shadows. Close by, she could hear Julia sobbing. With shaking legs she walked towards her bedroom, as the front door closed out the storm and the slave who had been pushed out into it.

Chapter Twelve - A Visit to Tryssa
June 15th (ante diem xvii Kalendas Julias)

When morning came there was still no sign of Marcellus.

At breakfast, Ondi stumbled about the dining room. He shivered as he worked, grey-faced. Lucretia lashed out as he spilt mead and dropped bread. Tears filled his eyes.

Camilla rose and followed him from the room. Stepping into an alcove to watch, she saw two of the other slaves step aside as he neared them.

'It's not my fault,' he said. They shrugged.

'You can wake our guest,' one said to him. 'See if he's survived the night. I'm not going in there. Not if there are spirits abroad.'

'You shouldn't be touching food,' said Lollia to Ondi as she came from the kitchen.

'It's all right, Lollia,' said the slave who didn't want to wake Gwil. 'We didn't let Ondi touch our own food. We only let him touch *theirs*.' He nodded towards the dining room.

'Fair enough,' said Lollia. 'It would take more than unclean hands to poison the Mistress.' She muttered something under her breath as she passed Camilla. It sounded like 'worse luck.'

Camilla caught up with Ondi as he entered the slave quarters. There was only one other person there, Lucco the gardener, hunting in a box.

'Ondi,' said Camilla.

He paused and turned, his shoulders slumped.

'Sit down,' said Camilla. 'You're exhausted. What happened? Why are the other slaves avoiding you?'

Tears started to fall. Shaking, Ondi wiped his eyes and then glanced at his hands and shuddered.

'I ... they sent me out to find the Master, Miss. Master Marcellus.'

Camilla stopped herself from saying that she knew already.

'And what happened then?'

'I found Briccio's body, Miss, half buried in a ditch, but I didn't find the Master and I came home and...'

'Yes?'

'They made me go back and see if the Master was under Briccio. I had to move the body. Touch it. Now the others say I'm unclean and that his spirit will haunt me.'

'They're fools,' snapped Lucco, slamming the lid of his box. 'They helped move and wrap him themselves yesterday. They put him on the horse for Ritonix.'

'Yes, but now they're saying, what happened to make his body fall? To make Ritonix sick? To make Marcellus, I mean the Master, disappear? They say it's the spirit of Briccio come to haunt them, and now he'll have followed me home. Besides, they fired up a sweat tent where you couldn't see yesterday evening and sweated out the pollution. I never got the chance. They say I'm cursed!'

'Ondi!' snapped Lucco. 'Stop wailing and go and get yourself in that sweat tent. If the gentry fire up the bath-house later, which I'm sure they might...' He glared at Camilla.

'Oh, yes, of course,' she said.

'Then you can finish off in there, but it's all nonsense. Nonsense, Miss. All these hauntings and cursings and goddesses no-one's ever heard of. I've seen birth and death and murder and neglect and if anyone was going to get haunted, it wouldn't be this poor lad here. I don't know why anyone wants to weep a tear for Briccio anyway. He was no good. No-one liked him apart from Blod, and that girl's a fool. Now all of a sudden he's everyone's best friend. And now I think of it, they didn't know him well enough to be able to describe him, let alone recognise him.'

'There wasn't enough to recognise,' pointed out Camilla.

It was hard to make out Lucco in the gloom of the roundhouse but his normal glare seemed to have deepened into a frown as he muttered to himself. 'Come to think of it, there was enough,' he said more loudly. 'When you spend your life at ground level, digging and hoeing like I do, you have a different view of people. I'm telling you it's all nonsense. All of it. But I'm saying nothing more. It's got nothing to do with me. I just want to find my spare leggings and they've gone. Thieving bastards.'

'Tell you what,' said Camilla, 'Ondi, I'll ask for you to drive us to town.'

'Don't make me go back down that lane, Miss!'

'You will have to do it sooner or later, you might as well do it now. You can take me, Poppaea, Fabio and Julia. Once we're out of sight, Fabio can take over the reins and you can rest. You can doze all the way there -'

'I won't be able to Miss! Not knowing down one of the byways is a ditch with -'

'You needn't worry about that, lad,' said Lucco. 'I know for a fact that someone buried that body properly. Word came up with the butcher's lad this morning.'

'And,' Camilla continued, 'you can sleep while we're in town and you can sleep most of the way back. While we're there, I'll get you something from the wise woman and we'll tip you so well that you can buy the other slaves a treat. I bet you a denarius to a sestertius that they'll forget how cursed you are the minute you have something to share. Oh, and I tell you what. Go and wash in the sacred spring of Diffis.'

'Oh that'll help,' muttered Lucco. 'Add a bit of visible mud to some invisible stains.'

'I was thinking we could ask for her help,' explained Camilla.

'To help,' said Lucco, 'you have to exist.'

'I'll pretend I didn't hear that,' said Camilla. 'Ondi, get yourself washed and ready. We will be expecting to leave at the ninth hour.'

***

Even before they'd reached the point where they'd intended to swap, Ondi had dozed off, helped by an infusion which Poppaea had made up for herself but given to him. Fabio, sitting beside him on the seat at the front, took over the reins and rolled Ondi into the back, where the women covered him over and pushed him under their seats.

'Why's Ondi asleep?' said Julia.

'He's very tired and needs a rest,' said Camilla. 'But we needn't tell anyone at home. It's very boring to hear about people going to sleep, isn't it? Mummy says you were very brave last night.'

'I was. I wasn't scared of the thunder really. Especially after you came in.'

'I'm not scared of it at all. Next time we'll watch it together. It's really exciting when you see the world for a second and then it disappears.'

'I don't like the noise. Nurse said it was Grandfather's spirit stumbling about looking for the wine flagon.'

'You shouldn't listen to Nurse if she's going to say that sort of thing. The woman's clearly an idiot. Your grandfather's spirit had already found it and was busy snoring in Gwil's ear. I think that's why Gwil

90

overslept. He was so tired from listening to the snoring that when the morning came and the snoring stopped, he just fell asleep. Like that.' she pointed at Ondi then winked up at Poppaea. Poppaea shrugged. Julia giggled.

'Where's Daddy?'

'Oh, I think he's gone hunting for the Muse who gives him poetry ideas.'

'Is that true, Mummy?'

'Yes, of course.'

Poppaea rubbed her eyes and swallowed her nausea. She kept her eyes averted from the byway which held the ditch where she believed Briccio had been dumped. She thought of the sleeping draft she'd given to Ondi and longed to sip it herself but she was unsure. So unsure. The night, full of light and sound, Julia sobbing in her arms and the cold, empty bed where Marcellus should have been, had drained her. She had lain awake until dawn and now she was exhausted.

They passed Vulpo rattling and muttering his way up to the villa.

'Coulda sold a load down in town today. Coulda sold more than just what they'll pay me, miserable miserly…'

He may have had a point. Pecunia was livelier than normal. The market place was full. Farmers' wives were there with butter, eggs and herbs, butchers slapped flies from haunches of meat and furred game, trinket sellers vied for custom waving painted and dyed goods, moving them too fast to be inspected properly before purchase.

'Have you heard?' Gossip flowed past them as they trundled towards a hitching point.

'Ritonix is dead. Tryssa said there was nothing she could do.'

'Haunted, they say.'

'Bashed on the head, they say.'

'Thrown by his horse, they say.'

'Caught a fever, they say. Come on sudden.'

'The goddess is angry, they say.'

'What goddess?'

'The new one, old one, Diffo, Diffa, you know the one I mean.'

'Diffis? Why?'

'Ritonix doubted her powers.'

'Ritonix did?'

Fabio hitched up the wagon and helped the others down. Conscious of stares and glances, Poppaea pulled her veil across her face and bade Camilla do the same. At the corner of the forum, she whispered in Fabio's ear and stepped away from the others. Julia turned to follow her.

'Now my sweet,' she said, 'here are two sesterces. See if Cousin Camilla and Cousin Fabio can help you spend it. I just have a little business of my own to attend to, and I will see you back here near the temple very shortly.'

'But -' said Camilla.

'It's all right,' said Poppaea, 'I'm not going far and and everyone knows me.'

'I'm not sure that's a good thing. Marcellus would not be happy to know you were walking about on your own.'

'It doesn't matter what he'd think. He's not here to think anything. Now, stop worrying, I'll be back in a moment.'

She turned down a side street until she found the house she was looking for.

It was small but neat, whitewashed, the thatch fresh. A rose was painted on the wall and pots stood outside filled with medicinal plants.

The door opened before she had a chance to knock.

'Come in,' said Tryssa, 'I'm pleased to see you. There is someone here for you.'

Poppaea frowned and followed Tryssa to peek behind a curtain. Fast asleep on a pallet was Marcellus.

'What…?'

'Shh, come and sit.'

Trembling, Poppaea found a stool and sat.

'We were so worried. They said that Ritonix is dead and we thought Marcellus -'

'It was Marcellus who found Ritonix. It took him a while as it seems Ritonix had dragged himself towards home and then collapsed. The pony was nowhere to be seen, although it turned up later, sweating and shaking. By the time Marcellus located Ritonix, the thunderstorm had started and his own pony bolted. It took him quite a while to carry that unconscious form on his back to Pecunia.'

'What had happened?'

'To Ritonix? He'd been thrown, perhaps.'

'Perhaps?'

'His head was hurt. It was a bad injury; perhaps his skull was thinner than usual. There was nothing to be done.'

'How could you tell?'

'I know when I hear the breathing of a dying man, especially those whose heads have been crushed. I have sat by enough of them as they passed through the veil. All I can do is soften the pain.'

'And speed the passing.'

'I would not speak of such a thing, Poppaea.'

Poppaea thought of Ritonix crawling through the dirt, and retched.

'Let me bring you some infused ginger,' said Tryssa. 'That will help with the nausea.'

'I am -'

'You are with child again.'

'Yes.'

Tryssa brought a cup filled with a sweet, spiced brew. Poppaea sipped. She turned towards the curtained bed, listening for the soft familiar snores. Her shoulders sagged and with her left hand, she touched her stomach.

'Is Marcellus ill too?'

'A chill and exhaustion. I gave him a draught to help him sleep. Take him home with you when you go.' Tryssa laid her own hand over Poppaea's. 'How long have you been with child?'

'I don't know. Perhaps four months? I am afraid.'

'Because you do not want to lose another baby.'

'My mother-in-law has never known. Never known how many were lost. It always happened so early. It was impossible to be sure if they were boys or girls. I gave Lollia extra money for the laundress to keep quiet. This one has held longer, but I am so sick. I was sick with little Lucretia and with Julia. What if this is another girl?'

'Then it is another girl.'

'Can't you check for me, Tryssa? They say there is something you can do, hang a ring over me, test me with something, and you can tell. Will you do that for me?'

'No. What would you do with the information?'

'I ... I don't know.'

'Then I will not help you with that. I will help you with the nausea, I will be sure to be there with the midwife when the time comes. I will speak to Lucretia.

94

She and I ran together once, before her father had ideas of grandeur. Before she married a fool.'

'When she was kind?'

'I did not say that.'

Poppaea folded in on herself and started to sob.

'What does Marcellus say?'

'I haven't had the chance to tell him. I was going to, but he rushed out after Ritonix to try and catch him before he buried the body.'

'Indeed? That much has been kept quiet. How interesting.'

'Interesting? That he was last seen chasing after Ritonix and now Ritonix is dead?'

Tryssa looked askance. 'Do you believe Marcellus hurt Ritonix?'

Poppaea stared. 'No! No, it's not that.'

'Were you afraid he had come to harm himself?' said Tryssa.

'Of course I was! He's my husband. And now there's this man…'

'Ah yes,' said Tryssa, standing and brushing down her robe. 'I heard.'

'How?'

'He was asking round the forum about the family. It's a bit of a novelty: strange accent, different clothes, a good-looking man and the possibility of stirring things up for Lucretia,' Tryssa grinned. 'I'm sorry to say it, but people talk. They like a bit of scandal, especially if it might bring someone down a peg or two. Still, I wonder if this Gwil saw anything to explain what befell Ritonix.'

'He just wants to usurp Marcellus. If he does, what will happen to us? Can you see? Will you see for me?'

'If I could, I would not.'

Poppaea sniffed and wiped her eyes. 'Perhaps I should pay more deference to Diffis. Perhaps having been woken, she is angry we are too slow to show her homage.'

'I doubt that.'

'Nothing has been quite right since she was rediscovered.'

'No, indeed,' said Tryssa. 'No, indeed.'

Chapter Thirteen – Lunchtime
June 15th (ante diem xvii Kalendas Julias)

While the small party returned from Pecunia, Vulpo had set up his brazier and was toasting garlic flatbreads to eat with honey and cheese. He seemed discontented and distracted, muttering as he turned flat cakes of sausage which smelt so strongly of spice, pepper and garam that it was hard to be certain what meat they contained.

Gwil reclined under the sun and looked up at the villa. The front, with a portico over a large oak door, was plastered and whitewashed, with flowers painted on it. It was effectively a sort of large porch built onto the rest of the house. Just within was an atrium in the Roman style, complete with plinths on which stood various gods and nymphs. The gods' faces were indistinct, neither Roman nor Celtic, as if they wondered who and where they were and why they had to put up with freezing in what was effectively an outhouse with a hole in the ceiling.

Beyond the atrium was a central dining room, various rooms tacked on one at a time over the years apparently as afterthoughts, and a damp courtyard.

'It is an unusual design,' he said aloud. 'I have never quite seen anything quite like this villa.'

'I'm sure your mother told you all about it,' said Lucretia.

Gwil smiled and sipped from his goblet. 'She never came here. And of course, father died before I was born.'

'How convenient. Let me get you some more wine.' She summoned a slave.

'No, thank you. It's only noon yet I'm still sleepy. It's very strange. They tell me there was a thunderstorm last night, yet I heard nothing of it.'

'How very peculiar. I assume then that you were not bothered by the shade of my late husband.'

'If he was there, then he was sleeping as soundly. Perhaps we shared the same wine.'

'My husband did not share wine. And when he was in his cups, his snores were louder than any thunder.'

Urbanicus came over, followed by a slave who proffered a platter of sausage cakes. Gwil picked one up, sniffed it and put it down again.

'After you,' he said.

'What is your real story?' said Urbanicus. 'Who are you, and what do you hope to achieve?'

'My father married my mother in Londinium.'

'I knew your father well. I don't recall his marrying anyone.'

'It was somewhat secret. But he registered her as his wife nonetheless. I have the paperwork.'

'Where?'

'Safe.'

'Surely you trust the people whom you believe are family.'

'Surely. But slaves, you know…'

'Indeed.'

'My brother would have told me if he had married,' Lucretia insisted. 'I was newly married myself and expecting Marcellus. We were close, Rhys and I.'

'Ah yes,' said Gwil. He sat up and stretched, putting his nearly full goblet of wine on the bench beside him. 'My mother told me that my father had two younger sisters. She said he described them thus: "Tullia dreams too much, Lucretia -" Now what was the phrase she said he used? It was something like "Lucretia plans too

98

much." Something like that. Maybe the word was stronger than "plans". We got the impression of dogged determination.'

'One has to prepare ahead.'

'Indeed. Incidentally, where is my cousin Marcellus? Was he so late home last night he's still sleeping?'

'Where he is is none of your business,' said Urbanicus.

'Quite,' agreed Lucretia. 'And when he returns, he will explain that this is my land and that I will one day leave it to him as the oldest male descendent of my father.'

'It is my land,' said Gwil with a confident smile. 'But even if it were not, doesn't the land belong to Marcellus now that his father is dead?'

'Marcellus does as he is told. My father left the land to me. And I will choose to whom it goes when I die. Which, may I point out, I do not intend to do with any alacrity.'

'Mmm. And this spring. In the town, they said a great deal about the spring. They were looking forward to the pilgrims who will come and worship. They'll make the town and everything around it prosper. It -'

'What made you come here now?' asked Urbanicus. 'You must be nearly forty.'

'My other grandfather withheld a great deal of information, wanting me to build up his business in Londinium. I wasn't entirely sure where my birthright was.'

'How convenient,' repeated Lucretia.

'When should I expect to meet Marcellus?' said Gwil. 'Perhaps we could agree something between us.'

Lucretia stood at the sound of wheels.

'Ah, here come the ones who went to town. I can't imagine what's taken them so long. Prisca has been sulking all morning because they went without her.' She walked away.

Gwil lifted the sausage cake again and sniffed it. He touched a little with his tongue, put it down again and called over one of the dogs. Not knowing him, the dog padded over slowly, her tail down, her ears pricked. She smelt the cake.

'Don't!' said Urbanicus, knocking it from his hand and picking it off the ground before the dog could eat it.

'Why not?' said Gwil, 'I'm not hungry, perhaps she is.'

'We do not feed our dogs while we eat ourselves,' said Urbanicus. 'It is not civilised.'

Gwil shrugged, stood, and wandered over to Pomponius, who was sketching on a piece of bark with some charcoal.

'This house,' he said. 'Its design is quite unique.'

'It started as a round-house,' said Pomponius. 'Lyn, that is my grandfather-in-law - Lucretia and Tullia's father - he was a crafty one. He was already rich in land and cattle and one day it occurred to him that he could be richer if he made friends with the Romans. His wife was half Roman of course. She died when Tullia was born. Anyway, when he Romanised the family he Romanised the house too, until he ended up with this monstrosity.'

'Did he do it because he liked the Roman style, or wanted to impress the Romans?'

'Mmm,' Pomponius considered. 'I think mostly the former. You know what roundhouses are like, dark and smoky and full of people.'

'Yes,' said Gwil. 'They're convivial.'

'But chiefly dark. Although this isn't exactly a classical villa, is it? I imagine it's something of an abomination to an artist's eye. Perhaps you don't see that.'

'It's certainly unique. But the atrium and courtyard don't seem very suitable for the climate.'

'Oh, that was Porcius.' said Pomponius. 'He had delusions of grandeur and Lucretia's money. I imagine you live somewhere very fancy in Londinium.'

Gwil shrugged. 'Not really. It's one upper floor of a large building. We can see a long way but it's not like countryside.'

'And you really are Rhys's secret son?'

'I am indeed.'

'And you think this land should be yours?'

They both fell silent and looked at the view; the valley sloping towards the town, mosquitoes twinkling over the marsh, the distant river, marking the boundaries of wind-bent trees, entwined hedges and shallow ditches, and the dark lumpy slopes leading up to the forest.

'Whatever anyone says, the forest belongs to itself,' said Pomponius, recalling the horror of the corpse in a shaft of dull rain-flecked light. Gwil frowned, returning his gaze to the cultivated land where slaves toiled in the sun to break and feed the clumpy dark earth into fertility.

'It's all my land, forest and all,' said Gwil. 'I am the eldest son of the eldest son. And if I weren't and anything happened to Marcellus, then shouldn't it go to Prisca's - I mean your son? Or perhaps to Tullia's son Fabio? Have you ever thought about that?'

'That's not how Lucretia's father left things.'

'So I hear. But how do you feel about it?'

'We have discussed it and I am content. I have other things on my mind. Lucretia says that the house and land will be Marcellus's, but the proceeds from the spring will be shared between Lucretia, Tullia and their children. Naturally in Prisca's case that means they will be shared with me, and maybe even come directly to me. But I intend to put my fair share in. I'm designing trinkets and amulets with the goddess's image on for the faithful to purchase and take home as blessings. I'll hire craftsmen to make them.'

'Really? How very altruistic of you,' said Gwil, peering at the charcoal scribbles in Pomponius's hands. 'What does the goddess look like, by the way?'

'Oh,' said Pomponius. 'Well obviously since Diffis has been lost, er, forgotten, er, *neglected* all these years, her likeness is not entirely certain.'

'But we're surrounded, according to Lucretia, by her female descendents.'

'Are we? Of course, I mean yes. I imagine the family resemblance has come down somehow.'

'Lucretia?'

Pomponius glanced over at his mother-in-law and shuddered.

'Or your wife Prisca? That is Prisca isn't it? The er … curvy one who's in, er, deep discussions with Tullia.'

'Yes, that's Prisca, but you'd need her to be thinking about gladiators to get a bright and hopeful expression.'

'Gladiators?'

'Don't ask. There's my niece Camilla. She's a girl. I'm not sure she'd stand still long enough to draw or sculpt though.'

Gwil watched the party climbing down from the wagon. Fabio helped Poppaea alight first. She was

102

drawn and grey, the smile she put on for her daughter forced. She was bundled in a dress which looked a little too large and a veil which was slipping from brown curls. Camilla was younger, little more than a child. Her hair was darker, coiled around her head with strands curling loose around her rosy face where the veil had disarranged it. She was chatting and singing to Julia, her face mobile and her expressions changing as she sang. Yes, it was hard to imagine her sitting still for long. The slave and Fabio together assisted a slim man in his late thirties to the ground. He appeared unstable on his feet, his head lolling.

Gwil raised his eyebrows. 'Who's the drunk?' he asked.

Pomponius frowned, 'It's Marcellus.' He watched Lollia step forward to usher his brother-in-law into the house. 'He must be ill.'

'Not fit to discuss things with?'

'Maybe not just now.'

'Ah well, It can wait. Come, Pomponius,' said Gwil, rising and stretching his arms. 'I'm not convinced about this street vendor's food, are you?'

'Well, now you come to mention it, it doesn't look so good today. I haven't had any yet. It doesn't seem as if anyone fancies it much. I believe a new cook is coming later to prepare a feast.'

'A feast? In my honour?'

'Er no. The Decurion's coming for dinner again. There are things to discuss.'

'Really, how intriguing. Let's take the wagon back to town, you and I. I will treat you to a meal at the tavern and you can tell me *all* about your wonderful in-laws. What do you think?'

Pomponius took in a deep breath which sucked in the smell of rancid sausage meat and coughed.

'I should probably stay here with the family.'

Gwil clapped him about the shoulders. 'Oh but I'm family, remember. And besides, I gather there's a troupe of dancing girls in town. We might be able to see them rehearse.'

'Really? Do you think we could?' Pomponius said. He put the piece of bark down and wiped charcoaled fingers on his tunic, then brushed off the black marks and smoothed his head. 'Well, I suppose it would be cultural.' He smiled. 'Come on then, let's go.'

Chapter Fourteen - Foreign Objects
June 15th (ante diem xvii Kalendas Julias)

It always seems a bit mean, giving the things we won't eat to the pig, thought Fabio, watching Lucco take Vulpo's sausage cake towards the sty. *Especially pork.*

It was peaceful. The men, and after them, the women had all bathed and retired to various parts of the villa. Camilla, fresh and fragrant, had wandered off in the direction of the orchard, where the pony was. *What's she up to?* Fabio mused. *She's never been interested in animals before.*

The evening was hot again and Fabio felt the benefit of his own bath seep away. The cool of the cold pool had been a short-lived relief, and now he had started to sweat again. He sat with his lyre and plucked the strings at random, waiting for a tune to come. The general ambience of the place did not help. Somewhere towards the back of the villa he could hear arguing and earthenware clattering as the new cook settled in.

'What's your song about, darling?' Tullia sat next to him, resting her head against the whitewashed wall. Her hair was down, still drying. In the evening light Fabio, not generally given to considering his mother as a separate entity, saw what Camilla would look like one day, if she lived until her late forties, and perhaps if some of her impatience was replaced by contemplation. Their mother's hair flowed in soft curls. It was mostly dark but white at the front and threaded with silver.

'I have an urge to write something about badgers,' he said.

'How very odd. Where's Camilla?'

'Feeding the pony.'

'Are you sure you haven't a fever darling?'

There was a crash from the kitchen and some harsh guttural shouting followed by a girl's sniffling and some low guttural growling.

'I do wish Lucretia would hire someone we could understand.'

'I'm not sure those words needed translation really, Mother. I expect he's swearing at Blod. Most people do.'

'Here come Anguis and Olivarius in the chariot. What a lot of dust it throws up.'

'That'll bring Camilla back from the orchard. She'll be galloping herself, rushing to put her best sandals on. As if he's interested in her sandals.'

'Who, the Decurion?'

'She'd rather marry the pig than Anguis.' He plucked a soft phrase, melancholy, trickling.

'Is that for Diffis?'

Fabio shrugged and put the lyre down, 'No. Diffis is … elusive. I can't quite feel her presence,' he said.

Tullia shook her head. 'Nor can I,' she said.

***

'I thought you might enjoy some entertainment this evening,' said Anguis, shifting his thin frame on the bench. 'I know that some of you like dancing and I felt that perhaps your female slaves, redoubtable as they are, might not be quite, er, trained up.'

He watched as Blod, red-eyed, sniffed her way around the dining-room with a platter of figs and then contemplated Lollia. He shrivelled a little under Lollia's glare.

'Oh yes, I like a bit of dancing,' said Pomponius, slicking the strands of his hair round his pate.

Prisca rolled her eyes.

106

'Not, I should add,' continued Anguis, 'those provocative squirmings that many might think of. I prefer something more classical.'

He clapped his hands and two musicians entered, one playing a high-pitched slow tune on a flute, while the other accompanied on a tambour at a rhythm not quite in time with his companion. Two sturdy women tiptoed in after them, waving silken scarves and whirling in opposite circles, jewelled feet pattering on the mosaic. They were followed by a slender young man whose gyrations made the women's scarves flutter into the dishes of garam, then stick to the linen dresses clinging to their matronly frames.

Anguis reclined with his eyes half closed. He tapped his fingers out of rhythm, a dreamy smile on his angular face.

'This place gets duller by the second,' murmured Camilla, and laid her head down on the bench.

'I'd hardly describe the last few days as dull,' said Poppaea. She was picking at slivers of fowl, wincing as a sticky scarf flicked close to her face.

Pomponius slumped. Fabio shook his head in despair and started to throw crumbs onto the mosaic.

With a squeak just one counterpoint above the music, a mouse ran across the floor and over the feet of the dancers.

The larger of the dancers shrieked, lifting her feet and kicking a dish of garum onto the floor. Her arms flailed until she caught the young man in the face and knocked him backwards into Prisca.

'Unhand my wife,' snapped Pomponius, as the youth struggled to right himself, slipping in the spilt anchovy sauce and floundering against Prisca's full breasts as she tried to help him stand.

The smaller dancer, scowling at the others, kept dancing. Then the cat shot across the room and the mouse, making a sharp u-turn, sped back across the floor. The larger dancer lifted her jewelled feet as if she was walking on burning coals and flung herself at the other two dancers, clinging to them like a drowning swimmer.

Anguis clapped his hands and waved the troupe out of the room.

Fabio applauded. 'I never knew the classics were so diverting,' he said, 'I should have studied them more.'

'Perhaps I should have considered the size of the available space before I brought dancers,' said Anguis. 'Never mind. That is not the only entertainment. I *could* ask Olivarius to recite some poetry. Classic poetry, that is. None of this modern stuff.'

He absorbed the frowning stares. Even Marcellus seemed annoyed. Perhaps it was the slight on modern verse such as his own. But he could say nothing, having lost his voice.

'So,' Anguis continued. 'I thought you might appreciate some mysteries.'

The family brightened up.

'I've brought some artefacts to show you, from my travels at the very edges of the Empire.'

He paused. 'I mean the edges of the Empire that aren't West Britain. Olivarius, go and get my bag.'

Olivarius stood up. 'Perhaps Lady Camilla would like to help me,' he said.

'I don't think so,' said Lucretia. 'Camilla, stay where you are and look after Poppaea. She is looking peaky again. Fabio, assist Olivarius.'

Camilla slumped and glared at Poppaea. Poppaea mouthed 'sorry.'

'And Gwil,' said Lucretia, 'while we are waiting, perhaps you can tell the Decurion our family history, going back to before the Romans came. After all, only a family member would know all the detail.'

Gwil smirked and opened his mouth. Pomponius, draining his goblet, grimaced.

'In the name of Diana of Ephesus,' cried Anguis, 'I do not want to hear another tale of woe and disgruntlement. I have been from shore to shore of this great Empire and let me tell you, there are few places where people complain more than here. I put it down to the weather. Try not to grumble about what is lost, but think on what you have gained: the drainage, a single currency, protection of legions trained to withstand the hounds of Hades. Emperors who are gods, gods who -'

'So you keep saying. But what about taxes, foriegn control, martial law, divine emperors who die a lot, mad emperors, gods who, immortal or otherwise, wouldn't last five minutes in a British winter dressed the way they are, and urbanisation separating us from the natural world which holds our spirits and our ... er -' Camilla burst out.

'Lucretia,' snapped Anguis, 'keep your niece under control. In particular, keep her away from unsuitable young men. I thought, young woman, you preferred life in Glevum, which you seem to consider a positive metropolis.'

'Well, it's got good tradespeople,' conceded Camilla. 'But I've been corrupted by city life so that I've lost my sense of the oak and stream, the -'

'Camilla. Desist.' said Lucretia.

'Anyway,' whispered Prisca in Camilla's ear, 'think of it this way: oak and stream is one thing, but a young man who's seen the eastern sea could be even more interesting and still take you shopping.'

She nodded towards Olivarius as he and Fabio returned carrying two bags, one leather bag, long and slender, and another smaller bag of some soft material.

'Ah,' said Anguis, 'Here we are.' He pulled an ornate box from the smaller bag and from within that, a fine gold pendant. 'This is an amulet from Egypt - or is it Palmyra? I can't quite recall. Either way, it holds the golden eyelashes of a goddess.'

'Didn't she want them?' said Fabio.

Anguis ignored him. 'They are so fine, they cannot be seen,' he continued. 'Holding this amulet will comfort the broken-hearted as their tears drop on this carving of a dragon - or is it an eagle? It's rather stylised. Anyway, this amulet is so rare that it cost half a month's salary and a small slave to purchase.'

'And does it work?' asked Prisca.

'Of course it does! Do you take me for a fool?'

There was half a beat of silence.

'So,' said Pomponius, as the Decurion's eyes narrowed. 'How did you test it? Were you heart-broken and wept on this and -'

'Well naturally nothing has ever broken my heart,' said Anguis.

'He'd have to have one for a start,' muttered Camilla.

'But it came with testimonials in Greek and hieroglyph, setting out the wondrous stories from centuries of comfort which are in its history. See! Olivarius can read them to you.' He waved some crisp rolls of parchment.

'They seem rather new to me,' said Fabio.

'Well they're facsimile, of course. The originals, which they showed me, were barely legible and crumbling.'

110

'Let's try the amulet on Blod,' said Prisca. 'Get her to weep on it and see what happens. All we'll have to do is mention Briccio.'

'It won't work for slaves,' snapped Anguis. 'They cry too much. Their tears would wear it out. And slaves tend towards cynicism, I find.'

'In other words, they are not easily deceived,' said Fabio.

'My boy, you are missing the point,' said Anguis. 'Lucretia, I sincerely suggest you do not allow this boy to get too involved in "rediscovering" artefacts for Diffis. I feel he is not showing the right level of -'

'Gullibility?' said Fabio.

'No, business acumen.'

'But you're the one who spent all that money on some invisible eyelashes inside a sealed box with scribbles on.'

'Who said I bought it?' said Anguis, with an enigmatic smile. 'I simply possess it. And now I am presenting it to you, dear Lucretia, as a token of my commitment to our joint enterprise, and in honour of the grief you must feel for poor dear Porcius.'

Lucretia took the amulet, and after a pause put it round her neck.

'Should you weep in the night...' said Anguis.

'I will find comfort in its golden allure,' said Lucretia.

Anguis nodded. 'And that is not all. Olivarius, show them the next thing.'

From the longer bag Olivarius pulled out a tube, around six feet long. Rope was wound at various points along its length.

The family exchanged glances.

Olivarius drew out some gloves and, donning them, pulled out a locked wooden box and a key.

'More magic, sorry, sacred relics?' asked Urbanicus.

'No,' said Anguis, 'watch. Only the foolish would touch these with bare hands.'

Olivarius unlocked the box and pulled out three darts. They were slender as arrows and nearly as long.

'And where do these hail from?'

'Ah now, this is very curious. They hail from a land beyond the west.'

The family exchanged glances. 'There is nothing beyond the west,' said Fabio, 'except Hibernia and beyond that, the Otherworld.'

'Well, according to the sailor from whom they were purchased, these come from wild and unimaginable lands so uncivilised they make Pecunia look like Elysium. Sailors speak of vast oceans, rivers the size of countries, and wild forests; trees full of creatures like jewels and plants which eat insects; snakes longer than a willow tree which eat birds. They tell of hot constant rains which make Western Britain appear arid and frozen. And in those lands, they say, are wild men who hunt monkeys with darts, blown through tubes. This is such a tube.'

'That's ridiculous,' said Pomponius. 'What damage would a dart like that do?'

'Let's try it on your pig and find out,' said Anguis, 'Have you a dispensable slave to do the blowing in case it goes wrong?'

'Not really,' said Lucretia. 'I've lost one cook already and don't want to lose the next. Ondi seems to have some kind of sleeping sickness at the moment. Blod would probably soak it with her drizzling. Lucco is essential for keeping all the others in order. And I wouldn't trust Lollia anywhere near any kind of weapon. She is lethal enough with tweezers. The rest of them are just plain useless. Here, Gwil, you can use it.

112

You're keen to show how you would fit in. Or are you scared?'

Gwil rose and went to stand with Olivarius. He checked over the tube and the darts. 'Do the people who use them use gloves?'

'I don't think so,' said Olivarius

'Then perhaps there's nothing to fear.'

Olivarius frowned. 'They say that the darts are deadly.'

Gwil shrugged. 'Come on then. Where's piggy?'

With some grumbling the others rose, gazing ruefully at the remainder of the feast. Lucretia summoned Urbanicus to take her arm, and sent Lollia to arrange for something to be put on the ground to stop her feet from being mired.

'Thank goodness for small mercies,' muttered Prisca. 'I am sick of my shoes being ruined. But I do think this is ridiculous. Has Snooticus ever seen a pig? How would a tiny dart like that even pierce its skin?'

'How do you know so much about a pig's skin?' said Camilla.

'I'm married to Pomponius, aren't I?'

'I'm really not sure about this,' said Tullia, pulling at Fabio. 'That poor pig. Why should we harm him?'

'Mother, the pig is being fattened up for slaughter. It's going to be harmed one way or another eventually.'

'Yes, but this bodes ill.'

'Well you're the one who understands boding.'

'Everything is wrong. Everything.'

'It's just a pig, Mother. And as Prisca says, that tiny thing will just probably bounce off. With any luck, the pig will be so annoyed it'll leap over the wall of the sty and knock Lucretia flat.'

'That's very disrespectful thing to say about your aunt.'

113

Fabio shrugged. 'In fact, I might line everyone up so the pig can knock them all down one after the other. Not you of course, Mother.'

They gathered near the sty, Prisca pressing her veil against her nose and lifting her skirts to keep them off any potentially dusty grass. Poppaea also covered her nose and mouth, her skin pallid. Gwil glanced at her, watching Marcellus put his arm around her. She remained rigid and looked steadfastly at the pig. It was rooting round the sty and grunting as it munched on scraps. Wandering in the grimy straw, it glanced at the entourage out of the corners of its small, irritated eyes.

Camilla's veil had slipped from her head and her hair floated in the breeze. It flowed unbraided down her back like a waterfall.

'Olivarius!' snapped Anguis. 'What are you staring at? Pay attention. Show Gwil what to do.'

'I've never done it myself,' said Olivarius.

'Then work it out.'

Olivarius, Gwil and Fabio all examined the pipe.

'Which end is which, do you reckon?' muttered Gwil. 'The stained bit or the really stained bit?'

'The bit which is easiest to hold, I suppose,' said Olivarius.

Gwil peered down the tube. 'Then you put the dart in here and hold it like this…'

'I think so.'

'Then you blow?' suggested Fabio.

Olivarius shrugged. 'That's what Anguis said they said.'

The first dart slipped out of the tube before Gwil could balance it, landing an inch or so away from Lucretia's foot and making her step onto Urbanicus's.

The pig stopped munching to watch. Its small eyes seemed to be narrowing.

Gwil managed to blow the second dart with mild force. It bounced off the pig's rump and landed in a pile of muck. The pig squealed and stared, first at the dart and then at Gwil. Then he backed up as if deciding what to do next.

The third dart hit the pig firmly between the eyes and trembled in his flesh, embedded for sixty seconds in which every heart could be heard pounding. Then it fell out.

With a roar, the pig ran towards the fence, crashing against the wicker, backing up and crashing again. The fence bent and bowed. Gwil backed away and knocked Anguis into the old straw.

'Told you,' whispered Fabio to Tullia.

'Piggy, piggy!' called Lucco.

The pig ignored him and squealed again.

'Piggy, piggy!' Lucco shouted louder and rattled a wooden box. Inside were the uneaten sausage patties.

The pig paused in his third attempt at breaching the fence and sniffed. As the patties landed at his feet, the pig touched them with his snout and then wolfed them down. He paused, dribbling. His eyes turned red, crossed, then glazed. Then he fell over, twitched once and was still.

'I knew I was right to avoid those sausages,' said Gwil. 'Either that tradesman needs locking up or the person who ordered the food does.'

He stared at Lucretia, who stared back, unblinking.

'Oh, any housewife can tell you how pork spoils when it's out in the sun all day,' she said, turning towards the villa. 'Come, Anguis, have you any other artefacts? This is turning into a fascinating evening.'

Chapter Fifteen - That's Entertainment
June 17th (ante diem xv Kalendas Julias)

Two days passed. Whenever possible, Marcellus sat in the bedroom, writing frantically in the light of the small window as if trying to work out a logic problem. When he regained his voice, he focused on Gwil. 'Show me your proof and I'll talk,' he croaked. Gwil shrugged, smiled his slow smile and replied 'I'll wait till you're better. It's all quite complex.'

Poppaea sat on the edge of their bed, then traced her finger along the frieze of stencilled lilies on the walls, then rearranged her pots and boxes on the shelf. After all these years of listening rather than talking, she didn't know how to tell her husband what worried her.

'Marcellus -' she said, but her words were drowned by his coughing. She poured him a draught of honey and goat's milk.

His smile was vague as he kissed her cheek gently and rasped out, 'thank you, darling.' After a sip, he said 'Poppaea...' But talking made him cough again. His eyes ran. Under her hand, his brow was still hot.

'Marcellus,' she said, 'I need to talk to you about something.'

'D-don't worry,' he spluttered. 'Gwil's an imposter.'

'It's not that. It's something else. I -'

Lucretia's raucous voice could be heard in the dining room, chivvying Lollia, demanding Poppaea.

'Oh gods, your mother -'

'Poppaea,' whispered Marcellus, trying not to start the cough again. 'Darling, I need to concentrate. See here...' He held out a piece of parchment, forgetting she couldn't read.

116

'It's lovely,' she said, staring down at it, wondering whether a fever would improve his poetry. Marcellus's hopeful look faded. She tried to force an eager smile. 'Will you read it to me?'

He shook his head, dropped his hand and slumped back in the chair.

'It doesn't make sense,' he said. His face was pale and thin, his eyes dark from headache.

Lucretia called more loudly for her daughter in law.

Still holding the parchment, Poppaea stepped into the gloomy hall. She collided with one of the slaves lurking outside the door. He was one of the more dim-witted ones, bundled in a cloak. He bowed in deep apology.

Another shriek came from the dining room.

'Give this back to Master Marcellus,' said Poppaea, passing the parchment to the slave. He grunted at her. Lollia would have her work cut out training this one up.

'Poppaea!' Lucretia was marching towards her. 'Stop dawdling. Are you deaf?'

'What do you want?' snapped Poppaea.

'I want courtesy to start with,' said Lucretia. '"How may I help you" would have been preferable. And when you are suitably polite, I want company. Everyone keeps wandering off, and I can't understand a word Marcellus is saying at the moment. Why does no-one think of me?'

She gripped Poppaea's arm and marched her towards the door. From outside came the distant bang, crash and profanity of building.

Work was now well underway. The two women made their way up the slope so that Lucretia could interrogate the mason. There was no hot spring on the land as there was at Aquae Sulis, therefore a significant hypocaust would be required.

'Trouble is, missus,' said the mason, 'the slope's a bugger and the water pressure isn't very strong. It sorta seeps when what we want is gush.'

'I'm sure you'll find a way round any issues,' said Lucretia. 'To begin with, the baths need not be quite as big or involved as the ones at Aquae Sulis.'

'Lotta water needed for three pools,' said the mason, sucking his teeth, 'and then there's changing rooms and latrines and presumably you'll need space for stalls where the faithful can buy wax tablets and bits of tin to write their prayers on, and little images of the goddess and wine etc. You know, the essentials to worship.'

The mason originated from Iberia. The west British hills and woods were alien to him, uncivilised in their wildness. In full sun, they felt open and exciting: birds chattered, streams trickled, the slopes undulated like sleeping giants and the local people chattered and gossiped and delved for information. When (quite possibly on the same day) the skies grew grey and rain started, the hills and woodlands were as secret and brooding as the locals after too much mead. Still, a job was a job and the one thing he knew was that where there's a god there's money. After all, he figured, the holier the place, the easier it is to make a pile of money.

But despite the morning sun, the workmen shivered. They were from further west and a little north, where the slopes soared and plunged and rivers raced. They eyed the spring with doubt and glanced at each other.

'Usually,' said one, 'where there's a sacred spring, there's tributes. Things people leave for the goddess. This is just dampness.' He whispered, as if afraid he would be overheard by the leaning trees.

'She was forgotten a long time,' said Urbanicus. 'I expect as you dig you'll find old things, things which haven't yet rotted. Probably tomorrow, when you come back to work.'

'If everyone forgot her, won't she be angry?' said another.

'Sleeping,' amended Lucretia, 'she has been sleeping. And therefore unable to bless anyone, but now I've found her again. She won't be angry. She will honour all who honour her,'

'What are her gifts again?' asked the foreman, popping a nut into his mouth.

'To the most faithful, she gives long life and second sight,' said Lucretia.

The workmen exchanged glances, rolled their eyes and hefted their shovels.

'Doesn't take second sight to know it'll take more than a sleeping goddess to give us slaves the chance of life beyond thirty,' muttered one. He turned his back and plunged his shovel into the earth.

Before lunch Marcellus saddled up the horse and left the homestead. His explanation was punctuated by so much coughing it was unclear where he was going.

'Will you join us in Pecunia later?' asked Poppaea. He shrugged and held her tight.

'It may take longer,' he croaked.

'When you come home, maybe we could walk in the orchard and talk,' she whispered. But it seemed he hadn't heard. Kissing her again, he mounted the horse and slumped in the saddle, rode away.

Alone in the orchard, Poppaea sat in the grass and hugged herself. She had never thought Marcellus's inattention would make her feel so lost. She closed her eyes and tried to recall some of his verse, but after ten years of tuning most of it out she could remember nothing, save something she'd once heard him whisper when she had been half asleep.

'*Oh quiet beauty,*
With soft, secret eyes.
My words fail me,
Unable to voice the love
That bursts my heart.
I cannot read
your smile and kiss.
Please let it be true
That your heart
Bursts with love for me as well.'

'You seem sad, Poppaea.' It was Gwil.

Poppaea opened her eyes and looked up. He stood against the sun so that it made him appear to glow. This man was so familiar, and so disturbing.

'Lady Poppaea Silvia if you please,' she said and stood up, pulling her veil over her dark coiled braids.

'Come now, we are cousins.'

'We are not,' she said, 'and you know it.'

'Then let's be friends. Walk with me.'

'No, I must go and play with Julia. '

'She could play hide and seek with her father. He's very good at being elusive.'

'He is still not over the chill he caught. It's not fair of you to badger him so. You have waited long enough.'

'Perhaps. And what will you do when I prove my claim?'

'You won't. Incidentally, there is a new pig. Do you think you could keep away from her? We would like to have pork in the winter. We have a sow this time and expect piglets. You may wish to note that in the case of swine, as in many creatures, the female of the species is not as weak as she appears.'

'It was not I who killed the previous pig.'

'That's debatable. You strike me as the sort to avoid taking responsibility.'

'Do you think so? Perhaps you're judging too soon. Anyway, it was nothing to do with that dart. The pig died after eating those rotten sausage patties. And if he hadn't, he would have been slaughtered eventually. In fact we could have eaten him after he died.'

'Would you have fancied it?'

'Well, no. Are you coming to the entertainment this afternoon?'

Poppaea could make out the workmen up the hill, digging and moving earth and stone. Even at this distance it was possible to hear an odd combination of rhythmic song and explosive swearing.

'Yes, I am,' she said.

'I'm sure Marcellus will join us later,' said Gwil. 'And this evening maybe I'll bring proof of my claim.'

'You have no proof.'

'And do not worry, Lady Poppaea Silvia. If Marcellus does not return, I will take care of you.' He stepped forward and reached as if to touch her shoulder. She shrugged and moved away.

'I can take care of myself,' she said. 'If necessary.'

***

The wagon had to make two trips to transport everyone to Pecunia. The pony's knees trembled as he arrived on his final trip, the wagon loaded with Lucretia, Urbanicus, Tullia, Gwil and Fabio. He all but leant against the hitching post as they descended. Ondi, his tremors under control, bustled to lead his masters to the makeshift theatre which had been created on hastily constructed wooden tiers.

It was mid-afternoon and the sun scorched through linen and cloth. Women fanned themselves and dabbed

121

at their faces with scented cloth. Make-up and perfumed oils melted and trickled.

The family sat on cushions in the place of honour with Anguis and Olivarius. The theatre was normally a sloping and therefore difficult patch of open ground off the forum. Later in the afternoon as the sun dropped, perhaps the buildings on the west might offer some shade, but at the moment it was stifling.

There was a screen behind the space left open for a stage. Hidden beyond that, invisible performers prepared. The gathering audience could hear little disconnected phrases and trills as singers and musicians tuned up. Snatches of song and random rhythms mixed with barely distinguishable verse, various animal noises and the rasp and clash of metal against metal.

Those in the lower, cheaper seats covered their noses as the stench of animals seeped from behind the screen.

As the audience settled it grew restive, fidgeting and muttering. Before it could grow too loud, a trumpet blasted and a lion roared. Or at least it was presumed to be a lion. Truth be told, the number of people in the crowd who had ever seen a lion could have been counted on one hand with two fingers missing.

'*Hail! Hail!*' bellowed a voice from behind the screens. '*Listen and attend, for soon you will see a spectacle fit for Emperors. A story nearly forgotten, of maidens, widows, heroes, ravenous beasts and beneficent gods.*' The voice dropped. '*Shhh, be very quiet ... who approaches?*'

There was complete silence, as the audience leaned forward to see what would happen next.

A lyre started to play off-stage. There no particular tune, just a simple repetitive sound reminiscent of drifting leaves or trickling water. From

122

behind the screen came a stream of girls dressed in green, who pirouetted and danced before forming a triangle and starting to dance in synchronisation.

'*We are the dryads, waving in the breeze!*' they sang.

All around, members of the audience started a running commentary.

'Daddy, what's dryad?'

'Shh, pay attention.'

Another group of girls appeared, dressed in grey blue, running with blue ribbons in between the others.
'*We are naiads, trickling through the trees!*'

'What's a snaiad?'

'Shh!'

'*Behold*!' The unseen speaker made them jump. '*A maiden is lost in the woods!*'

Aurelia, her hair redder than before and wearing a mustard coloured dress which stretched across her full breasts, slipped from behind the screen and danced between the dryads. She mimed her woe and terror as she skipped and spun.

'Maiden my ar - aunt Bron.'

'Have you seen the colour of that hair?'

'Must be foreign.'

'Or Iceni.'

'Or she got it out of a plant.'

'Is there a plant that turns your head red, Mum? What plant? Can I get some?'

'No you can't, no daughter of mine is going to dye her hair or paint her face like that.'

'It's not fair. Eira's mother lets her paint her face. You're just so -'

'*Beware fair maiden! The forest holds danger! Here comes a lion!*'

123

A large creature bounced out from behind the screen and ran circles around the maiden. It was nearly chest height, its coat a similar colour to her dress and a large shaggy mane of black obscuring its eyes. Its long, shaved tail was tipped with a brown tuft. Loud roars sounded but it was hard to think they were coming from the lion, who was jumping up at the girl with its tongue hanging out, and wagging its tail furiously.

'Is that a lion, Daddy?'

'Must be, son. Never realised how much they looked like deer hounds.'

Aurelia waved her arms and wailed. Bits of her wobbled.

'I'll save you!' shouted someone from the lower seats.

'No you won't, you peasant!' yelled Pomponius, half-rising. 'Don't be scared, Aurelia!'

Prisca pulled him back down. 'Sit still, you stupid slug.'

The audience stamped and yelled.

'Run girl, run!'

'Scream for help, darling, let's see you inflate those lungs!'

'Eat her up, lion!'

The lion bounced more enthusiastically and pulled at the dress, which Aurelia clasped tightly to avoid losing it. She staggered a little under the assault but continued to bellow out her song of terror:

I am lost and on my own
Surely am I doomed to die
A virgin maiden, all alone
Will anybody hear my cry?
A ravenous beast attacketh me!
Get down you moron!'

124

The lion woofed, jumped down, ran off, cocked its leg against the edge of the screen then started to race round the arena, its tongue lolling, saliva spraying and the mane sliding over its right eye.

'I didn't know lions barked, Daddy.'

'Educational, that's what this is.'

'Is a moron a kind of lion?'

'*Never fear!*' boomed the offstage voice. '*Help is at hand!*'

Another voice, this time high-pitched and female, accompanied by a tingling bell, said '*I am Diffis, goddess of this sacred water! I will send aid and you will be blessed with long life and second sight!*'

A heavily-armoured man on a pony burst from backstage. The pony sidled sideways, its legs skittering under the weight.

'Hastorix!' sighed Prisca. 'What a man! What muscles! What thighs!'

'Be quiet, woman,' snarled Pomponius. 'Have you no dignity?'

'I wish he could rescue me!'

'It's not rescuing you want him to do.'

'You have no romance. He'd have to rescue me first.'

Hastorix jumped down from the pony in one fluid spring and stood for one moment like a statue, his muscles flexed, his sword held about his head. The horse staggered off in relief and leant against the screen, which started to buckle.

'Oh he's just gorgeous,' sighed Prisca.

'What, the horse?' snapped Pomponius.

The gladiator swung his sword as if drawing a celtic knot, thereby severing the ribbon and nearly the head of a passing naiad.

125

He then pumped his biceps, cast off his helmet and breastplate, shook out his braids and rippled his abdomen.

Others in the audience gasped.

'Oooh, look at that firm slab of -'

'Isn't the lion supposed to be doing something frightening?'

The lion was by now on its third circuit of the arena.

Aurelia interrupted her song to issue a sharp whistle through her fingers and the lion changed course and bounded towards her, his mane now hanging from one ear.

'What made his hair come off, Daddy?'

'Probably small children asking questions.'

'Really?'

'It'll be the heat. It's too hot. I bet lions don't like the heat.'

'Don't they, Mummy?'

The lion lolloped back to Aurelia and jumped at her again. It licked her face.

'Go on! Eat her! Eat her!'

With a roar louder than anything coming from behind the screen, Hastorix rushed towards Aurelia and the lion flailing his sword. The lion, swinging round intent on biting out his throat, or possibly licking him to death (it wasn't quite clear to the audience), unexpectedly caught the flat of the sword on his rump. With a yelp, he ran off and looking back as he did so, collided with the horse, which was minding its own business making deposits on the ground. Whinnying in disgust it kicked out, missed the dog and caught a dryad in the back. She overbalanced and fell against another dryad.

'Ooh Daddy! They all fell over! It's just like skittles! Can the lion eat them better if they're lying down?'

'*RESCUE ME!*' shrieked Aurelia. Hastorix, pushing his sword into his leggings in a way which made every man wince, whisked her up in his arms and kissed her passionately.

'Hey! Steady on!' said Pomponius and Prisca together.

'Never mind snogging! Feed her to the lion! He could do with a square meal!'

But the lion had lost interest in attack. He ambled back, flopped himself out at Hastorix's feet and stretched out his legs.

Seizing his moment, Hastorix, while somehow simultaneously pressing Aurelia against his pectorals, pulled out the sword and made as if to plunge it into the lion.

'No! He's the best bit!'

'Daddy, don't let him!'

The lion lifted his head, farted and lay back down again.

'*You are safe! My darling!*' shouted Hastorix. '*Now we will live out our lives together as lovers!*'

'*I knew this would happen!*' declaimed Aurelia. '*Ah the goddess was right! We will live long lives and I can see beyond.*'

'Beyond what, Daddy?'

'Erm…'

'*Into the void, beyond the veil, into the Otherworld.*'

'I wish the lion would wake up.'

The dryads picked themselves up. Encircling Hastorix and Aurelia, they started singing again as the naiads wove in and out, trying not to trip over the lion.

'*Oh lovers, together forever will you be,*

127

Brave hero, from terror you will never flee,
Saving the beautiful virgin maid!'
'As if,' said Prisca.

'I wish that heathen would put her down,' said Pomponius.

'It's her, she's got her arms round his neck so tight he can't let go.'

'Daddy, how can those two grown-ups breathe? They've been kissing a very long time.'

'Oh wild and savage beast
Oh wicked lion, no more to roam
Oh vanquished foe, you will not feast
The hero takes his maiden home!'

'Woof!' said the lion, and farted again.

Spiralling away, the naiads and dryads with the lovers in their midst wafted behind the screen. After a pause the horse ambled after them, and the lion, opening one eye to find himself alone except for a hundred strangers staring at him, got up, shook the mane from his head and followed.

'And now for the clowns!' declaimed the voice behind the screen. A group of brightly dressed men tumbled out into the arena and started juggling and playing the fool. Somewhere out of sight, a band played tunes everyone recognised. Toes started to tap and people started to laugh and sing along.

Anguis took his head out of his hands and leaned forward to tap a young man in front of him on the shoulder.

'What do you think you are doing?'

The young man was scribbling on a wax tablet as if his life depended on it. He paused and turned round.

'What, me? I'm trying to make a history of what really happens here. Everyone I've ever met from

128

abroad thinks we're a bunch of savage yokels who sacrifice each other.'

'And?'

'Well, I'm trying to write something more accurate. Today, I'm writing about our rich cultural... Anyway, I've written up everything that just happened.'

Anguis leaned forward a little further and scratched a long fingernail down the shorthand.

'I think you may have misspelled that bit,' he said, handing over two denarii. 'I think you should have written "Today we saw a wonderful classical Greek tragedy in one act".'

'But I want my art to reflect truth.'

'Very noble,' said Anguis, 'but I think you'll find fiction pays better. Have another denarius.'

'Excuse me, excuse me,' Pomponius had risen and made his way down the terrace to the rear of the stage. Prisca had already left on the pretext of powdering her nose in the shade.

'Here,' said a stage-hand, 'you're not allowed back here. The magic happens out front.'

'Out of my way,' said Pomponius.

At the back of the tents he found Aurelia touching her lips and humming.

'Kitten!' exclaimed Pomponius. 'That kiss looked very real.'

'Oh, but am I not a great actress?' said Aurelia, her eyes filling with tears. 'Besides, I am alone with no-one to care for me...'

'But I -'

'You have a wife. Albeit a false one.' Aurelia nodded towards a tent. Inside Pomponius saw Prisca, her arms around Hastorix, plastering his sweating chest with kisses.

129

'This is all quite enough!' snapped Lucretia from behind them. 'We are going home now. Prisca and Pomponius, you will both come back in the first journey with me. Urbanicus here will remain with the others until the wagon returns.'

***

A few hours later, as they waited in the dining room for the evening meal, Camilla and Fabio replayed the performance. Poppaea felt herself smile for the first time in days. Surely Marcellus would be home soon. It was a shame he'd missed the show, but maybe he'd laugh when she described it.

Breaking into the antics, Lucretia rapped her goblet and snapped 'Where's Prisca? Lollia, go and fetch her.'

Everyone gazed at Pomponius. He shrugged and motioned for more wine.

Lollia came back. 'She's not in her bedroom, Madam.'

'Go and search again,' ordered Lucretia. 'Look outside in case she's mooning about under the stars. She's heading towards a peculiar age.'

'Prisca's only thirty, dear,' said Tullia.

'Mmm. Well we can't talk without her here. I want all of my heirs to listen. It's a shame Marcellus has been called away on business, but I've explained it to him already.'

The family shifted in their seats, and waited.

Lollia rushed in and knelt to whisper in Lucretia's ear.

Lucretia's face became expressionless. She sat up.

'Pomponius, come with me. Lollia, get Ondi, you know what he needs to do.'

She led Pomponius out of the room. The others sat up, and after a moment followed. They saw Lucretia and her son-in-law silhouetted against the night where a

130

slave stood with a torch, before stepping out into the darkness.

Lollia returned, wringing her hands.

'What's going on?' whispered Poppaea.

A wail sounded from beyond the walls.

'It's Mistress Prisca, Madam,' said Lollia. 'She's been stabbed. She's dead.'

Chapter Sixteen - A Culprit
June 18th (ante diem xiv Kalendas Julias)

'You should have called me earlier.' Tryssa stood, arms crossed, and looked down on Prisca's corpse.

'Nothing happened until last night,' said Lucretia.

'This is the third unexplained death in a week.'

'Four, if you include the pig,' said Lollia.

'Be quiet, Lollia,' snapped Lucretia. 'The pig died from accidental food poisoning. And it was a pig. There have been no other deaths, Tryssa, I have no idea what you are talking about.'

'There was the body in the woods...'

'Briccio? A slave? What relevance has the mauling of a runaway to the murder of my daughter?'

'Wolves don't attack people in summer, and even if the wild boar were not deep within the forest, an able-bodied man could probably overpower one. And then there's Ritonix.'

'The druid? Why would his death concern me?'

'No-one knows how his head was so badly injured. We only know it happened when he was taking away the body of your slave -'

'The body of my *runaway* slave. An irrelevant being.'

'And since then Marcellus has been disturbed.'

'Why do you say he is disturbed?'

'I surmised it. I have been asked for more salve for his throat and yet his chill should be gone by now. His usual nonchalance has gone. There is a rumour that Rhys had a son, and that Gwil has rights to this land. I wonder why you are keeping it quiet.'

'I am not keeping it quiet,' said Lucretia, leaning across Prisca's body to stare into Tryssa's face. 'I am simply not broadcasting it.'

'Aren't you concerned?'

'No. I have left the matter in the hands of my brother-in-law Urbanicus. He assures me that all is well. And it has nothing to do with either the fact that my slave allowed himself to be eaten by wild creatures who didn't know runaways were out of season, or the incapability of a druid to ride a small, slow pony without falling off. *This*, however.' She indicated Prisca's form. 'This is of concern.'

Tryssa unfolded her arms and with care, drew down the thin sheet covering the woman beneath.

In death, Prisca could have been someone else. The vibrancy and restrained passion were gone. Still, white, what little blood remaining in her body now drained from her upper frame, she lay as if she were a sculpture, her eyes weighted with coins and her chin bound. The full figure which only a few hours before had been pressed against Hastorix now seemed smaller, deflated, pathetic.

Tryssa pulled the sheet further down, parted the jagged slash in Prisca's dress, and with gentle fingers probed the entry wound beneath her ribs.

Lucretia drew in her breath and swallowed. The scowl deepened on her face. 'That is my daughter.'

'I'm aware of that, Lucretia, although I have to say you're very calm for a bereaved mother.'

'It's not necessary to bellow like a cow. I just don't understand what you're doing.'

'It's an unusual wound, but the thrust was upward and straight into her heart. She would have died very quickly. I hope that is of some small comfort to you.'

Lucretia nodded. She reached out as if to touch her daughter's hair, then withdrew her hand.

'Her idiot of a husband wants her to have a Roman-style funeral. A cremation.'

133

'Is that what she would have preferred?'

'She would have preferred to be alive.'

Ondi burst into the room and seeing the body, blenched and gulped. Tryssa covered Prisca's face once more.

'What is it, you oaf?' snapped Lucretia.

'I think I've found the weapon that killed her, Madam.'

'Did you bring it?'

'No, I ... I didn't want to touch it.'

'Foolish boy! Go and -'

'No!' said Tryssa. 'Let me see it where it is. Will you come, Lucretia?'

'I will not. I will stay here with my daughter.' Lucretia remained standing by the bed, her lips pursed. She made no move to touch the body, running her eyes from the head to the toes in silence.

After a few minutes Tryssa returned with Ondi and a sharp, stained, long-tined fork. 'It was cast into the marshy ground along the lane,' she said.

Lucretia frowned. 'I recognise this fork,' she said. 'Ondi, go and get Master Urbanicus. I imagine he's in the study.'

Urbanicus walked in, his eyes sidling from the covered body to Lucretia.

'What is it?' he asked. 'Ondi said it was important. I've sent Lucco for the priest and the guard. I am not sure what else I can do.'

'Look,' said Lucretia, 'this thing appears to be what killed her.'

Urbanicus took the fork and winced. 'It's from the kitchen, I presume.'

'No,' said Lucretia, 'not from ours. Poppaea and I did the inventory before the new cook's arrival. We are woefully short of ginger, and due to Blod's incompetence, earthenware. But I recognise this implement.'

'Really?' said Tryssa. 'Where from? I can't imagine that you frequent many kitchens.'

'Hardly,' said Lucretia, 'but this was what that fool of a street trader used on his wretched brazier.'

'Vulpo!' exclaimed Urbanicus.

'Vulpo?' said Tryssa.

'Yes!' said Urbanicus. 'And now I think of it, he was the one whose sausage patties poisoned the pig. They were supposed to be for us, but no-one ate them because they smelled so terrible. And Vulpo went off in a temper. We gave the patties to the pig and then the pig died. And now Prisca has been murdered.'

'Vulpo?' repeated Tryssa.

'We dismissed him, you see,' said Urbanicus. 'We told him not to come back because we'd found a proper cook. He bore a grudge, accused me of underpaying him. Ondi! Get the other pony and go down into town. Tell the guard to arrest Vulpo.'

'But what about the body in the woods?' asked Tryssa.

'Who? The slave? That has nothing to do with it unless Vulpo led him astray because he wanted the cook's job here.'

'That makes no sense. Vulpo is a free man. Why would a free man want to slave for you?'

'The lower orders don't think very clearly, Tryssa. You should know that, since you mix with them more than we do.'

'And Ritonix?'

'An old man who fell off his horse,' said Urbanicus. 'Coincidence. Never mind, my dear,' he said to Lucretia. 'Justice will be done.'

135

Chapter Seventeen - More Questions
June 19th (ante diem xiii Kalendas Julias)

Tryssa returned to the villa the following morning. She brought news from the guard that Vulpo's trial would not take place for five days. Hearing of the arrest Dondras, as a prominent townsman, had insisted that an independent magistrate be brought from Isca because there was so much conflicting evidence. Anguis had judged it politic to agree. While Urbanicus was adamant his argument was plausible, several witnesses, including prominent locals, had come forward as soon as they heard to say they had seen Vulpo in the tavern long after the family had returned home.

'It's not just the gentry,' Tryssa told Lucretia. 'The ordinary folk are arguing his innocence on principle.'

'I can't imagine why. He's an outsider, of the Dobunni. I am of the Silures, the same as they are.'

'Perhaps the townsfolk like Vulpo more than they like you, Lucretia,' said Tryssa. 'Odd as it may seem, a man who sells scraps and leftovers to the poor at a discount tends to be more popular than a family who offers to buy your children as slaves when times are hard.'

'How ridiculous.' Lucretia narrowed her lips and pulled her black veil over her curls. 'I'll make them sorry if my daughter's death is not avenged swiftly. What are you doing here again, anyway? I hope you are not defending Vulpo too.'

'I simply seek the truth,' said Tryssa. 'As yet, I have no view on the matter, but I would like to see the spring of Diffis.'

'Indeed? I'm glad you're taking it seriously, but today...'

'I know, I'm sorry. You're grieving. How is Marcellus taking the death of his sister?'

A slight frown cracked the paint on Lucretia's face. 'He is still away.'

'Since yesterday? Where did he go?'

'He has gone to Aquae Sulis to look into how they do things.'

'Oh,' said Tryssa. 'I'm surprised he was well enough.'

'He knows his duty. Still, if you wish to interrupt my mourning to go and see the building, I suppose you won't rest until I take you.'

'Perhaps the goddess can bless you.'

Lucretia grunted, then bowed her head. Waving the slaves away, she led Tryssa up the slopes.

The workmen were doing well. They had prepared an area level enough for the hypocaust and laid the necessary pipes to draw water into the baths. It was possible, the mason said, that there was even more water available if they could dig enough. But none of it was hot.

'I could do without the muttering, though,' he said to Lucretia. 'The men drive me mad. Two of them walked off site and I'm having difficulty getting anyone to come up from town and work here.'

'Because of my daughter's murder? How absurd,' said Lucretia. 'As if anyone would injure them. They have nothing to do with any of it. Besides, we've found the culprit and before long he'll be executed.'

'It's not that, Missus,' said the mason. 'It's the forest.'

Tryssa and Lucretia looked up at the trees. The building team had felled a few and the timber was being prepared for use. Beyond the piled timber,

137

however, the woods towered and rustled. It was a grey day, still warm, but with a hint of change.

'They're Ordovices aren't they? They should be used to forests,' said Lucretia. 'Or are they worried about whatever attacked Briccio? It's quite possible, of course, that Vulpo did that too. Tryssa here is convinced no wild animal would bother a human at this time of year, and while I don't suppose anyone has told the animals that, she has a point.'

'I tell 'em they should work harder,' said the mason, crossing his arms and glaring at the nearest slave. 'If they made more noise, no animal would come anywhere near.'

'It's not animals,' burst out one of the slaves, putting down his shovel. 'It's the face.'

'What face?'

'The ghostly face.'

Tryssa and Lucretia exchanged glances.

'Some think it's Briccio's spirit,' said another slave, miming struggling through the undergrowth. 'He's trying to get the help which never came.' The mason shivered.

A third workman shook his head. 'Nah, it's not that. It doesn't look like that. Its face is determined and calm.'

'It?' said Tryssa. 'Does that mean you're not sure if it's male or female?'

The men conferred. 'We don't really know,' the first man muttered.

'Come now,' said Lucretia, 'it's hardly difficult to tell male from female, unless it's a child.'

'N-no it's not a child... It's just a face, half-hidden by a hood. It peers out from behind the trees when we're arriving and when we're packing up. It's just eyes, really. We can't see anything but eyes. Glinting.'

138

'It's a woman,' said Lucretia, lifting her chin and crossing her arms. 'The goddess Diffis is watching to see that you, er, show the appropriate respect at her sacred spot. So mind your language. But remember this: she will show honour and blessings to those who do behave appropriately, whereas those who desert their post can suffer the consequences of their heresy.'

The men muttered, raised their eyebrows and with a glance at the woods, went back to work.

'Good thinking,' said the mason.

'I beg your pardon?' said Lucretia, pulling herself up to her full four foot six. 'The goddess watches you as well.' She walked away to stand bolt upright by a tree-stump.

Tryssa came and stood next to her. 'Why are you doing all this, Rhee?'

'Don't call me that.'

'It is your name. Your real name, before your father changed allegiance.'

'He didn't change anything.' Lucretia stared down on the villa. At the back of it, laundry sagged in the breezeless air. Lucco toiled in the vegetable plot, presumably digging in the old pig's manure.

'When your father saw which side his bread was buttered, then,' said Tryssa.

Lucretia, without moving her head, turned her gaze on the other woman.

'There is nothing wrong with wanting to provide for your children. It is called planning.'

'Scheming,' said Tryssa. 'It was what he was good at, old Lyn. And it was a skill he passed down to you.'

'I find that very offensive.'

'I doubt it. I don't think you're offended by anything other than the risk of poverty, or losing face,

139

or not being the centre of attention. I remember when we were all young.'

Lucretia grunted. 'You only came here to moon over my brother.'

Tryssa continued. 'All the local children ran together. Every one of us had a local name except for Tullia. In your family, there was Rhys, then Bryn, then you Rhee, then Mor. But little Tullia was named after your half-Roman mother with all the connections. The word was that when she died, the connections threatened to disconnect themselves unless your father sweetened things by bringing her children up as good Romans, scheming until he got his citizenship. By then Bryn and Mor had died, as is the way of things. But he gave Latin names to you and Rhys. I imagine you thought it was a good omen being called Lucretia. But Rhys refused to change.' She sighed. 'We were very close, Rhys and I. He refused to be called Regulus, didn't he? Rhys suited him better. Meanwhile, little Tullia, the girl with the Roman name, turned out more Briton than you and your father put together.'

'How you do go on,' said Lucretia. 'I'm quite worn out with listening. It was a long time ago, Tryssa. You and I are in our fifties now. Some would call us old women. What has the past to do with anything?'

'This spring. I don't remember anything about it. What are these baths all about really?'

'It is in my blood, Tryssa. One day, I was communing with the gods and -'

'You? Communing with gods?' Tryssa snorted.

Lucretia raised her chin, her eyes on the villa, and continued. 'I recalled the old tales my father told me, *long long ago*. I went for a walk and I found the spring and Diffis ... spoke to me.' She cleared her throat. 'And now I will honour Diffis as she deserves and

140

build baths which will bring pilgrims from far and wide. And none of it has anything to do with my daughter's death. I don't understand why you're asking about it and doubting me.'

'This place reminds me of something,' Tryssa paused, taking in the trees and the forest depths. 'Rhys,' she said after a while, 'it's to do with Rhys. Do you recall the day he was found, killed by a wild boar?'

'How can I forget, Tryssa?'

'It was very near here, wasn't it?'

'Yes. No. I don't know. I wasn't on the hunt, was I?'

'It was unexpected. He was a fine young man, a great hunter. It was the middle of summer, just like this. Very strange. Everyone was so shocked.'

'Well, it was shocking. And you were very emotional from what I recall, which means I doubt you remember it clearly. However, he has been dead nearly forty years and now this Gwil has turned up saying he's Rhys's son. Which is absurd.'

'Is it? He looks very familiar.'

'He is not of my blood.'

'No. I believe you're right. I knew Rhys, you know. Hiding a wife would not have been the sort of thing he'd do. Besides he and I ... as I say, we were close. Let's go down and speak to the slaves.'

'Whatever for? They're all beyond stupid.'

'That's as maybe. They are not, however, blind.'

***

In the kitchen the new cook was teaching Blod to bake better bread. His arms waved and his eyes rolled and Blod, head to toe in flour, cried into the dough as she pummelled it with small, red hands.

'If that girl gets any wetter, she'll dissolve,' muttered Lucretia.

'I don't know why she's crying this time,' said the cook. 'It's not as if if she's at risk. I mean I know she was fond of your former cook, but he ran off weeks ago and got eaten by wolves - oh shut up, girl - and then the druid got attacked when he was carrying the cook's body and dumped it in a ditch. It's obvious that cooks are the ones who are in danger. It should be me who's crying. But no, I'm just getting on with my job.'

'You seem to be forgetting who was killed last night. My daughter was hardly a cook,' said Lucretia, in tones cold enough to freeze fire. The slave shook his head and brought a cleaver down onto a slab of meat.

'No, Madam, I haven't forgotten, and I am truly sorry. Mistress Prisca seemed nice enough when she came to speak to me earlier. She was outside the door when I'd gone outside for some air.'

'When you were supposed to be working?'

Tryssa put her hand on Lucretia's arm. 'I imagine it gets very hot in here.'

The kitchen was barely big enough for the cook, Blod and the utensils, let alone an additional two people. Although the bake-oven was outside, and the small stove had not been lit, the room was already hot and heavy with scents of herbs, spices, cheese and meat. The previous evening, when things were being seared and boiled, it must have been unbearable.

'It does, Madam, but I am used to it,' said the cook. 'However, I needed some herbs from the pot outside. Blod should have brought them in but forgot, and I could hear someone moving about. I thought it must be a wild dog or something, but I don't know, it made my skin crawl.'

'I said I'd get it,' sniffed Blod. 'But he wouldn't let me.'

'You'd be crying a lot harder if you'd been murdered,' muttered the cook.

'I'm sick of all this weeping,' said Lucretia. 'I may have to sell her.'

'Nooooo!' wailed Blod. 'I have to stay here!'

Tryssa patted Blod on the shoulder and turned back to the cook. 'You said your skin crawled. What do you mean? Is this to do with the ghost of Porcius or the slave, Briccio?'

'Well, I never knew Master Porcius,' said the cook. 'I suppose Briccio might haunt me if he thought I was misusing his implements, but on the other hand, if he liked them so much, why did he leave them behind? Besides...'

'Besides what?'

'I don't know. I just had a feeling there was something very much in the here and now out there. Like I said, a wild dog or something. Maybe even that lion from the play Lollia told us about. They're supposed to be pretty fierce.'

'If you're scared of being licked to death,' muttered Lucretia.

'But anyway, I went outside and there was no-one there. Or at least, not as close as it had felt, and then I saw Mistress Prisca.'

'Yes, and...'

'She came over and asked what was for dinner. There was a little light coming from the kitchen and the sun wasn't completely down, so I could see she'd been crying, but she was smiling too. I was glad. I mean, I barely knew her, Madam, but she hadn't seemed the sort to be low for long, and I was happy if whatever had upset her was resolved.'

'Did she talk to you?' asked Tryssa.

'Just about dinner. I told her what was for dinner and she said "That sounds delicious, I'll come in for it in a moment. I just want a bit more fresh air first." Then she walked off behind the house. I thought "Nice for some", got my herbs, and came back into the kitchen. Blod was drizzling into the onions and I thought of sending her outside just to stop her from annoying me, but I needed her help.'

'What happened then?'

'Well, we were getting everything ready for service when Lollia came in asking if we'd seen Mistress Prisca and I told her and off she went. You know the rest. And I'm sorry. Perhaps she was mistaken for me in the dark. Like I said, it seems to be cooks they're after. But when they found her, me and Ondi and Lucco went out to see if we could find who'd done it but there was no sign. All the same,' he waved his cleaver in the general direction of the outside, 'there's a lot of world out there and plenty of places to hide.'

***

Lucco muttered as he mulched pig muck and straw into the claggy earth. Lucretia and Tryssa, their noses covered, stood at a little distance.

'Lucco,' said Tryssa, 'did you see or hear anything last night?'

Lucco slammed his fork into a wet pile of muck with a squelch and stood up, arching his back and stretching his arms.

It was hard to tell how old he was, sinewy and weathered. He appeared aged. Tryssa, like Lucretia, had survived against the odds into her early fifties. When she'd been a little girl Lucco had been a young lad, learning his trade while she and Rhee (before she became Lucretia) were running away from weaving to steal apples and hide on the edges of the woods.

'There was a lot of commotion when they found Mistress Prisca. But that's to be expected, I suppose. Poor girl.'

'What were you doing then?'

'It wasn't me!' Lucco was indignant. 'Why would I hurt her? I've known her since she was a babe. Known you two since you weren't much more. Most annoying things Mistress Prisca ever did was want flowers for her hair when there were none to be had. Otherwise she was kinder and more polite than most.' He glared at Lucretia.

'No-one is suggesting it was you,' said Lucretia. 'We have the culprit in chains. We simply need you to confirm that you saw -'

'We need you to tell us *what* you saw,' said Tryssa. 'Cook was in the kitchen. Blod and Ondi were going back and forth with dishes. Lollia was awaiting orders in the dining room. You, of course...'

'Not allowed in the house on account of the dirt, eating scraps outside the kitchen door, same as I always do.'

'Come, now,' said Lucretia, 'you are provided with good food in this house. Usually. When we have a cook.'

'Time was, a chieftain's wife and daughter knew how to cook a simple stew.'

'Well times change, and we are more sophisticated now.'

'But if you'd stayed unsophisticated you wouldn't have starved, would you? And old Porcius wouldn't have got poisoned by some fancy muck.'

'Mind your insolence,' snapped Lucretia. 'The only poisoner round here is Vulpo. Whether by intent or incompetence is yet to be determined. Either way, it may be simpler to execute him.'

145

'Vulpo? Pah! What you want to do is find the bastard who keeps stealing my things.'

'What things? You don't have things,' said Lucretia.

'I have spare leggings and I have a cloak. Or at least I should have. My little bit of savings for when *someone* finally gives me my freedom, that's safe. But I didn't think anyone would be so desperate or mischievous as to take *my* clothes.'

'Strictly speaking,' said Lucretia with a curl to her lip, 'since you are mine, the clothes are too.'

Lucco snorted.

'Could Ondi be playing a trick?' asked Tryssa.

'Pah. Briccio was the sort to play tricks, not Ondi.'

'Briccio has been dead for over a week,' snapped Lucretia. 'See, Tryssa, I told you the slaves were beyond stupid.'

'Pah!' spat Lucco.

'Oh, really!' said Lycretia. 'I am going for Urbanicus. This man needs flogging.' She walked back towards the house, straight as a staff.

'I want a simple answer, Lucco,' said Tryssa. 'What happened here yesterday, from the time you got up till the time Prisca's body was found?'

'What, all day? I was gardening. Cleaning out the pig, collecting the dog and pony muck, checking the latrines. You know, all those things that make you glad you've spent your life supping at Diffis's stream and living a long exciting life.'

Tryssa frowned. 'So you knew Diffis? I don't recall her at all.'

Lucco closed his eyes and slammed the heel of his hand against his head.

'Why would I want a long life if it's this one, Madam? Why would I drink from that turgid little bit of bog water? Why would a goddess keep quiet? It's

146

not what gods are renowned for, is it? Smiting, that's what gods do.' Lucco bent to his work.

'Well there has certainly been a lot of smiting around here recently,' said Tryssa. 'Briccio, for example...'

Lucco shook his head. 'Briccio was never eaten by wolves.'

'Well he was eaten by something. Who passes up a free meal? But killed? I'm not so sure.'

'He was never killed by them either,' said Lucco.

'You believe he fell and died of his injuries first? Well that's the merciful hope, I suppose.'

'Pah,' Lucco spat into the soil and straightened his back before continuing. 'Like I said, when your back's bent and your eyes cast down all day, you get a different view of people. Which is why I didn't notice much yesterday. The family went out, taking Lollia and Ondi. It was nice and quiet. Those of us left cleaned up. We all had lunch in the sun. We wished we'd been allowed to see the show. We cleaned up a bit more. The family came back. Mistress Prisca and her fat husband argued out the back. Mistress Camilla's young man waited in the orchard till dusk like he always does, but this time in vain. Mistress Prisca stormed off to my pig. Why they have to bother my pig with their problems I'll never know, especially after what they did to the last one. Master Pomponius stalked round the house a few times before going in through a different door. Cook was shouting at Blod. Blod was crying, no change there, only her wailing was louder than normal. Ondi put the pony in the orchard. Then Lollia...' The old man's face softened, 'Lollia came and had a word. She sat down on the grass and told me about the show. She's a wonderful describer. It was like being there. A

147

lion, imagine. I wish I'd seen a lion. Though Lollia said...'

'Yes?'

'They left before the magician. Something about Mistress Prisca and Master Pomponius and their never-ending arguments.'

'And then...'

'Then it was all quiet and I put my tools away and thought, *it's getting colder, I'll get my cloak.* I was hunting for it a long time and then I heard the screaming. I went to see what was going on. Then me and Ondi and the cook, we searched all round with torches, but it was too late. Nothing to be seen. At least she wasn't murdered near my pig. After what they did to the last one, I don't want another one upset.'

Tryssa thought for a bit. 'About the other pig,' she said. 'Tell me what happened.'

***

Lucretia went through the villa, through the tiny courtyard and into the hall. The latter was only marginally darker than the former. She was intercepted before she could seek out Urbanicus.

'There are some strange men here, Madam, and they won't go away,' said Lollia.

'Are they here from the priest?'

'They don't appear remotely holy, Madam.'

'What do they want?'

'To speak to you, Madam.'

'What sort are they?'

Lollia considered. There was a hammering on the doorframe.

'Solid,' she said.

'Well, I feel unable to deal with them. Where's the master?' snapped Lucretia.

148

'Which master?' demanded Lollia, her arms crossed. 'There are three. And if you count Master Gwil -'

'I don't.'

'Or Master Porcius's ghost...'

'Lollia, stop being insolent and attend. Porcius was no use in life, there is no hope of his support in death. I repeat, where is Master Urbanicus?'

'I can't find him, Madam.'

'Have you searched?'

Lollia glared and took a deep breath. 'Yes, Madam. He is nowhere in the house or the garden. I do not know where he is. Shall I get Master Pomponius? He is the next oldest.'

'That fool? If anything, he's less use since my daughter died than he was before. Tell whoever the persons are that I will meet them on the threshold, and find someone, if it's at all possible, who looks as if they can protect the household. Although there is not much to choose from.'

'That'll be Master Gwil and Master Fabio then, Madam.'

'Not Gw -'' Lucretia paused for thought. 'Very well, but tell Gwil that protecting his host's family is not the same as being family.'

***

Lucretia stood behind the door and took a breath. She slapped at Lollia as her dress and veil were realigned, and straightened her back as the door was pulled open. On the threshold were two men. They were so massive they made Slab and Lump seem weedy, but on the other hand they were better dressed. Lucretia tried to gauge whether they were a better class of slave, or a lower class of person. Either way they

149

were certainly uncowed, regardless of how coldly she stared.

'Sorry to bother you, Lady,' said one. His face was high-cheek-boned and clean-shaven. Of the two, he had the more refined stance and clothing. His hands, while broad, were undamaged, whereas those of his companion were scarred and tattooed. The companion didn't so much have hair as bristles. It looked as if someone had planted iron filings in his scalp to see what would grow and you could have sanded oak with his jaw. From his posture, it appeared that his thighs were too thick with muscle to allow his knees to do anything but wave to each other from a distance. He did not look as if he would know what do with a polite conversation if it was handed to him on a golden platter.

'I am Novus and this is my friend Septimus,' said the clean-shaven one.

'That's fascinating,' said Lucretia, 'but you're at the wrong villa. I did not order bodyguards, though perhaps I should.'

'We are not bodyguards,' said Novus, 'although we have been known to guard bodies.'

'Yeah,' added Septimus, his voice garbled through lack of teeth. 'We guards 'em till we can chuck 'em in the river.'

Lucretia's brow cleared. 'Oh you'll be the torturer and executioner,' she said. 'If you're after the prisoner, he's in town under lock and key.'

Septimus peered at the ground and shook his head.

Novus spread his hands in appeal. 'You've hurt Septimus's feelings, Lady,' he said. 'There's no need to call us names. We're clerks, that's what we are. We've got a good friend called Primo. He likes things tidy. We organise things for him. And we take care of his

150

accounts. It's very important all his scrolls are up to date. He's a great philanthropist. For a small sum, he can guarantee no-one will steal from your little business or burn it down. Of course if you don't pay, we can't promise nothing. Tragic what happens sometimes, isn't it Septimus?'

Septimus nodded solemnly while leering through shattered yellow teeth. Then his brow furrowed as Gwil and Fabio appeared on either side of Lucretia and crossed their arms.

'Now don't be like that, lads,' said Novus. 'We're strictly townsfolk. Primus isn't interested in a one-chicken town like yours. We're here on city business.'

'That explains very little,' said Lucretia. 'Which city in particular? The only person here at present with city connections is...' She turned to Gwil who shook his head.

'It's nothing to do with this gent,' said Novus. 'It's to do with another one. Our friend, Primo isn't just a philanthropist. He has other businesses. They chiefly involve entertainment.'

'The circus? If you're after that, you are again in the wrong place. You need to go back into town.'

'Nothing so energetic as the circus, Lady,' said Novus. 'Games for gentlemen this is. Knucklebones, dice. That sort of thing.'

'We are not interested,' said Lucretia, and indicated to Gwil and Fabio that they should shut the door.

Septimus put one booted foot against the hinge and stood the other on Fabio's foot.

'Well the thing is,' Novus continued, inspecting his nails and digging out dirt with a narrow dagger. 'We've been checking the accounts and deary me, I am sure it must be one big mistake, but your Urbanicus appears to owe Primo some money. Little bets between friends on racehorses. That sort of thing. Only Primo doesn't like his scrolls untidy. It's taken so long to track Urbanicus down, we are quite worn out. So if you'll just lead me to him, we can have a nice little chat and sort things out.'

'Dear gods!' shouted Lucretia, making everyone jump. 'Is there a single man in my life who is NOT an idiot?'

'Well, er -' said Fabio.

'You're an idiot, you're just not fully fledged,' snapped Lucretia.

A rattle of wheels made Novus and Septimus turn. Lucretia looked round their shoulders.

'Ah,' she said, 'I will add to my previous statement about people who have no apparent need to be here and yet, somehow are. Here come my groom, the priest, the Decurion, his secretary and, for no reason I can think of right now, slaves from the circus.' She gazed further into the dust being kicked up. 'And just to make things even better, here comes the hot-head on his knock-kneed pony. Normally I would tell my slaves to say I was not at home, but today I welcome them as they, or at least most of them, represent sufficient muscle here to put yours to shame.' She crossed her arms. 'Now, Septic and Numbskull, or whatever your names are, I have to tell you that I have no idea where Urbanicus is. He has ... gone away on business and I do not expect him back any time soon. In case you were unaware, he is in fact my brother-in-law and has no real reason to be here, although this is also true of many others.' She glared at Gwil. 'However, in a gesture of goodwill...' She rummaged in her bosom, to the consternation of all watchers. 'I will hand over this amulet which, as you can see, is of beautiful and rare design and also very very holy and extremely lucky. Take this in payment of

152

my brother-in-law's alleged debts and I will settle with him on his return. If you can't sell it on then melt it down. And if you're having difficulty understanding me, perhaps my friends can help explain.'

Novus and Septimus exchanged glances, considered the men bristling around them, and shrugged. Novus picked his teeth with the dagger.

'Well,' he said, throwing the amulet into the air, catching it then tucking it into a pouch. 'We may hang around town to see if Urbanicus comes back and have a chat for old times sake, or we may not. Thanks, Lady.'

They turned, and nodding at Slab and Lump, made their way back down the lane.

***

Minutes after they had gone, Camilla shrieked from the bath-house. She came out inadequately bundled in her clothes, carrying a scrap of cloth. Olivarius stepped forward as if to take her in his arms and was elbowed out of the way by Budic. She ignored both of them and waved the cloth, her eyes lit with fury.

'I nearly fell into the hypocaust. The bricks are all loose and this was covering them.'

'It looks like Lucco's old cloak!' said Ondi. 'Why would anyone stuff it down there?'

'It's just as well the hypocaust isn't lit at the moment,' said Anguis. 'It might have caught fire.'

'What is the matter with all of you?' shouted Camilla. 'Why are you worrying about the cloak and not me? What if someone's been crawling about underneath when I'm in there having a bath? The dirty old -'

'Will everyone get their priorities straight!' shouted Lucretia. 'This is obviously from when Vulpo lay in wait to kill Prisca. Can't you all see you should be searching for more evidence? Camilla, pull yourself

153

together. I know that all the men surrounding us are useless, but they are not blind. Go and put some clothes on immediately.'

Chapter Eighteen - Searching
June 19th (ante diem xiii Kalendas Julias)

The villa settled into something approaching normality. The priest had struggled to make sense of anything Pomponius had to say, but now he had left on a nostril-flaring pony. At an appropriate distance behind him, an acolyte's wagon rattled towards the cremating grounds on the outskirts of town with the bundled form of Prisca rolling in the back.

Pomponius slumped on the veranda, mumbling into a cup of wine and twiddling his wife's ring, which he'd put on his own little finger.

Budic and Olivarius both tried to comfort Camilla, one with honeyed words and attempts to brush her damp curls from her face, and the other with offers to kill the lurker and bring back his head for Camilla to pickle. She endured five minutes of this before stalking into the house to slam her bedroom door.

Slab and Lump stomped around the perimeter grunting at anyone they came across.

'Rsn Hstrx?' said Slab.

'Sorry?' said Ondi.

'Rsn Hstrx?'

'Er…'

'Rlr?' said Lump.

'Er…'

'Nwy,' said Slab and slammed a fist into his palm.

'Tgthr,' said Lump and smirked.

'To..geth..er..?' said Ondi.

'Yeah..' Slab slowed down as if speaking to a small child, somehow making himself even more incomprehensible. 'Hstrx n Rlr nwy tgthr. Bg BG trbl.'

Ondi thought for a bit.

'I expect you're right,' he said and went off to groom the pony. Guessing the wrong response seemed more dangerous that looking stupid.

In the garden, Anguis bowed and kissed Lucretia's hand.

'I have come to pay tribute to your daughter,' he said. 'And comfort you in your grief.' He paused. 'I am concerned, however, that the wrong man is in custody.'

'Prisca was killed with Vulpo's fork,' snapped Lucretia.

'That's doubtless true,' interrupted Tryssa. 'But Vulpo had told the world and his dog that the fork was missing from the first day he came here.'

Anguis nodded in agreement. 'That is what I've been told too.'

'Then he planned ahead,' said Lucretia.

'To kill Prisca?'

'Yes, no ... perhaps he's insane.' Lucretia crossed her arms and glared.

'It's quite possible that Vulpo's a little unhinged,' said Tryssa, 'but not in the homicidal sense. Decurion, why are those two, er thugs here? Have you brought them to protect Lucretia and her family?'

Anguis raised his eyebrows and scratched his nose. He scanned the area to see who was listening. Only one person appeared to be in ear-shot. Camilla was indoors. Poppaea and the nursemaid were distracting Julia in the orchard by making daisy chains. Cook and Blod could be heard arguing in the kitchen, and Lollia was out of sight. Presumably she was about her business somewhere within the house. Loud voices and cursing from the bath-house indicated that Olivarius and Budic were rummaging in the hypocaust, pushing each other about and getting dusty. Gwil was talking with Lucco who was tending vegetables in the garden as usual.

Tullia was a distant shape apparently made of floating linen, tacking up the slopes like a ship at fullsail. Only Pomponius was nearby, but he was barely conscious, his goblet slipping from his hand, the tip of his little finger white where Prisca's ring was jammed on it.

'Where's the boy?' said Anguis.

'Which boy?' said Lucretia. 'Oh, Fabio. I imagine he's composing music and waiting for lunch. You know what boys are like.'

'And Marcellus?'

'He's on an errand.'

'And Urbanicus?'

'He is away.'

'It seems rather unlike Urbanicus to leave without explanation,' said Tryssa.

'He left a message with Pomponius. It was almost as hard to decipher as his instructions to the priest. Urbanicus was concerned that Marcellus might be too unwell for his errand. He decided to follow him so that together they can learn from Aquae Sulis how we can make our baths better.'

Anguis considered. 'If Pecunia was on a major route it would help.'

'No matter, Urbanicus was certain that we could overcome that.'

'And now Urbanicus has gone,' said Tryssa.

'Urbanicus, as you will recall, does not live here,' said Lucretia, coldly. 'He simply visits as a welcome guest. He's at liberty to come and go as he chooses. Although I must admit that I've been relieved to have his company and counsel during this trying time.'

'His sudden absence would have nothing to do with those rather peculiar individuals, would it?' said Anguis.

157

'Certainly not. He was gone before they arrived. And on the subject of peculiar individuals, why have you brought those two trolls from the circus?'

'It's not a circus,' snapped Anguis.

'It's as near as makes no difference,' argued Lucretia. 'Why are they here?'

Anguis looked round. Behind them, Pomponius still lay on the bench. His eyes moved under their lids. It was not clear if he was dreaming or listening.

Anguis dropped his voice. 'They're searching for that moody ex-gladiator and the painted singer,' he said.

'Both of them?' said Lucretia.

'Together?' asked Tryssa.

'Well, that much is unclear. Certainly at the same time. They've both run off. Given the, um, interest which Prisca and Pomponius had in their, er, professional development, Contractes thought they might have come here. In fact...' Anguis glanced at Pomponius again. The eyes had stopped rolling under their lids and his hands were clenched. His chest did not move. 'Perhaps we should move further away and leave poor Pomponius to his grief,' said Anguis.

He drew the women to the front of the house where they could see down into the valley. The air was close and still. There was still no sun to speak of, but the greyness glared and the atmosphere was thick. Pomponius, now out of ear-shot, appeared to roll over and snore.

'In fact,' repeated Anguis, 'I regret to bear bad news, dear Lucretia, but Pomponius, it has to be mentioned, did have grounds to divorce Prisca. If he has resolved matters in another way and is brought to law, he would be found quite justified in er ...

158

satisfying his honour. His wife was after all his property, to do with as he chose.'

'She was my daughter,' said Lucretia very slowly, 'I do not care what the law says. She ... was ... my ... daughter.'

She pointed at Pomponius. 'If for one moment I thought that fool had the capability to kill Prisca, I can assure you that he would wish I only had a sharp fork to avenge her with and a - what did you say, Tryssa? - an upward thrust which meant instantaneous death.'

'The point is, my dear Lucretia,' said Anguis, taking a step backward, 'the girl with whom Pomponius is besotted has run away, and whether she has gone off with Hastorix or is waiting here for Pomponius's attention, no-one knows. There remains no evidence against Vulpo whatsoever.'

'His sausages were poisoned,' said Lucretia.

'Poisoned sausages did not kill Porcius,' argued Anguis. 'And Vulpo has been been given an alibi for every single unfortunate death, apart from Briccio's which is anyone's guess.'

Lucretia gritted her teeth. 'Porcius choked to death on his own greed. If Vulpo is not guilty then someone else is. But it can't be Pomponius. Look at him, he's a gibbering fool.'

'Gibbering or acting?' said Anguis. 'I need you to understand that when the magistrate gets here, Vulpo is likely to be released. This is, after all, supposed to be a civilised country. Having said that, Pecunia has turned into a hotbed of crime recently. My house, among others, was broken into last night. Nothing appears to be missing, so presumably the level of local incompetence remains as low as ever.'

He walked over to the bath-house door and peered into the hypocaust.

'Dear gods,' he said, brushing invisible dust from his tunic, 'I am amazed this heats anything, and more to the point, doesn't suffocate anyone.' He glanced up to the roof. 'Although you have plenty of ventilation. I do hope that the heating system at Diffis's spring will be an improvement on this.'

'Of course it will be,' said Lucretia. 'This bathhouse is only for the family and at the end of the day, what kind of person can't bear a little bit of cold? You've lived here for many years, Decurion. Britons do not require pampering. The cold air makes us strong and determined. For generations our ancestors bathed in streams and barrels. A little bit of cold water makes a man of you. In fact, I blame all this degeneracy,' she waved her hand at Pomponius, 'on the obsession with hot baths.'

'That doesn't accord with your desire to build some,' pointed out Tryssa.

'That is entirely another matter,' said Lucretia. 'The baths will honour Diffis. Diffis will honour us. It is all quite clear. The plans are coming together very well.'

'Whose plans?' said Tryssa.

'Why are you still here?' Lucretia's glare caused more flakes of cosmetic to fall from her brow.

'Lunch!'

They all jumped. Blod stood at the kitchen door hitting a block of wood and shrieking.

'That girl will have to go,' muttered Lucretia.

She glanced around the villa. Tullia was making her way back, Poppaea and Julia, holding hands, were walking towards them, Lucco was in deep discussions with Slab, or at least, he appeared to be working while muttering and Slab was nodding his head. Camilla had come out into the daylight, her hair braided and her head held high. Budic who had been waiting, rose to greet her but with a toss of her head, Camilla stared in another direction. Shrugging, Budic straightened his shoulders and headed for town. Lucretia rolled her eyes Camilla made a point of ignoring Olivarius too. She shook her head and bade goodbye to Anguis as he was handed into the chariot.

Slab and Lump ambled back with a sideways glance at Pomponius and addressed Lucretia.

'Cn fn m. Bg trbl.'

'I'm sure you're right,' said Lucretia. 'Anguis, when you return to town, perhaps you could ask Contractes if he would let these persons return here and guard us. Just in case there is the smallest possibility that you are right about Vulpo.'

'Gn dhn sk.' said Lump. He and Slab clambered back into the wagon, offered a place to Tryssa and clicking the reins, trundled away.

***

By evening neither Urbanicus nor Marcellus had returned, but the funeral could not wait. The remainder of the family went down to the cremating grounds outside the town walls and watched the priest's acolytes undertake the funeral rites for Prisca. Pomponius, swaying on his feet, stood with head bowed, his eyes everywhere but on the wrapped, flower-laden body.

After the cremation, they returned in silence to the villa. It felt as if a century had passed since the entertainment two days ago. By dusk, the rumble of thunder lifted all headaches but Pomponius's. When the rain came, it was a blessed relief. Then it stopped. And the mosquitoes, roused from ditch and swamp and boggy ground, streamed out of the night and attacked.

Chapter Nineteen – Attack
June 20th (ante diem xii Kalendas Julias)

'What is it now?'

Lucretia's mood had worsened. Her night had been broken by the whining onslaught of mosquitoes. Her throat was hoarse from shouting at Lollia to destroy them. Her hands were sore from slapping at insects and batting away Lollia's attempts to destroy the attackers with more force than seemed proportionate when they landed on Lucretia.

She could feel lumps forming on her body everywhere, even where she thought she'd wound herself up like a corpse. How long were the mosquitoes' proboscises? And what, given her reaction to the bites, had they been biting first?

In the shuttered gloom of the bedroom Lucretia could hear sniffing. She wondered why Blod was in attendance, and what she was crying about now. It was not until she tried to open her eyes that she realised a bite was half-closing her eyelid. She dreaded to think what she looked like.

She squinted as best she could and realised the sniffing was not coming from Blod, but Lollia. Tears ran down the slave's face and she was doing nothing to stop them. Lollia stood silent but for the occasional sob, her usual defiance crumpled by visible grief.

'What is it now?' repeated Lucretia.

'He's gone,' said Lollia.

'Help me sit up,' said Lucretia, indicating a pillow to be put behind her back. Lollia, at first did not move, then obeyed, for once without 'accidentally' catching Lucretia's ear or hair in the process. 'Who's gone?'

'Lucco.'

Lucretia let out an exasperated sigh.

'Well I hope he hasn't run into the woods, in case the wolves are back. What was the old fool thinking?'

'No, he hasn't run away.'

'Madam.'

'He hasn't run away, Madam. He's dead.'

'Well, I suppose he was getting on a bit,' said Lucretia, straightening up and wincing as the bites tingled and itched at the rasp of cloth against them. 'It's hardly unexpected. He was considered quite a marvel, living till sixty-five or whatever he was. People say I am too soft on my slaves because they live so long.'

Poppaea stepped into the room and, putting her arm round Lollia, took her out.

'Where is my morning drink?' demanded Lucretia to the emptiness, 'and a small honey cake? Really, have people no consideration?'

She scratched her leg in irritation. Blod, more red-eyed than usual, covered in scratches and oozing bites, with snot running down her face, wandered in to deposit a small tray on the side table and scurried out before the cushion Lucretia threw could strike her.

Poppaea returned. The greyness in her face had been replaced by a clear skin and bright eyes. Her hair, loose from its braids, fell down her back in thick dark waves. The mosquitoes seemed only to have bitten her arms. She still appeared a little bundled in her nightclothes, but otherwise stood straight and calm. Her face was flushed and her eyes angry.

'How can you be so cruel?' she demanded.

'I? Cruel?'

'Lucco is dead and Lollia is distraught.'

'Why? He was an old man. It's hardly unexpected. What was unexpected was that he lived so long in the first place. Most slaves barely live past forty. Most *people* barely live past forty. Porcius, may his spirit

163

stay away from the wine store, was younger than Lucco. Death is in the nature of things. You of all people should be aware of that.'

'Lollia was his wife.'

'Slaves don't have wives.'

'You know perfectly well what I mean. They were a couple, they loved each other. They had children together whom you sold.'

'Lollia would have been distracted when she should have been concentrating on Marcellus and Prisca. And I only sold two children. There was a third, but it died before I needed to take any action.'

'Do you think she has no heart?'

'She's never shown the remotest signs of having one. Two weeks ago her master died almost in her arms, choking on whatever it was, and she showed nothing but irritation at the stains on her clothes. Her mistress died outside only two nights ago, and she did, I admit, appear to wipe a tear or two away, but that could have been something in her eye. And how am I to manage if she's unable to wait on me today? Perhaps it's time to sell her on. Although who would take an old woman like her, I can't imagine. It does make you wonder how she'd react if I were to die. I, who have given her a living and shelter.'

'Oh, I'm sure she would have a huge emotional reaction,' said Poppaea, scratching at her blotched arm. 'You should have freed them both years ago, and they could have lived out their days on a little small-holding.'

'Well, I didn't,' said Lucretia, swinging her legs out of the bed. 'And she ought to put aside her feelings to care for me. I'm doubly bereaved and now injured. Instruct someone to bring the salve and apply it.'

'We have nearly run out. I will have to go down to Tryssa for more ingredients. Everyone is sorely affected. And poor Lucco, it must have been too much for him.'

'What?'

'The mosquitoes. He is covered in bites. Lollia thinks he went out to light a smudge fire to keep them off the slaves' quarters.'

'Off the slaves' quarters? Why not off us?'

'He could hardly light fires all round the house. And I think he preferred the slaves. I can't imagine why. Anyway, one of the bites has reacted worse than the others. It's desperately swollen and he seems to have just dropped down dead in the garden. Lollia, of course, was in here with you, and he wasn't found till Ondi started his duties this morning.'

'Well, it's all very inconvenient. Send Blod with what's left of the salve, but make sure she wipes her nose first, and get Ondi to take you and an escort to Tryssa's as soon as possible. I am very weary of all this upheaval. In a house of mourning, too. Which reminds me, you should still be in black. Although your black robe did look rather snug yesterday. Is there something you need to tell me?'

'Is there anything you need to tell me?' said Poppaea.

'I?'

'About Marcellus. Where is he?'

'Aquae Sulis.' Lucretia tried to uncurl her fingers and cursed as the bites on her swollen knuckles cracked open. She forced her expression to one of smug nonchalance. 'I thought he told you.'

Poppaea frowned. 'I'm sure that's not what he said.'

'Well, you can't have been listening properly.'

'Is it what he told you Lucretia?'

165

Lucretia frowned, then winced as the motion set off the itchiness on her eyelid. 'He left a message for me,' she said. 'He was too busy talking to you, even though you weren't listening, to speak to his own mother.'

'Why didn't you tell me about the message?' The healthy glow in Poppaea's face was now an angry flush. She stepped forward, but Lucretia met her glower for glower.

'I don't see why I should tell you anything when you tell me nothing. Besides, he and Urbanicus will be back soon. It's not so far to Aquae Sulis. I always thought you indifferent to Marcellus. Are you missing him?'

'Of course I am, Lucretia. He is one of the few people who makes any sense. And talking of people who don't, when are you going to send Gwil off with a flea in his ear?'

'When I can discredit him.'

Lucretia stood up and wrapped herself in a shawl, knocking a bite she hadn't known she had. She cursed again. 'Don't just stand there, Poppaea. Go to Tryssa's and get whatever ingredients you need. Be off with you. I am sure you don't feel like breakfast. You haven't for some time.'

***

It was still early when Poppaea and Fabio arrived in Pecunia and hitched up next to the temple. Only kitchen slaves and housewives were in the market, buying fresh goods for the day. A crudely-chalked drawing on the wall indicated a forthcoming performance by Contractes' troupe. It had presumably been drawn before Hastorix and Aurelia's disappearance, since they both figured in the sketch, including exaggerations on various parts of both anatomies. In another sketch a furious lion roared through a laurel wreath. It was unclear why.

Ondi walked a few steps behind as usual. He was red-eyed and silent.

'I'm sorry about Lucco,' said Poppaea, stopping at a baker's stall to buy some hot rolls. She passed one to Ondi and after a moment's hesitation, he sniffed and took it.

'He was like a father to me, Madam,' he said. 'It was horrible, finding him like that, his face all swollen, crushing the cabbages.'

Poppaea wondered what was for dinner later and her stomach, which had been behaving, lurched. Glancing sideways at Fabio, however, she realised he felt the same.

The door of Tryssa's roundhouse was open and Poppaea peered inside. In the gloom it was hard to make anyone out, but as her eyes grew accustomed to the darkness, she picked out nothing but the loom and the fire and the various sleeping and eating areas round the edges. The odour of ashes mingled with herbs, wax and honey. Small sounds, of mice perhaps, caught Poppaea's ears as she stepped back into the sun to make her way to the smallholding and the little shelter where Tryssa worked in the summer.

The older woman jumped when Poppaea spoke to her, and blinked. She had been muttering to herself. 'Oh Poppaea!' she exclaimed. 'I wasn't expecting to see you today. Is everything all right? How is Lucretia? Any more trouble from those strangers?'

'No, it's not that.'

'Has Urbanicus returned?

'No, nor Marcellus. But I'm in desperate need of beeswax and calendula oil. We're all suffering. Look!'

She showed Tryssa the swollen bites on her arms and indicated Fabio and Ondi. Ondi stood sniffing, his eyes downcast.

'Of course,' said Tryssa. 'I'll get them for you now. But otherwise, you're well? I couldn't speak to you yesterday but you seem better. Blooming. Is your…' She glanced at Fabio who, sensing imminent women's talk, sidled off to inspect the fruit trees, taking Ondi with him.

'It's holding, I think,' said Poppaea. Her solemn face brightened. 'I felt quickening today. In the midst of everything, I felt quickening.'

There was a noise from inside the round house. A hiss, or perhaps an indrawn breath. Poppaea turned.

Tryssa made no sign that she had heard it too. Poppaea shrugged. Perhaps the cat had found the mice. Then she frowned.

'Tryssa, these bites are very sore. Are they dangerous too?'

'Dangerous? Well, who can say? Some say that fever comes after mosquito bites and others say it comes from drinking the marsh water. I can only treat the symptoms. But you appear well and so does Fabio. Is Lucretia suffering?'

'Lucretia? Of course she is. Worse than anyone. No-one suffers worse than Lucretia suffers.'

Tryssa bit back a smirk and glanced over to the two men. 'Ondi looks sad. I hadn't thought he would be so fond of Prisca that he'd weep over her.'

'He wasn't,' said Poppaea, taking the small earthenware bottle and pot from Tryssa. 'He's mourning Lucco.'

'Lucco?' Tryssa put down the pestle and mortar she had just picked up. Her voice was sharp. 'Lucco is dead?'

'Well he was fairly old.'

'He seemed fine to me yesterday. Did his heart give way? He didn't look like someone who was about to die like that.'

'I'm not sure,' said Poppaea. 'That's why I was asking about the mosquito bites. Lucco had a terrible reaction to one. It seemed to have paralysed him so that he couldn't breathe. Poor Ondi is very upset. He was the one who found Lucco's body in the garden.'

'That's a very unusual reaction. Very unusual. We must go back to your house. I need to find out for myself. And as for you, I think you should take Julia and go back to your parents.'

'What nonsense! Over a few insect bites?'

'No, because I fear someone is trying to kill you. Someone is trying to kill you one by one.'

Chapter Twenty - Camilla
June 20th (ante diem xii Kalendas Julias)

Camilla walked through dewy grass of the orchard and headed towards the spring. The workmen had started early, and already the stone and brick was forming into a small building surrounding a pool. Its angularity was all at odds with the asymmetric slopes and frayed edges of the forest. A soft warm breeze flowed from the south and curled itself around her face. She paused and surveyed the scene. It was nice to get away for a few moments. She thought of her cousin and wiped her eyes with the edge of her veil. Poor Prisca, one minute arguing, laughing, flirting and now just ashes. And then funny old Lucco, swollen like an overgrown marrow.

Introspection came as naturally to Camilla as wearing last year's hairstyle or doing her own laundry. Inner voices, in her view, were for poets, dreamers and lunatics, but the last few days had made so little sense that for the first time in her life she tried to imagine what went through her mother's mind to see if there were any answers. The countryside around her ranged from the forest-topped mountains to the boggy slopes, down to the shrubs and hedges and trees studding fields and meadows, the unseen river, the imagined sea. According to Budic and to Tullia, the natural world was whispering: 'You are part of us. The city is just a veneer, a veil, hiding us from you. In the end, we are and we will be, and you will be part of us.' Camilla listened, but could hear nothing except the usual things, birds of some description, rustling leaves… She ran out of knowledge. Her sandalled feet were tickled by grass and it made her shiver, wondering what was crawling over her. There was little risk of slugs in the city, other than human ones.

But it might be worth it if she could talk to the spirit of the hidden stream which trickled under mossy earth, concealed among the trees. Camilla loved the town and felt lost in the countryside, but Budic said he felt the opposite. How would Diffis, who was so elusive that everyone had forgotten her, feel to be trapped in stone and brick, her image transformed from Briton to Roman and sold with the promise of what Lucretia said she could do?

Could Diffis, while she was still unfettered, tell Camilla what her future held? What she should do? Camilla didn't mind riches but wasn't entirely sure about longevity. At seventeen, a thirty year old seemed ancient. If she'd had to live for more than a month with the husband they'd chosen, she would have longed for an early death. And it was hardly as if her mother's life had been unending joy. Camilla knew that Tullia had put up with years of failing to produce viable children, with a mother-in-law nagging, nagging, nagging, until she had finally produced Fabio at the advanced age of twenty-eight.

Camilla's grandmother, evil in her senility, was now the impossible age of sixty-one and still nagging.

Life wasn't all it was cracked up to be. Camilla was young, fresh and flexible but even that held its problems. She was still at risk of being married off without consultation.

The wagon was coming back up the lane. Presumably Poppaea was returning with the means to make more ointment. Camilla's mosquito bites tingled at the thought and she resisted the urge to scratch. Her arms were covered in small red lumps but she was not as badly off as some and at least nothing had bitten her face. She thought of poor Lucco, his body rigid and his face swollen, his eyes open in surprise, and shuddered.

He must have been bitten by millions of insects in his time, and yet just one had finished him off.

'Hello, Pretty,' said Budic, coming out from under the trees.

Camilla's urge to scratch her bites made her fingers curl, and she hoped the one on her ear was not visible. She pulled a strand of hair forward in an attempt to hide it.

'Hello,' she said. She forced her voice to stay cool but she could not stop her face from flushing as she gazed at him. His long-lashed eyes, his dark curls, his full lips. A sigh escaped her.

'I want to apologise for grabbing you yesterday,' he said, putting on a sad face like a naughty puppy. 'I was angry that you had been frightened. And when that gilded Roman -'

'If you mean Olivarius, he's neither gilded, nor Roman,' said Camilla, rolling her eyes and scratching a bite after all. 'I wish you'd stop arguing with each other and just talk to me properly. How can I choose between you when I don't really know either of you? Or perhaps you and Olivarius should just go off together. You already bicker like an old married couple.'

Budic bridled, then drew a breath. 'You seem sad, Pretty,' he said, reaching to stroke her cheek. 'I suppose you're still missing your cousin.'

'Yes. And the gardener died last night,' she said.

'The old chap who didn't approve of anything?'

'That's him. Well, he didn't approve of that.' She waved her hands at the building works. 'I'm not sure he believed in the goddess.'

Budic bridled again. 'Why? Because she's British and not Roman?'

'I don't think he thought much of Roman gods either, to be honest. Although it's hard to tell with

172

slaves, since you don't see them worshipping. I always wondered whether he and Lollia belonged to that sect.'

'What, the foreign one?'

'More foreign than Romans?'

Budic grunted. 'Well anyway, he was old.'

'Yes, but it's still sad. He was a bit of a curmudgeon, but he was kind underneath. He was really upset when the pig died. All the slaves are miserable today, expect the cook. He just carries on as if nothing has happened.'

'When you marry me, we will just have one slave and be very kind.'

'Just one? Who will do everything?'

'We will. You will cook and I will garden.'

Camilla snorted. 'I don't think so. Besides, you're a scribe. You won't be able to dig and scribe. And I can't cook. You are being ridiculous. What can you offer me? A life in Pecunia with two trips a year to Isca?'

'Is that so bad? Here you are among the mountains where your ancestors hunted and flourished.'

Camilla paused. 'I tried to hear the land speaking to me like it does to Mother, but either it was keeping quiet or I couldn't hear it.'

'Never mind that. If you marry me, I won't be scribing when I have you by my side. We will head into the mountains and carve our living out by hand, listening to the spirits of the wood and stream, building our round house, hunting, planting...'

'I have absolutely no idea how to do any of those things,' said Camilla. 'Have you?'

'We can learn. We can tame the wildness, live like our ancestors before the Romans came.'

'Oh that sounds so wonderful,' snarled Camilla. 'I can't imagine why I don't run away with you right now.'

173

'What can Olivarius offer which is better than that?'

Camilla crossed her arms. 'Londinium. The Empire. The sea. He wants to go back to Tarsus. Live like *his* ancestors. Somewhere hot and dry.'

'I can take you to see the sea. It's not that far away: a day's walk.'

'I've seen it, remember. The sea here is fairly muddy. And I live in Glevum, at the top of the estuary. Every spring, the river rolls down over the incoming tide in a huge curl. It's incredible, but it's still muddy.'

'With me, you won't be in a strange country. We'll stay forever in our own land with our own gods, waiting for the day when the invaders will leave.'

Camilla stared back down at the villa. Something was going on in the kitchen garden. A group of people was standing among the neat rows of vegetables and soft fruit bushes, a little away from the tethered pony under the wormy apple trees, the mongrel villa and the lane leading down towards the eastern road. Not so long ago, she had been longing to head back to Glevum and a decent forum. Now, it occurred to her that Glevum held Grandmother and more plots in the way of husbands. But her stray thoughts were interrupted by activity at the villa.

'What is it, Pretty?' said Budic reaching to stroke her hair.

'Something's happening,' she said and pushed his arm away. 'I can't stay here. And neither should you. You spend so much time in these woods, Budic, I'm surprised you still have a job.'

'Maybe I'm getting used to living in them, shaking off my town shackles and -'

'Well, I don't want to be eaten by a wolf. I saw what Briccio's body looked like. I am going back.

174

Something is going on down there. You can come with me or stay, it's up to you.'

'So you haven't decided yet?' urged Budic. 'When will you choose between us?'

'When one of you offers me something I like the sound of.'

* * *

'I know it's hard for you, Lollia, but it's important someone shows me where he was found,' said Tryssa. She was with the guard and had gathered Gwil, the family and slaves to search around the spot where Lucco had been found. Lucretia grumbled all the while from a chair which had been brought for her to sit on.

Lollia rubbed her eyes with the heel of her hand and pushed her white hair back from her face. Ondi, supporting her with his left arm, pointed with his right to an area of disturbed ground in the vegetable patch. The withies supporting the beans were askew, and the cabbages were at an angle. Nearby a small pile of compost waited, trowel sticking from the top, for someone to dig it into the claggy, black earth.

Tryssa went over and crouched. It was clear that Lucco had fallen as if struck down. There was little sign that having done so, he had squirmed or struggled. He had fallen like a tree. She had looked at his body and shaken her head. They were two things: stroke and allergic reaction. It made no sense. None of the numerous bites on his arms had reacted much, but on his jaw a tiny red puncture wound was surrounded by greenish-white skin stretched over his unrecognisable swollen face. Only his startled brown eyes were the same. They were trying to tell her something.

'Is all this necessary?' said Lucretia. 'I really do need that salve and Poppaea is taking an age to do it.'

'This is no usual death,' said Tryssa. 'Lucretia, I thought it might be suspicious. That's why I've asked the guard to come. This man was poisoned.'

'What nonsense,' said Lucretia. 'Who would poison him, difficult old man that he was? And how? The slaves all ate the same food, and more to the point, it was the food we had left over. Is that not so?'

Ondi nodded.

'Furthermore, I am covered in more bites than he is and no-one seems to care. It stands to reason that a person will react more to a mosquito's bite if the mosquito was previously biting an animal's backside. Lucco was working between an incontinent mule and a runny pig, so it's no wonder he's all swollen up like an oak apple.'

'I don't know,' said Tryssa, 'but there is something wrong. Nothing's been right since you announced that you'd found a goddess no-one could remember forgetting.'

'Perhaps she didn't want to be found,' said Fabio. 'There's nothing like being disturbed after a long nap to make you fractious.'

Everyone stared at him.

'Even Lucretia doesn't kill people after being awoken unexpectedly,' said Tullia.

'Not yet,' muttered Poppaea.

'A disturbed goddess has not brought about this death,' said Tullia. 'I don't recall Diffis at all, but surely a water goddess would drown someone, not attack them with insects. Although all those old gods were supposed to like human sacrifices. What a pity Ritonix isn't here to explain how that worked.'

Tryssa lifted the trowel. The pungency of pig-muck spread and everyone recoiled. With her scarf over her nose, Tryssa went to replace the trowel and then paused. Digging a little more, she uncovered a slender piece of wood with feathers glued along the edge.

Ondi leaned forward to pull it out.

'No!' said Fabio. 'Don't touch it. Not without gloves.'

'Why?' said Tryssa.

'It's one of those darts. I thought Olivarius had taken them all away.'

'What darts?'

'The ones Gwil shot at the pig before it ate the gone-off sausage patties and snuffed it.'

'But they were harmless,' said Camilla, coming up with Budic in tow. 'It was all showmanship. And Gwil oversaw those darts being packed up and given back to Olivarius. Didn't you, Gwil?'

She looked up and into his eyes, this man who seemed so familiar and yet so hazy, who said he was her cousin. His eyes were glazed, wet even.

'I did,' he said.

'Is there anyone who can prove that?' said Lucretia. 'Did you kill my slave somehow and try to hide the dart?'

Lollia's fists clenched, and tears streamed down her face. She burst out: 'you went out to talk to Lucco. I remember. You went out to talk to him while I was fetching something for the mistress in the middle of the night. I saw you. You passed out through the kitchen.'

'I needed to talk to him, but I did no harm, I swear!'

'Arrest him!' Lucretia commanded the guard. 'This man has attempted to defraud me and he's attempted to frighten me, and now it's clear he's destroyed my property.'

'Your property?' shouted Lollia. 'Your property? He was a man! My husband. My man.'

'No, Lollia, no!' said Gwil. 'You've got it wrong!'

177

Lollia glared at him with reddened eyes, her fists still clenched.

'Lollia, believe me!' cried Gwil. 'Of all the people in the world I would kill, I would not kill Lucco. Not after all this time. Not ever.'

'Take him away!' shouted Lucretia. 'Take the imposter out of my sight.'

'No!' Gwil yelled, grabbing Lucretia by the shoulders and shaking her. 'You unspeakable monster. This is all your fault. I -'

Before anyone else could move, Lollia struck him over the head with a spade.

'Is he dead?' she sobbed.

Ondi lashed out a kick, and the crumpled form twitched.

'No,' the guard said. 'But he's out cold.'

Lucretia let out a long breath and assumed an expression which might have been a smile. 'Thank you, faithful servant.'

'I didn't do it for you, you old witch,' snarled Lollia, throwing the spade to the ground and rubbing furious tears away with muddy hands. 'I did it for my man Lucco. And if they don't execute *Master* Gwil for killing a *mere* slave, I'll do it myself with my own bare hands.'

Chapter Twenty-One - Secrets
June 20th (ante diem xii Kalendas Julias)

'Of course, Tryssa,' said Lucretia, as Gwil's unconscious form made its way down the lane in the back of the guard's wagon, 'I would normally have sent you back with them, as I'm fed up of your interference. But as you've rid me of that tiresome imposter and have brought some salve, I've ordered a *quick* lunch, after which I'll make sure you get back to town, where I dare say you're very busy.' She paused. 'I don't suppose you know of any gardener slaves? And perhaps a body slave, since Lollia is being impossible. Now, at last, we can get back to what passes for normal.'

They sat under the thatch as ointment was applied to Lucretia's bites.

'I don't think it's that simple,' said Tryssa.

'I suppose you're right. It's hard to get a slave hereabouts.'

'No, I mean *why* would Gwil kill Lucco?'

'I imagine he was trying to destabilise my household,' said Lucretia. ' I suspect he'd been planning ahead. He had encouraged Briccio to run away and talked Vulpo into poisoning us and killing Prisca. Why else would he turn up pretending to be the heir to this property?'

'Why did you let him stay if you thought he was an imposter?'

'I wanted him where I could see him.' Lucretia frowned again and pursed her lips. The cracks in her white make-up made her face look like a mosaic with pinkish grout. It was hard not to try and make sense of the pattern. 'There is something about Gwil....'

'Something that reminds you of Rhys? I can't see it, Lucretia, and I knew your brother very well even though it was so long ago. But something about Gwil has been nagging at my mind for a while.'

'Well, naturally. He's up to no good.'

'Perhaps.'

'And in cahoots with Vulpo.'

'I doubt that very much. Lucretia, where is Marcellus?'

Lucretia scratched her arm and ran her fingers along her swollen eyelid. 'Do you think your salve is safe near eyes? I don't want to blind myself.'

'It will be fine, but Marcellus? It is unlike him to be away for so long and I am worried for Poppaea and Julia.'

'You're worried about them, but not me.'

'You're the last person I'm worried about. Rhee, where is your son?'

'Don't call me Rhee.'

'Then tell me what's happening.'

Lucretia sighed and readjusted her veil.

'Blod!' she shouted. The girl came out from the kitchen, wiping her hands on her apron. Her eyes as usual were damp, her blotchy skin further emblazoned with insect bites.

'What do you want, Madam?'

'You mean "Yes, Madam", Blod. Go to my room and find the little oaken box with the knotted-rope carving.'

'The dark one with the twisty, knobbly bits what are hard to get the dust out of?'

'Probably.'

'And when I've found it, what do you want me to do?'

'Gods this girl is hopeless. Bring it here. Be careful, it's heavy. Don't pry and don't drop it.'

'Yes Madam, No Madam.' Blod shuffled back indoors.

The two women sat in silence. Tryssa put the lid on the ointment, pulled a spindle from her bag, and started to pace the veranda as she spun wool.

'Do you never sit still?' said Lucretia.

'Being busy and useful helps me think,' said Tryssa. 'Perhaps you should try it.'

Blod returned with the box. White finger-prints were plastered all over its polished surface. Lucretia slapped at the slave's floury hands and snatched the box away, waving Blod back towards the kitchen.

She undid the complicated catch and peered round to check no-one but Tryssa could see what she was doing. Satisfied, she ran her nail down the inner edge to pull out a lining which to all appearances was joined to the main part of the box. Beneath an section full of bangles and rings was a small piece of parchment.

'Marcellus has gone to Aquae Sulis, as I keep telling everyone. But as you so repetitively pointed out, he wasn't very well and Urbanicus was concerned enough to follow. My brother-in-law didn't want anyone to know Marcellus was going originally, in case someone stopped him from finding out about our plans to compete.'

'Who would care about your plans to compete with Aquae Sulis? It'll be years before your baths could possibly pose any kind of threat.'

'What utter nonsense,' argued Lucretia. 'You simply have no comprehension of business. All the plans were going well and -'

'Apart from Porcius dying.'

Lucretia waved her arm to indicate her husband's death had, if anything, made life simpler. 'I repeat, everything was going well. But when Gwil turned up, I felt certain that someone was trying to stop us from making a success of -'

'Making money out of an imaginary goddess.'

Lucretia stamped her foot. Her veil slid from her hair and more flakes of make up fell from her face, exposing a red and slightly sweaty section of cheek. 'Diffis is not imaginary. How can you say such a thing? You of all people. I worship one whose name means happiness and -'

'Oh, what nonsense.' Tryssa stopped pacing and shook her head. The spindle slowed. 'When have you ever cared about worshipping anything but wealth, Rhee?'

Lucretia stood and stabbed her finger at the other woman. 'When have you ever stopped being obnoxious? You've been getting at me ever since the day I stopped Rhys from marrying you.'

Tryssa paled but only a slight flutter of her eyelashes showed she was less than calm. 'And how did you do that exactly, Lucretia?'

Lucretia shrugged and turned her gaze elsewhere. 'I explained that he would be better choosing someone with more influence.'

'You mean someone with more money.'

'Is there a difference?'

'Well,' said Tryssa, starting the spindle off again, 'if he was swayed by your words, then he was no loss to me, perhaps.' She sighed. 'Coming back to the present, I repeat that leaving little notes and rushing off to be adventurous sounds unlike Marcellus.'

Lucretia swallowed. 'Perhaps he felt like a change.'

182

'No, there's something you're not telling me. What is that piece of parchment, anyway?'

Lucretia turned it over in her hands and bit her lip. 'It's a note from Marcellus. Urbanicus read it to me and told me to keep it safe till he returned.'

'You're worried.'

'Urbanicus has everything under control.'

Tryssa shook her head. 'Why would Marcellus use parchment rather than a wax tablet? And why not send the message to Poppaea?'

'Perhaps he thought that if she could keep secrets, so could he,' said Lucretia. 'And besides, as his mother I take precedence.'

'I thought Marcellus had told Poppaea he'd worked something out and not to worry.'

'You see?' Lucretia shouted, then dropped her voice. 'The minx didn't tell me that. I imagine he has some sort of artistic plan and wants to check if they do anything similar in Aquae Sulis. But then of course he was injured on the way.'

'Injured?' Tryssa stopped spinning, and stared. 'But you haven't told Poppaea!'

'If she was remotely respectful I might have, but since she's nothing but insolent, I thought I'd let her stew.'

'How long have you known?'

'A day after he left he sent this to the inn and Ondi brought it home. It says that we must not follow them.'

'That really doesn't make any sense.'

'Nevertheless, that's what it says.'

'Does it? Read it to me.'

Lucretia picked up the piece of parchment and peered at it. Her half-open eye watered and her other squinted.

'It says *"Attacked on road. Continuing to A Sulis. Don't search."'*

'Rhee, I can't read, but I know you're holding that parchment upside down.'

'My eyesight … I memorised it.'

Fabio passed and nodded at Tryssa. She snatched the parchment out of Lucretia's hands and gave it to him. 'What does this say?'

'It says … oh what awful writing… *"oh nibbled bones, how like a chicken's leg is your ankle with its bitten flesh, yet we will recall your chicken legs of bliss with joy…"* What?'

'Thank you,' said Tryssa, taking the parchment back.

Fabio shrugged and went indoors.

Tryssa turned to Lucretia, who straightened her shoulders and lifted her chin. 'Well, I never learnt to read any more than you did.'

'So why were you lying?'

'I wasn't. Or at least,' Lucretia frowned, 'it's what Urbanicus told me it said. He must have been trying to reassure me. And even though it said, or rather I thought it said that Marcellus had been attacked, maybe I misunderstood. I just knew I must keep it from falling into the wrong hands.'

'Whose hands? Only the free men in this house can read.'

'Yes, and Gwil was one of them.' Lucretia thought, then brightened. 'Ah, I understand. We don't know where Gwil came from, only where he *said* he came from, and he turned up the night Ritonix was killed. Marcellus was trying to work something out. He must have found proof of Gwil's guilt, and he went to Aquae Sulis not only to find out about the baths but also because it's where Gwil comes from. I *thought* that

184

imposter's accent didn't sound like a Londinium one. And wasn't Gwil away for a few hours when we were at the entertainment? He must have attacked Marcellus that afternoon on the road and left him for dead, but somehow Marcellus managed to send a message to Urbanicus and Urbanicus has gone to find him and that's why he wasn't here to sort out the misunderstanding with those thugs. Although, I'm not quite sure why the words make so little sense. It must have been quite a blow to the head.'

Tryssa swallowed and ran her hands through her hair. 'I hope so, I really hope so. But the whole thing worries me immensely. It sounds too neat, and I'm desperately worried for Marcellus. You must tell Poppaea. She'll be distraught.'

'Oh, that girl. Marcellus is my son. She never cared for the marriage, you could tell from the outset. Why aren't you worried about my feelings?'

Fabio returned with Poppaea. 'Olivarius is coming up the lane in the chariot. He's driving it himself.'

'You'd have thought Camilla would like to see that,' said Poppaea. 'And yet as soon as I told her, she rushed off to do something to her hair. I really can't imagine why.' She grinned.

Olivarius swept to a halt in a wide circle, the horse barely sweating, dust in a swirl around them. He swung down from the chariot and flicked back his auburn hair. Fabio rolled his eyes.

'I have a message from Urbanicus, Lady Lucretia,' Olivarius said with a bow. 'It came with someone who's heading for Nidum.'

'It's a bit of a detour coming up here,' said Fabio. 'Pecunia is hard enough to find when you're looking for it. Did the messenger get lost?' Olivarius ignored him and glanced around, straightening his tunic and smoothing his hair again.

'What does it say?' said Lucretia. 'Read it to me.'

Olivarius unsealed the roll.

He read, "'*I'm in Londinium. Don't worry. Keep up the good work. I will be back when the baths are*"- there's something crossed out -"*nearly ready to open. Keep faith in Diffis and all she can achieve for us. Also to tell you that I have seen Marcellus and he is well. He was injured, but do not worry, dear lady, I have left him in good hands and he is nearly well enough to return. Your humble brother-in-law Urbanicus.*'"

'Londinium?' said Lucretia.

'Marcellus?' said Poppaea.

'LUNCH!' shrieked Blod.

Chapter Twenty-Two - A Proposition
June 20th (ante diem xii Kalendas Julias)

'I want you to come away with me,' said Olivarius, leaning close to Camilla as she gripped the reins.

Lunch was over, and Olivarius was keeping his promise to show her how to drive the chariot. Lucretia had suggested Fabio as a chaperone but Camilla's narrowed eyes were enough for Fabio to plead a prior engagement with the Muse. He played the lyre in the sun just out of the way of anyone likely to ask him to do anything.

Camilla, glaring at the horse, which seemed disinclined to obey instruction, half-turned and forced her glare into a simper. It was frustrating to have to behave coquettishly while concentrating on something more interesting. Boudicca's success must have been due to the fact that no-one expected her to flirt at the same time as burning Londinium down. Couldn't Olivarius just let her get on with driving?

Camilla tutted. The horse took this as a command and started to canter towards the orchard. The chariot wobbled and rocked, throwing Camilla against Olivarius. He held her round the waist with one hand and grabbed the reins with the other to slow them down. Camilla didn't know whether to be thrilled or irritated. If only people would let her try things which didn't involve matrimony.

Olivarius steered the chariot round so that it was facing the lane. The horse champed the bit and stamped its hooves, but did not move until Olivarius chivvied it into a walk.

'I want you to come away with me,' he repeated.

Camilla forced a smile and gave him a gentle push to unhand her. She just wanted to take the reins and make the horse gallop. She wanted her hair to fly in the breeze, the exhilaration of speed to race through her veins. She wanted the dust of the lane to scour away the memory of poor Prisca and swollen Lucco, of repulsive Porcius choking on dormice all those days ago, and the stinking form of Briccio under the sacking.

'Do you really think I'm that silly?' she said. 'I'm not just going to wander off into the bushes like a village girl.'

'That's not what I mean,' urged Olivarius. 'I mean, I want to marry you.'

Camilla blinked. She felt herself falling into his soft green eyes, her gaze focussing on his firm lips and straight jaw.

'But first, I want you to come away with me.'

She shook herself. 'What do you mean?' she demanded. 'You want to try the goods before you buy them? Never! I'm not doing that. If you want me that badly, you'll have to marry me first. Or do you think if I'm ruined, they'll marry me off cheaper? No, that doesn't make sense. But ruined, no-one else would want me, would they, and you'd get my dowry. Turn around.'

'You need to come away now. Just listen to me. You don't understand.'

'Turn around!'

Camilla grabbed the bridle, making the chariot wobble again. Olivarius reached for her again but she pushed him away and tried to turn the horse.

Glancing back at the villa, Camilla realised that her raised voice had even woken Fabio from composing. He had put his lyre down and stood up to watch. From the orchard came the familiar shape of Budic, running.

'Listen, Camilla, you've got it wrong,' said Olivarius. 'I want to take you away from here. Away from these horrible people.'

'They're *my* horrible people!'

'Yes but you're -'

'Get off me and take me home. I mean, back to the villa.'

'I'm worried about you. Look what happened to Lucco. Tryssa found one of those darts, didn't she? I think that was what killed him.'

Camilla blinked, then her eyes widened. 'Well who had the darts last?' she said. 'It was you. You had them.'

'No, Anguis told you. We had a burglary.'

'He said nothing was taken.'

'I didn't check the bag at the time, but when I did this morning, there was a dart missing.'

'A likely story. My grandmother told me never to trust a man with green eyes. What did you want to kill that lovely old man for? Fabio, come and help me!'

Camilla hitched up her dress and, letting go of the reins, jumped down from the chariot. She fell, twisting her ankle as she landed in the dirt. Pulling herself up, she limped as fast as she could back to the villa.

'Camilla, stop being ridiculous,' hissed Olivarius, leaning over the edge of the chariot as he kept pace with her. 'I'm not trying to seduce you, I'm trying to rescue you.'

'That's what they all say.'

'All who? Who else has been trying to get you to go away with them?' Olivarius looked up and saw Budic striding closer. 'Oh, him. You'd rather live in a house made of mud with that idiot than in an apartment in the city, would you? I could take you to see the world. He's offering you a forest full of wolves.'

189

'They're *my* wolves.'

'Camilla, listen. Please listen. You'll only be safe if you come with me. I can't promise otherwise…'

As they neared the villa, Budic ran up and swung himself onto the chariot. Before Olivarius could regain his balance, Budic punched him in the face and dragged him off onto the ground. The two men rolled and wrestled in the dust.

'Leave her alone.'

'No, *you* leave her alone.'

'Both of you leave me alone!' shouted Camilla. 'And you,' she snapped at her brother, 'you're supposed to protect my honour. Hit both of them!'

She limped towards the villa fully intending to slam the atrium door. *All I wanted to do was drive the chariot.* She turned. Budic and Olivarius were laying into each other and swearing. Fabio, leaning in to separate them, was felled by a flailing leg and the three of them started punching and kicking each other.

The horse stood a little to the side, nibbled some grass and glanced sideways at Camilla. She was sure it raised its eyebrows. Slipping past the shouting men and ignoring the women gathering on the threshold, Camilla climbed back onto the chariot and took up the reins. *I'll show them.* Summoning the blood of her ancestors, Camilla gave a blood-curdling cry to tell the world what she wanted to do with any man who got in her way. The horse, whinnying in excitement, stretched out its neck and broke into a gallop.

Camilla's braids loosened, her veil fell from her shoulders and she raced towards Pecunia. Risking a peek behind her, she saw the men stand up and stare then one by one, run fruitlessly down the lane behind her.

Chapter Twenty-Three - Under the Trees
June 21st (ante diem xi Kalendas Julias)

Pomponius left the house at dawn the following day, carrying a spear and small bow he'd filched from a chest. He was sick of the house. His bedroom still held Prisca's comb and mirror, her little pots of perfume. What was left of the family was barely speaking to each other, and they were mostly women. He wanted something male to do, to prove that he wasn't just a useless city man.

Hunting couldn't be that hard if a daydream like Marcellus could do it. Pomponius tried to recall that day, what felt like a year ago, when they had gone searching for boar or squirrel and come back with Briccio.

Ondi, preparing the wagon for a trip to town, glanced up in surprise. Pomponius, stumbling towards the hummicky slope, ignored him.

At the edge of the forest Pomponius could hear trilling, and for a moment wondered if the melody was bird-song.

He stepped into the still shadowy trees as if slipping under a curtain. It took a while for his eyes to adjust. Around him, as before, small noises eked and trickled and slid in the undergrowth and in the branches. The grey-green gloom was like dipping your head under water in the river. He almost expected a salmon to swim past, or a water nymph or an otter, or maybe a dolphin. Pomponius had a very thin grasp on natural history.

The song continued and he made his way towards it, feeling for twigs through the soft leather shoes on his feet to avoid making a sound, raising his spear until he caught its end on a tree and nearly fell. In a clearing he

191

saw that leafy branches had fallen against a hefty trunk in a shelter. From it came the smell of something cooking, and the song. Propping the spear's shaft against his side, Pomponius applauded while in a low voice he said 'bravo'. The song stopped, and from within the leaning branches came Aurelia, wrapped in a cloak, her scarlet hair hidden by a brown scarf.

'Kitten!'

Aurelia pouted and then sighed as if a pout was simply too much effort. Her face dropped to a frown.

'You are tired, thin! I have been so worried about you.'

'Have you?' said Aurelia. She pulled the cloak tighter and glared.

'See, I have some bread.' He handed over a bag.

'Yesterday's. It's stale.'

'Blod hasn't started baking yet today, but I could bring some later. I can bring anything you want.'

'What I want is what you promised.'

'I d-don't quite know... Come here, Kitten, let me hold you! We could climb into your shelter and pretend to be little bunnies. It must be lovely snuggled up in there.'

'Lovely? I don't think so.'

'Don't be angry, Kitten, come and cuddle me. Where's my little kitten smile?'

Aurelia made no movement. 'I want what you promised,' she repeated.

'Er...'

'Marriage. Freedom. A home. Slaves of my own. Never lifting a finger. Remember? All those things you promised me once you'd divorced that old witch of a wife of yours. Now you don't even have to divorce her and you didn't come to get me. Well, if you won't give me those things, I'll get them another way.'

'Don't be like that, Kitten. There has to be a decent interval of mourning. And my children ... they've lost their mother and don't even know yet. If you'd just stayed with the troupe a little longer... Go back. Go back and I'll vouch for you.'

Aurelia snorted. 'When I heard she'd been murdered, I thought at last! He's done it for me. Someone has done something for me for once. And I waited, and waited.'

'Why would I kill her when I could divorce her?' said Pomponius.

'Speed. Or honour, since she'd cuckolded you. She was your possession.'

'Yes but ... my children! Come now, Aurelia, let me take you back to Contractes. I can't believe you like living like this. Aren't you afraid of wolves?'

'I have protection, thank you,' said Aurelia, turning her head away. 'We only stayed long enough to give you the chance to do what you always said you would.'

'We?'

Pomponius felt the softest of breaths on his neck, the tiniest pressure of air behind him and spun to find himself staring into the impassive face of Hastorix.

'You?'

Hastorix said nothing. The two men stood eye to eye, the same height. If you had averaged them out, they might have been the same width. But whereas Hastorix's torso was a triangle with shoulders broad enough for a sheep to recline on, bulging pectoral muscles stretching the meagre cloth of his tunic and a narrow waist within a studded leather belt, Pomponius's torso was more of a trapezium - if a trapezium can curve and slop as it protrudes through a slipping cloak.

193

In the forest Pomponius's wealth was meaningless. His clothes were too fine. Through snags from the undergrowth, little bits of white flesh peeked. His leggings, slung under his belly, were loose on his thin legs. Staring at the gladiator, his spear dropped further.

Hastorix, still and silent, throbbed with power. His clothes were rough and the leggings, like his tunic, strained against his muscles. His arms were crossed, his hands red, and there was a knife tucked into his belt. Pomponius let the spear's shaft slide through his hands so that the blade would be easy to thrust, but the shaft jammed into the ground behind him. Still, Hastorix hadn't moved or spoken. He simply stared into Pomponius's eyes as if considering a beetle, and the beetle's fate.

Pomponius pulled his stomach in as far as he could. He pointed in Hastorix's face. 'You turned my wife's head!'

'What does that matter?' said Aurelia. 'You didn't want her. You told me she didn't understand or appreciate you.'

'That's not the point. She was still mine.'

Aurelia's half-hearted pout was grotesque on her grubby face, smeared with the remains of make up , and with grey bags under her eyes. 'You should've been glad,' she said. 'It gave you cause to discard her for me.'

Hastorix uncrossed his arms and clenched his fists, 'I did not touch your wife.'

'Well you were touching her last time I saw you.'

'No. She held me and kissed me. I did not kiss her back. I did not want her.'

'How dare you! She was a lady, the wife of a citizen. She was worth ten of -'

'Ten of who?'

194

'Ten of many.'

'Ten of me?' snarled Aurelia.

'No, no, Kitten. You're very refined. No I mean the sort of trollops this barbarian is used to.'

'He is used to trollops like me.'

'You can't mean it, Kitten! You and he - no! I thought you were saving yourself for me!'

'Well *that* was worth it,' said Aurelia, rolling her eyes.

'I go north,' said Hastorix. He rolled his shoulders and flexed his muscles. 'I want to go. She asked to stay to see you first.'

'Well?' said Aurelia. 'I stay and you take me as your wife, or I go with Hastorix.'

'You can't want to go north. They say it gets colder and wetter and you can't understand people, and eventually it's full of Picts who've got over the wall to corrupt the locals.'

'I will go past the wall,' said Hastorix.

'How? You are runaways. You have no papers. Contractes might guess you are heading to Caledonia.'

Hastorix shrugged. 'I might fight to the death on the wall. I do not want to die a fool in a show.'

'You can't want to go north,' Pomponius repeated to Aurelia. 'Let me take you back to Contractes and explain that Hastorix kidnapped you. I'll sort something out.'

'Pay for my freedom and marry me?'

'Well, er, I'd have to talk to my mother first. It might take a while to persuade her. And Lucretia too.'

'What has that old besom got to do with anything? Her daughter is dead. You are no longer part of her family.'

'But my children are and their inheritance -'

195

Aurelia threw her arms up. 'I should have guessed it was all for nothing. You weren't the only one in Isca, you know. I just picked the wrong one to back, didn't I? Goodbye, Pomponius. I will take my chances going north with Hastorix. I too would rather die swiftly than to have to sing for my supper till I'm too old and get thrown on the midden. There are plenty of girls waiting to take on my role.'

Pomponius reached out for her, but her stare was cold. His hand dropped.

'This forest is dangerous,' he said. 'You should get out quickly. There are wild animals here and they attacked someone a few weeks ago. Aurelia, won't you -'

'No.'

'But you are right,' said Hastorix.

Pomponius brightened, reaching out for Aurelia again.

'These woods are strange,' continued Hastorix. 'It is not just us here. A thing walks.'

'A thing?' Pomponius shivered and peered sideways, reluctant to turn his back on the gladiator.

'Human, god, beast ... I am not sure. It pads and sneaks and spies. It smells of earth.'

'Go now,' said Aurelia. 'I don't want to see you any more. Go back to your family and your life as a citizen.'

For the first time Pomponius saw her face stripped of paint and artifice. There were tears in her eyes, but whether it was hurt, regret, fury or exhaustion, he could not be certain. He wondered how old she really was, what her past had been. Her future could be... He saw his mother's narrowed eyes, heard Lucretia's scornful dismissal, felt his life of fine food and cloth falling away.

'I wish you well,' he said. 'If you find a way, please send word that you are safe.'

'We cannot write.'

'Then just a picture of a songbird and...' He glanced at Hastorix and heaved a sigh. 'A sword.'

'No,' said Aurelia, 'we will send nothing. Goodbye.' She turned and ducked back into the shelter.

'Go now,' said Hastorix.

'I won't tell,' said Pomponius. 'I promise.'

Hastorix shrugged.

Pomponius hesitated, then turned away. He wasn't sure if the sounds he heard were sobs, forest sounds, or both. His back prickled, knowing that Hastorix was behind him, in dagger's reach. The trees all looked the same, and he could not recall the way he had come. After a moment he stepped forward. His foot snapped a twig and panicked birds shot up from the branches above. He walked away, glancing back once to the small clearing. Hastorix had gone.

Pomponius stumbled on. The woodland seemed to be getting darker, not lighter. He must have gone round in a circle, because he could see the shelter propped against the tree, could smell smoke. He swallowed. Would he have to ask for help to leave the forest? His shoulders slumped, but he already felt a fool; one more proof of it made little odds. He opened his mouth to call out and a movement caught his eye. Someone bundled in a cloak, near a tree to his left. He squinted into the gloom and frowned, wishing his eyesight was better.

'Hello.'

He stepped towards the tree. There was no-one there.

He felt the air above him shift and ducked but the lump of wood struck him just the same. His last thoughts were how soft the ground was, and wondering what it felt like to have teeth sink into your soft, fat, pampered flesh.

Chapter Twenty-Four - Discovery
June 21st (ante diem xi Kalendas Julias)

Pomponius would have been found earlier if everyone hadn't been distracted. To Lucretia's irritation, she arose with no-one but Blod to wait on her.

'Where's Lollia?'

'Gone out, Madam,' said Blod, standing with a basin of petal-strewn warm water, flanneling Lucretia's face and hands.

'Why?'

'Mistress Poppaea has gone on the wagon to visit Mistress Tryssa.'

'It's beyond me what she needs now,' muttered Lucretia.

'Well apart from anything else, Madam, I suppose she'll bring Mistress Camilla back after she ran away to Tryssa's to get away from all them suitors.'

'I do wish everyone would concentrate,' said Lucretia.

'If I had lots of suitors,' said Blod, 'I wouldn't run away. Especially if they looked like those two. I'd -'

Lucretia waved her hands at Blod to be quiet and frowned. 'Now you've stopped wittering, I've realised I can't hear anything from the slopes. Haven't the workmen started yet?'

'I believe they did Madam, but I think they've stopped again. The mason is having terrible trouble with them.'

'Don't tell me they still think a ghost is watching them. It's the goddess giving her approval.'

'Is it, Madam?'

'Of course it is.'

There was a hammering at the front door. Lucretia glared at Blod. Blod glared back.

'Well, I dunno who it is,' said Blod.

'Go and find out, you stupid girl.'

At the door was the mason, muscled and tanned. He was sucking his teeth and had his hands on his hips. Blod held the basin against her hip with one hand and twiddled a strand of hair with the other.

'Is your master in?' asked the mason.

Blod frowned. In the absence of Marcellus, who was Master? Urbanicus would have been her next thought, but he was gone too.

'I think he's in Londinium.'

'Londinium? Don't be ridiculous. He was here two days ago. Takes more than two days to get to Londinium.'

'Well that's what they said.'

'Never mind love. Just get your missus. Is she in?'

'Where else would she be?'

'Don't get pert with me, girl.'

'What in the name of whatever god happens to be awake is going on now?' demanded Fabio, appearing at Blod's elbow and rubbing his eyes.

'The mason wants to see the Master, but I dunno who the master is. Is it you? You're about all that's left. Anyway, then the mason said he'd see the Mistress but I'm afraid to ask her. You know what she's like -'

'And how would that be?' said Lucretia. She was robed and regal, standing with her arms crossed and her nose up.

Blod squealed, dropped her basin and ran to the kitchen.

'What is it, mason?' said Lucretia. 'Why are the men not working? I had hoped to have this ready by the end of the month.'

'Well, the thing is,' said the mason, glancing at Fabio, 'is it possible to have a word in private?'

Lucretia waved Fabio away. 'He is of no consequence. What did you want to say?'

The mason sucked his teeth, then breathed out. 'When's Urbanicus returning from... wherever he is? That girl said Londinium, but that's ridiculous.'

'My brother-in-law can command the finest horses.'

'Can he now? The thing is, I've still got problems on this job. The men don't like it. Things staring at them from the woods, things going missing. I've got men refusing to work and slaves legging it.'

'Is anything technical hindering the building?'

'Nooo, just uneasiness. They're worried they've offended Diffis.'

'I thought we'd resolved all this.'

'Well, they say we should have started with a temple and built the money-spinner afterwards.'

Lucretia pursed her lips and said: 'That's what I told you to do in the first place.'

'No it's not, you...' The mason met Lucretia's stare and drew in breath. 'We will rectify that immediately,' he said. 'Once you pay me some of the wages due.'

'It's not the end of the month yet.'

'It's not just wages. I've still got expenses that Urbanicus promised to pay. And now I hear he's disappeared.'

'He hasn't disappeared, he's away on business. Anyway, why can't the expenses wait? Your men are mostly slaves.'

'Mostly, yes, but not all. And either way they've got to eat. So have I, come to that.'

'Very well,' said Lucretia. 'Stay there.'

Shutting the door in the mason's face, Lucretia went into her room and, checking that no one was watching,

201

uncovered a loose flagstone under her bed and drew out a small chest. She braced herself for its weight, and fell backwards. Frowning, she unlocked it and opened the lid. Inside was nothing but a tarnished bronze bracelet in the shape of a dragon biting its tail. Slowly she closed the lid, locked it and replaced it under the bed. Her heart thudded. Two days ago it had been full with bags of denarii and the more valuable pieces of her jewellery, which she didn't keep in her trinket box. She touched her ears, checking that her gold earrings had not been taken in the night also. Standing up, she felt sweat forming on her face and wiped it off. Her eyes darted around the room, and her heart raced. Forcing her breathing to slow and her expression back into haughty grandeur, she wondered how to put the mason off. Perhaps she could offer a bottle of Gaulish wine. That would suffice. Maybe a small bag of raisins or pepper. Maybe a tiny jar of Iberian oil.

She opened her mouth to call for Blod.

No, she thought, *it would all take too much explanation. Best wait until Poppaea is back. She has a way with the slaves.* Lucretia's ears strained for the rattle of the wagon coming up the lane.

She sailed back towards the front door and motioned Fabio to open it.

'Ah, there you are!' she said, as if surprised to see the mason there.

'Like that, is it?' he said. 'I thought -'

They were interrupted by a yell from the slopes behind the house, simultaneous with the thunder and clop of the wagon as it pulled up in front of the villa.

'What?' the mason yelled towards the spring, stepping back from under the thatch.

The shouted words were still indistinguishable to Lucretia, but the mason frowned and turned to Ondi as he pulled on the reins.

'Here you. Can you get that wagon up the slope over the grass?'

'Maybe, if the ground's hard enough. But the pony's knackered.'

'Well, have you got some sort of stretcher or litter?'

'Kind of,' said Ondi, glancing at Lucretia.

Lollia, Poppaea and Camilla climbed down from the wagon.

'What's going on?' said Lucretia to the mason. 'Why do you want a stretcher?'

'There's a body up on the grass,' he said. 'My foreman's just found it.'

'A body?'

Ondi blanched. 'Master Pomponius?'

'Why would he be out and about?' said Camilla. 'It's barely the ninth hour. He's rarely up before noon.'

'He went hunting at dawn, Madam. At least that's what I thought he was doing.'

'Pomponius?' said Lucretia and Fabio together.

There was another yell from the slope.

'Quick!' said the mason. 'It sounds like he's still alive. But we might not have long.'

'I'll get him,' said Ondi, unhitching the pony. 'It'll be quickest to bring him back on the pony's back. Come on girl, you'll be fine.'

'No,' said Poppaea. 'Ondi, go back to town for Tryssa and the guard. Mason, get your men to carry Pomponius down here. Camilla and I can help. We'll do our best till Tryssa arrives. It's just as well I stocked up on medicines. Ondi...'

'Yes, Madam?'

'Hurry.'

'Yes Madam.'

***

Under Tryssa's supervision, Poppaea and Camilla cleaned and packed the stab wound in Pomponius's side with moss and linen. Pomponius had muttered just a few words, 'I hope your teeth aren't blunt,' and then fell silent. His was breathing better now, but he remained grey and his pulse low. As soon as she arrived Tryssa had given him a small dose of poppy water, and he slept.

'It was too much for him, wasn't it?' said Blod, picking up the bloodied scraps for burning. 'The thought of living without his beloved wife. Decided to finish it all. So romantic.'

'Really?' said Camilla, 'I didn't think they could stand each other.'

'Oh sometimes that's how married couples get when perhaps they weren't the best match, Madam. Underneath it all, I'm sure he loved her. I mean - he tried to kill himself for grief.'

'And how do you think he did that?' said Tryssa.

'Well it's obvious. Stabbed himself,' said Blod. 'Just didn't do it in the right place. He was from the city, wasn't he? If you've never really killed anything, I guess you don't really know where to do it, and he was a bit ... erm ... round. Perhaps that was the trouble, Madam Tryssa, it must be hard to get through all that flesh. What do you reckon Madam?'

'That's an interesting theory,' said Tryssa. 'But I'd like to know how he managed to hit himself over the head, stab himself in the back and lose the knife.'

'Well ... maybe he fell after he stabbed himself, knocked some sense into his own brain, changed his mind and dragged himself out of the woods while still conscious, and then probably fainted or something.'

Tryssa pointed at the ruined clothes they'd cut off Pomponius, and the soiled rags they'd used to clean him with. 'No matter how desperate he might have been, I don't think he could have dragged himself face-down and backwards, so that his face got covered in mud and leaves went up his nostrils. This is not a suicide attempt.' Tryssa paused. 'But as a murder attempt, it's very odd that the murderer did not simply leave him in the woods to bleed to death.'

'Second thoughts?' said Camilla.

'Or warning?' said Poppaea.

'Or something else altogether,' said Tryssa.

Lucretia looked down at her slumbering son-in-law. 'When he wakes up -'

'*If* he wakes up,' pointed out Tryssa.

'If he wakes up, he can tell us.'

'You need to keep him under guard, Lucretia. And you need to release Vulpo and Gwil. They had nothing to do with this. Nothing whatsoever.'

Chapter Twenty-Five - Doubts
June 22nd (ante diem x Kalendas Julias)

Poppaea stepped out into the garden wiping her bloody hands on a rag. Although her morning sickness was all but gone, the sight of Pomponius would have been enough to make a statue feel nauseous. Tryssa said his breathing seemed good. There was none of the snoring she associated with a cracked skull. And the wounds seemed clean since, so far, there was no fever. Perhaps he would be all right. Perhaps he would wake and when he did, his story would explain everything. There was nothing further Tryssa could do, so she had gone home. Poppaea hoped that wherever Marcellus was, someone was caring for him as well as they were caring for Pomponius. It would be so good to see him again.

'Poppaea.' Lucretia's voice made her jump.

'Yes, Lucretia.'

'I don't understand why you're smiling. It's been a very trying few days.'

'I'm sorry. I didn't realise I was. I'm glad Pomponius may be saved. Looking forward to Marcellus coming home.'

'I need to ask you something, Poppaea. Did you tell Gwil where the money was?'

Poppaea paused in her hand-washing and stared. 'Whatever do you mean? I don't even know myself. You have never seen fit to tell me. Not in ten years of my living here.'

Lucretia threw her hands up. 'Is everyone determined to think of themselves all the time? My money has been stolen and rather than comfort me, all you do is to imagine yourself slighted. I am doubly bereaved and need support, yet all Lollia cares about is some wrinkled old slave who smelt of manure.'

206

'She was his -'

'Yes, yes. So you say. And not only has the building work stopped, but Pomponius has to make it worse by disturbing the workmen further.'

'I'm sure when he comes to, he'll apologise.'

'Lunch!' shrieked Blod.

'I don't suppose for one minute you inquired about new slaves in town this morning.'

'No, I was busy.'

'Doing what?'

'Deciding whether or not to go back to my mother's.'

Lucretia was silent for a moment. 'Without Marcellus?'

'I hope he will join us when he returns.'

'I really don't think he'd leave me for you. I am his mother.'

Poppaea shrugged. 'I will join you after changing,' she said. 'Then I will ask Fabio to read this out to us. It was waiting at the town gates for you.' She waved a sealed roll of parchment.

'That is Urbanicus's seal.'

'Yes.'

'Give it to me.'

Poppaea stepped sideways. 'I'll bring it through to the dining room in a moment.'

***

Clean, fresh, and clasping the scroll, Poppaea reclined alongside Camilla. The younger woman was silent, eating nothing and staring into her goblet. The rest of the family picked at the bread and cheese. The cook had threatened to find a better employer if their appetites didn't pick up, but it was hard to feel much interest while everything made so little sense. Lollia stood by Lucretia, wringing her hands.

207

'What is it, woman?'

'Madam, is it true they will release Gwil?'

'Apparently so,' said Lucretia, picking a grape pip from her teeth. 'Apparently it turns out that he is a citizen and has rights.'

Lollia smiled.

'What are you grinning about? What's it to you that he's a citizen? I'd have thought you'd be annoyed. I still maintain he is behind all this trouble.'

'No Madam. No. Not Gwil.'

'You wanted to kill him yourself two days ago.'

'I was not thinking straight, Madam. I was blind.'

'You certainly are, that's the second time you've overfilled my goblet. Poppaea!'

Poppaea jumped.

'Pass that parchment over to someone who can read it.'

Poppaea gave it to Fabio. 'There was other news in town,' she said. 'It slipped my mind, what with Pomponius being found.'

'They've recaptured Hastorix and Aurelia?'

'No, it wasn't that. They're still at large. They haven't been seen on the roads. Contractes thinks they must have tried to put people off their scent. Certainly no dogs can find them. He thinks they went up river or down towards the sea.'

'Or they could have gone into the forest.' said Fabio.

'Without being seen?' asked Tullia.

'Other people's clothes, someone else's pony,' suggested Fabio. 'All the same, I wouldn't fancy their chances.'

'Surviving in the woods with all those animals?' said Camilla.

'It was the animals I was thinking of.' Fabio sipped some wine. 'Hastorix could probably bite the head off a wolf if he wanted to.'

'Stop wasting time,' said Lucretia. 'Read my letter.'

Fabio broke the seal and scanned the parchment. His face went red and he said nothing.

Tullia broke the silence. 'You were saying there was other news, Poppaea.'

'Oh, that's it,' said Poppaea. 'Lucretia, you remember those strange men who were here the other day, seeking Urbanicus?'

'Who told you about them?'

'I'm not deaf.'

'Well, what about them?'

'They fell in the river and drowned. Washed downstream.'

'How very odd.'

'They were seen drinking with someone under a tree shortly beforehand. Apparently they were all staggering about the place, drunk as Bacchus. They must have gone off the road where the riverbank is crumbling and ... splash! That river's faster than you'd think and full of weed.' She shuddered. 'They must have got tangled up in it, and couldn't get to the surface.'

'I don't suppose anyone will miss them, although I wonder if whoever found the bodies retrieved my amulet,' said Lucretia.

'Why did they have your amulet?' asked Poppaea.

Lucretia flushed. 'Stop asking irrelevances. Now come along, Fabio. What does that scroll say?'

Fabio's face was redder than ever. 'Aunt, perhaps you'd like me to read it to you privately.'

'Don't be absurd.'

Fabio took a breath and glanced round at the family. What seemed like a million weeks ago there had been a dinner party for Anguis and a room-full of reclining people, eating Briccio's specialities. Now, including Tryssa, there were just six. That evening was when it had all gone wrong.

'Get on with it,' snapped Lucretia.

Fabio bit his lip, then started reading.

'"*Greetings dear sister-in-law, most beauteous Lucretia.*"'

Lucretia preened herself. Lollia, behind her, pulled a face as if nauseous.

'"*Londinium, for all its magnificence, has not the beauty which you possess. Nor do the finest ladies here have your refinement or culture.*"'

'Good gods,' muttered Camilla. 'I really don't believe he's in Londinium if he can't find anyone more refined than Aunt Lucretia.'

'"*And may I say that the baths in Aquae Sulis are not as fine as those which you will build on your land, bringing wealth and blessings to your loved ones.*"'

'If she has any loved ones,' muttered Lollia.

Poppaea glanced at her and frowned. Lollia returned an impassive stare.

'"*I will return the day after you receive this.*"'

'Wonderful!' said Lucretia.

'Impossible,' muttered Camilla.

'"*And I will bring news and...*" there's something scratched out, I can't make it out - "*and.... something... will replenish your coffers to overflowing.*"'

'Replenish?' said Tullia. 'Were the coffers empty?'

'Of course not,' said Lucretia, avoiding Poppaea's gaze.

'"*Since one must speculate to accumulate, it is now that our ship has come in to fruit.*"'

Everyone squinted as they tried to visualise this.

'"*And once I return, with my investments blossomed, I will oversee the building of our baths, I mean, dear beautiful lady, your baths but I hope, I am not mistaken, that you have a warm regard for me and hope, that once your broken heart has recovered from its grief at the loss of my brother, you will consent to be my wife.*"'

Poppaea watched Lucretia's face squirm as she tried to combine grief with bashfulness and smugness. It was an unpleasant sight.

'Do you suppose,' Lucretia muttered to Poppaea, 'Tryssa could make up a potion which would enable me to have a child? I am, after all, only fifty-three.'

'No,' said Poppaea. 'She can do difficult but she can't do impossible.'

'Obnoxious girl.'

Poppaea shrugged. 'Does he say anything about Marcellus?' she asked.

'No. He finishes: "*I hope we will have many years of living like kings before us. Yours until we meet again, my something throbs -*' oh it says heart, thank the gods for that, "*my heart throbs with longing for you. Your loving and supportive suitor, Urbanicus.*"'

The room fell silent. Into the pause, Lollia said, 'Madam, I am begging you. Get a guard here. Bring Gwil back.'

'Gwil? He was trying to defraud me.'

'But I don't think he meant you any harm, Madam. Not physical harm. But everything is amiss and he is at least young and strong.'

'Lollia, you cannot tell me what to do. You forget yourself.'

'But Madam, he is young and strong and can protect us.'

'I will think about it. But all that aside, Fabio, tomorrow I want you to go to the slave market. Mention Blod.'

There was a wail from the hall. Lucretia raised her voice.

'Not the the slave market in Pecunia, but the bigger one further downstream. I am rather tired of all the inbreds here. Blod, stop crying, I'm not selling you on. Yet. I would get too many complaints. But maybe Ondi can choose a child to assist in the kitchen, so that you can be released to learn from Lollia. And Ondi, bring back some muscle as the new gardener. It's rather a shame we didn't think of buying Hastorix before he escaped. Although perhaps that would have been cruel to Prisca's memory.'

Blod came in, red-eyed, to clear dishes.

'Have you looked in on Master Pomponius?' said Tryssa.

'Yes, Madam. He's muttering.'

'I'll come.'

Tryssa rose and went out of the room. Poppaea followed.

In the cool of his bedroom, Pomponius groaned. He was very pale and when he squirmed, blood seeped through the bandages.

'I may have to stitch it,' whispered Tryssa. 'I will need the men to hold him down. I am just afraid of doing it until I'm sure the wound is clean.'

'Pomponius,' said Poppaea, 'it's Poppaea. You're all right. You're home.'

'I have been very cruel.'

'I'm sure you haven't.'

'I did it for the children, you see. In the end, I did it for them.'

'Did what?'

212

'My poor children.'

'Your children are safe in Isca.'

'Yes, but their inheritance. Prisca's inheritance. I couldn't risk losing it. You know what that old witch is like. I don't want it for myself, but for them. Just for them.'

Poppaea turned to make sure Lucretia was out of earshot. 'What did you do?' she muttered.

Pomponius stirred and his eyes flickered. He squinted up at Poppaea and then Tryssa.

'Am I still in the woods? Will the wolves eat me?'

'No. You're in your room,' said Poppaea. 'You're quite safe.'

'I couldn't see,' whispered Pomponius. 'I couldn't quite see.'

'Well it's very dark in the forest, I imagine,' soothed Tryssa.

'It wasn't that. It wasn't too dark. But he was too close. I can't see people so close.'

Tryssa exchanged a glance with Poppaea and said: 'Who?'

'It was very strange,' Pomponius murmured..

'What was?' said Tryssa. 'What was very strange?'

'How could he do that?' The words were barely audible.

'Who?' said Tryssa. 'Who did what?'

Pomponius closed his eyes and his breath faltered, rattled, then stopped.

213

Chapter Twenty-Six - Tullia Decides
June 23rd (ante diem ix Kalendas Julias)

The following day, after lunch, Tullia wandered with Lollia towards the site of the spring. Imprisoned in channels, it trickled from the edge of the forest. The trees were heavy with leaf and the beginning of fruits and nuts could just be seen.

Tullia, pausing just far enough from the water to avoid muddy feet, peered into the woodland.

'It's very dark,' she said to Lollia. 'I don't remember it being so gloomy when I was little.'

She stepped into the wood and felt rather than heard the tiny scurryings of small creatures in the undergrowth, and wondered if it was the Sight or imagination which made her sure that bigger eyes were watching. A bush in the middle distance, dark and shaggy, seemed to move as if padding from side to side. So little light could penetrate the branches that it could have been brown or grey or black. A shape could be a shrub or a wolf or a bear, or a person? Tullia shook herself and blinked round at the slave, standing silent in the sunshine.

'Perhaps you weren't here then, Lollia, although I'm sure you were,' she said, 'but we used to play here, me and Rhee, that is Lucretia, and Tryssa, though of course I was a lot younger and used to tag along after them. I even followed Rhys and his friends. We were all just children, of course. The boys were shocking. They used to hide behind trees and jump out on us. They'd threaten to tie us to trunks so that we'd be eaten by something. But all the same, it didn't do to let on we were scared. And at least we girls didn't have to do what they had to do; go into the wood one day and kill a beast on their own.'

214

Lollia grunted.

'Yes, of course, I forgot. You were born a long way away. Perhaps your boys don't have to do such things…'

'They do,' said Lollia.

'Well, it was always the way among our people, wasn't it? Long before anyone tried to tell us we weren't civilised. And despite what Lucretia says, there were only so many of the Roman ways our father would put up with. He said Romans tried to teach us reason and by doing so took our spirit. Rhys served in the army, as an auxiliary. He had no real issue with that. But there were still things he expected us to know about our heritage: an awareness of the land, of the trees, of the sea, of the western skies. How to listen to silence, how to respect our foe. How to mourn the animals we hunted and be grateful for their spilt blood. I see you know what I mean. The Romans have lost much of this, don't you think?'

Lollia nodded.

'How long have you been in my sister's service?'

'Thirty years, Madam.'

'It is time to free you then.'

'That's up to Madam Lucretia.'

'I'll speak to her, I promise. But you see, I remember this place and what it was. I remember what our father said about everything. About making the most of what was offered, but not losing what we knew. And then the boys died, one by one. Perhaps you don't remember Bryn and Mor, but I'm sure you recall Rhys being killed. It was such a shock. And shortly afterwards, Lucretia married Porcius. Once Father died, I suppose Porcius thought he could make the most of Roman law and claim this land through his marriage, but he should have known he wouldn't get past

215

Lucretia. She was always cleverer than all of us. She always gets her way no matter the cost. But she can't *see*. Only *I* could see. And yet I am confused, very confused.'

Tullia closed her eyes and opened her arms, as if trying to embrace the breeze , the musky, animal scent of the wood, and the dank muddy smell of the spring.

'I remember all Father said, but I don't recall him mentioning any goddess in this place. Not even a string of memory is plucked at the name Diffis. I suppose I was the youngest. I was only five or so when father died, but even so...'

She opened her eyes and smiled beyond Lollia, who turned to see Fabio ascending the hill with long strides.

'Darling!' said Tullia. 'What a surprise to see you!'

'We were having lunch half an hour ago.'

'Yes, but I thought you were composing music for Poppaea, based on Marcellus's poems.'

'Well I've escaped,' said Fabio. 'Have you actually heard those poems?'

'Yes indeed, I am so happy that such creativity has come down from Mother to so many of her family. Marcellus, and you, and of course me in my own small way. I still have hopes for Camilla, and who knows what Julia may become. Prisca, I fear, was always a lost cause.'

'Yes but Mother, have you actually *listened* to Marcellus's poems? They're terrible. I'm not sure I can bring myself to associate my music with them. I was coming to see if you'd intervene. On top of that, there was something in a footnote of that awful letter which means that Aunt Lucretia keeps burbling about me going into the army. Can't you come down and get them to leave me alone?'

216

'Not just now dear, I need to work something out. But I wonder if you could take Lollia back down to the house and help Lucretia sort out the manumission paperwork. It's about time she was free, don't you think?'

'Madam,' said Lollia, 'you shouldn't stay up here alone.'

'Nonsense. I will follow shortly.' Tullia fluttered her hands to wave them off down the hill.

She stood watching them go, looking down on the villa as it glinted in the sun, and the marshy ground below it. She could see figures, family, slaves, outside the walls, in the garden, busy and fussing. She tried to work out who was who, but they were distant and fuzzy.

Tullia walked over to the abandoned half-built bath-house. It was square and incongruous and, she felt, quite possibly rather small. She stepped inside to find where the spring had been piped into the basin.

She crouched near its source, reaching out to touch the water with her finger and taste it. She waited to feel the divinity of a goddess ancestor come to life in her veins, hear her voice perhaps, but there was nothing. Her blood pumped as normal, her ears heard nothing but skylarks and songbirds and the secret rustling of the woodland.

'It's very strange,' she said aloud. 'If you are here, Diffis, I don't understand why you'd make yourself known to Lucretia and not to me. She has never been interested in the spiritual at all. I believe I should take the children and go home. I don't really believe in mixing money and religion. It seems to miss the point somehow. That nice sect, that one about love and forgiveness - have you heard about it? It was considered a terrible nuisance a while ago, what with people arguing with the emperor and saying that one person was as good as another in the sight of their god, and that money couldn't assure a good afterlife. Now some people say it will be the next craze. It's very curious. Well, all I can say is that it seems very kind now, but I hope no-one decides to mix it with money and power, because then it'll be just as bad as any of them. Well, Diffis, you are still silent. I really don't approve. I think I'll have to tell everyone what I know, and if that means falling out with Lucretia then so be it. Fabio and Camilla will just have to make do with their other grandparents' wealth, such as it is. I am decided, Diffis - no, not Diffis, for you do not exist. I am going to tell everyone that this whole thing is nonsense, and when I return to Glevum I will ensure everyone knows it is rubbish. People can make of that what they will. If it fails on account of what I say, perhaps it will be for the best.'

She started to stand, finding herself stiffer than she'd expected. She was conscious that someone was beside her and turned, half expected to find Diffis and ready to beg forgiveness for her lack of faith. But it was not Diffis. The figure was against the sun and hard to discern. Tullia's eyes struggled to adjust.

'Oh! How did you get to be here?' said Tullia. 'Could you help me up? Who is that with you? No! That can't be. Whatever are you doing with that piece of brick?'

The blow knocked her into the basin and as her eyes closed, the water flowed red as it soaked into her white dress and the muddy stone.

Chapter Twenty-Seven - Wig
June 23rd (ante diem ix Kalendas Julias)

Lucretia peered into the bronze mirror again. She had not survived into her fifties by being nice, and it was an effort to raise her eyebrows enough to eradicate the deep frown lines, in order to appear simultaneously coy and alluring. Apart from that, however, with a little subtle make-up she could surely pass for less than thirty, especially with the new wig.

Lucretia was proud of the wig. It was fashioned in the latest style with ringlets and braids made from black Indian hair threaded with golden German hair. It piled in effusion over a face she had been painting for an hour. Her cheeks bore rosy circles. Admittedly it gave the impression of fever rather than bashfulness, but that was the modern style and presumably men realised that. Her eyelids were bluer than a summer sky, her lashes blackened into sooty sultriness. It was a shame that the kohl made her eyes water, but provided the day remained cool, the whole effect should not melt.

Arranging pearls and scarves around her very slightly dry neck, Lucretia thrust out her bosom and practised forming her lips into a kissable pout.

The door opened and Julia sidled in.

'Ooh Grandma, can you show me how to do that?' she said. 'You've made your mouth look exactly like the cat's bum-hole.'

'You loathsome child!' Lucretia threw a pot of ointment at her grand-daughter, but Julia fled giggling. The pot struck the closing door.

'Blod!' shrieked Lucretia, rising to push Lollia out of the way and wrench open the door. 'Round up Julia and take her to cook! Tell him to roast her for dinner and serve her up with radishes.'

219

She readjusted the wig and sat down. With a struggle she forced her face back into a welcoming smile, and practised a gentler pout. She glanced sideways at Lollia.

'You've heard of women having babies late in life, haven't you?'

'It's rare, Madam, but not unheard of.'

'Still,' said Lucretia, 'I doubt Urbanicus really wants a legitimate son or he'd have married years ago. I'm sure he'll be happy to adopt Marcellus. It's somewhat of a relief. I don't remember anything delightful about pregnancy and childbirth. Do you?'

Lollia stiffened as she tidied the dressing table. 'No, Madam.'

'I've always thought it was a shame a freeborn woman couldn't get a slave to do it for her. I suppose that's an option, if necessary.'

Blod burst in and opened her mouth to speak. Then, looking at Lucretia properly, she gawped. 'Have you got a fever, Madam? And did you know your hair's all wonky?'

'On the other hand,' said Lucretia, 'perhaps not. Go away, Blod.' She picked the mirror up again and stared into it.

'I remember when you got that mirror,' said Lollia. 'Your brother Rhys gave it to you, just before he died.'

Lucretia blinked.

'You haven't forgotten him, have you Madam?'

'No, of course not. Why does everyone keep talking about him? It's a long time since he died.'

Lollia rearranged the pearls round Lucretia's neck and tidied the wig's curls. 'I don't know why anyone else would mention him Madam, but…'

'But what? Will you spit out whatever it is you want to say.'

220

Lollia paused.'You never went to the woods after he died. Not the part where they brought out his body, anyway. And then one day you did and you found the spring. And since then, you've talked in your sleep.'

'What nonsense.'

'I remember back when your father changed things.'

Lucretia grunted.

'It wasn't long after he bought me to serve you. You were Rhee and your brother was Rhys. And then your father changed your names and built a villa. But your father and brother never really became Romans, Madam, did they? Master Rhys never kept his Roman name. Not like you.'

Lucretia stared into the mirror and tried to make out Lollia's face in the reflection. It was hard to see. Lollia was simply an indistinct bronze image, ageless, passive, unreadable.

For a moment it was if the slave was still a girl, and it took Lucretia's mind back to herself at fourteen or so, with a new name and a world of sophistication opening up to her. Rhys had been a fool. He'd had the chance to go out in the world and yet he couldn't be doing with all the Roman stuff. When Father changed their names, it was as much a surprise to Rhys as to anyone in Pecunia. He didn't want a villa and reclining and being waited on. He wanted hunting and farming and mucking in. He didn't mind having slaves. That was how things got done. If you had no money, you were a slave. If you had some, you owned a slave. After a while, the owner might free the slave with a pot of cash to add to whatever they'd earned on the side over the years. And their children would be free. Rhys was fine with that, everyone was fine with that. It was the way of the world. Rhys would have worked alongside the slaves when need be. Lucretia didn't want any of that.

'Who would want to be a farmer's wife?' Lucretia said, unaware she spoke out loud.

'I wouldn't have minded,' said Lollia.

'Well, I would,' said Lucretia. 'Porcius was a citizen and offered a life of being treated like a princess, nay, a goddess. He had connections.'

'Shame about the land.'

'What land? He didn't have any.'

'Of course, Madam. He didn't, did he? I had quite forgotten. But you had.' There was a smirk in Lollia's voice.

'Anyway, what nonsense is this about talking in my sleep? I am not fanciful like Tullia.'

'No, Madam. That's why it's been so strange to hear you dreaming about Rhys and the boar.'

'He went into the woods to catch a boar and the boar won. It was a long time ago, but he was my brother. It was a terrible shock seeing his body.'

'And you were waiting just inside the forest for him.'

'How do you remember that, after all this time?'

'I was looking for you. And you were the one who found him and raised the alarm.'

'I needed to speak to him, Lollia. And, none of it was then, nor is it now, any concern of yours. Rhys died, and it was very sad. But it was also a long time ago. At least the land stayed in the family. I never let that flatulent fool of a husband take control. My father would have been proud of the wealth I've accumulated.'

She put the mirror down and turned to narrow her eyes at Lollia. The slave stood, calm as ever, white-haired, cold-faced. Too old to sell on, too observant and useful to pension off.

222

'I am sure you know already, because I daresay you were eavesdropping as usual, that I was talking to Urbanicus about the old days. I do not usually dream, but that night I dreamt about Rhys, and the next day I went to pay my respects to his shade. And when I was there I found the spring, and I remembered about Diffis.'

'Mmm.'

'What do you mean, "mmm"? Anyway, going back to children, as soon as Marcellus is back I need to explain that he must put aside the poetry and concentrate on making a profit. I can see that I have been lax in training him. Perhaps with the help of Diffis -'

'Mmm.'

'There you go again. I've rediscovered a holy spring in a place so far off the beaten track that the locals don't even know there *is* a track. And here we are in the land of the Britons, who are so bored of Roman gods and goddesses with their inadequate clothes and patrician noses, but are forgetting their own. Yet we all retain the urge to sacrifice, don't we?'

Lollia said nothing.

'And the thing about a sacrifice, if you remember,' Lucretia continued, 'is that it has to be worth it. It has to be the best. Not the worst. The highest born. Not the lowest.'

'What if it is the wrong sacrifice to the wrong god, Madam?' said Lollia. 'What if it isn't worth it all along?'

'Please don't tell me you belong to that peculiar sect with a god who makes furniture or fishes or something. The one who says everyone is the same really and money means nothing. Fool. That sect needs to be stamped on. There is nothing more important than money. Nothing. You're a slave, you of all people should realise that. Pour me some wine.'

Lucretia turned back to peruse herself. She half closed her eyes to check that the mosquito bite on her eyelid had disappeared. Then she closed them completely. In her mind she saw Poppaea with her secrets and silences, pulling Marcellus away. Porcius drinking their savings. And Urbanicus, wise and travelled, leaning close to whisper, '*no-one appreciates you, my dear. No-one but me.*'

And she heard the wine being poured into the goblet and she thought of the spring trickling over her feet as, so many years ago, Rhys's blood had once trickled.

Chapter Twenty-Eight - Revelations
June 23rd (ante diem ix Kalendas Julias)

'Madam! The snooty Roman bloke is here,' said Blod, putting her head round the door.

'Anguis?' Lucretia patted her curls and bit her lips. 'The only person I was expecting today was the priest, about Pomponius. I'm not fit to see the Decurion wearing this hideous black again. It makes me look sallow. Where is Lollia?'

'Just come in from walking out with Mistress Tullia.'

Lucretia glanced into her mirror. How many years were there between her and Tullia? Six or so? Surely not. Surely she looked younger than the little sister of the daydreams and vague worries.

'Arrange the seating so that Tullia sits in the sun. It will improve her pallor.'

'She is not back yet, Madam.'

'Well, settle Anguis somewhere sunny and I'll be there shortly. Where is Camilla?'

'Mooning about in the orchard, Madam.'

'That is very disrespectful, Blod. Make sure she stays there.'

'I don't think that'll be hard, Madam, she's arguing with that Budic again.'

'Dear gods. I hope she isn't losing her head.'

'She hasn't kissed him yet.'

'Don't spy. And good. Don't let her. I am still hopeful she might marry Anguis. Although...' - she fluttered her blackened eyelashes at herself in the bronze mirror - 'he might prefer a *real* woman. Go on then, off with you. And send Lollia to me. I will go against tradition and change into white. I never liked Pomponius anyway.'

Blod, looking appalled, left the room, colliding with Lollia in the doorway. Lucretia stood as Lollia arranged the folds of her dress. How tiresome of Lollia to be so emotionless. Nothing showed on her face. Nothing. She was worse than Poppaea. The slave was thin, her elbows and shoulders bony and her hair white. She had gone white so young that Lucretia could not recall its original colour, although she had an image of bronzed sunshine when she thought back. Lollia's skin rarely burnt, but the skin around her green eyes was lined. Her hands, required to care for Lucretia, were kept soft with the lotions Poppaea made, but her knuckles and fingers were twisted. It would be nice to have a body slave who was more decorative and less sulky. Not too decorative, of course, and at least Lollia made a nice contrast with real beauty.

'Stand next to me when I am outside,' commanded Lucretia. 'Make sure I'm in a shady spot with just a little light trickling onto my hair. What?'

'Nothing, Madam.'

In the garden, Anguis waited. He started at the sight of Lucretia, walking with more deliberation than was usual, the wig heavy on her head.

'Good afternoon, Anguis,' she said.

'Good afternoon, dear lady. You appear quite...' His eyes swept her from head to toe. 'Quite breathtaking.'

Lucretia tried to remember how to simper.

Anguis kissed her hand. 'I have come to offer my apologies for Olivarius's somewhat over-enthusiastic courtship of your niece. Perhaps it's what happens if you employ the child of a freedman. I had no idea he would cause you such anguish.'

'I understand he will be returning later to make his own apology.'

'So I believe. I am concerned, however, that he knows rather too much of our plans. That is, your discovery and its potential.'

Lucretia considered. 'That had not, I confess, occurred to me.'

'You don't suppose he brought Gwil here? Although having said that, they never seemed to have much to do with each other. I don't even recall them standing very close together. Do you?'

Lucretia frowned as she pictured them.

Anguis continued. 'However, I am minded to keep Olivarius in my employ so that I can keep an - er ... encourage his support. I will also arrange for the remaining darts to be burnt.'

'Do you think that's necessary?'

'Accidents can happen.' Anguis tapped the side of his nose.

'I suppose you're right,' said Lucretia. 'But I'm sure everything has settled down now and we can progress. And we need to marry Camilla off to someone whose influence will benefit us all. Someone who can help ensure the bathhouse, I mean shrine, is very well attended by the best people.'

'Building has ceased.'

'I have been assured it will restart tomorrow.' Lucretia nodded to emphasise her point and felt the wig move. She straightened up and wiggled her head to reposition it. 'I'm sure you agree, Decurion, that Camilla needs a mature husband who can keep her in line. Perhaps a Roman official ... wise and cultured. Unless of course that official wouldn't prefer an older wife of mature years.'

She fluttered her eyelashes and Anguis blinked.

'Still no Marcellus?' he said.

'No but I'm sure when Urbanicus returns, all will be clear.'

'And that will be...?'

'People coming!' shrieked Blod.

Lucretia rolled her eyes. 'Lollia, will you please train her properly?'

She took Anguis's arm and they stepped towards the front of the house and saw what appeared to be a cavalcade coming up the lane. Urbanicus was on a fine horse weighed down with saddle-bags, and beyond him was a small group in a cart which might or might not be the villa's. The dust made it hard to tell.

Urbanicus pulled up and dismounted. Lucretia dropped her eyes without lowering her head, for fear the wig would slip again, and blinked up at him under her eyelashes.

'My dear Lucretia,' he said, 'you appear quite ... I am amazed. And by the way,' he rummaged in a pouch, 'I think this is yours. I came across it when we took our horses to drink at the river. However did it get there?'

He handed over the golden amulet.

'Were you burgled too, Lucretia?' said Anguis. 'I hadn't realised. Pecunia is turning into a den of thieves. I must apply for more guards.'

'Indeed, Anguis,' agreed Lucretia. 'That might be wise. But for now, welcome Urbanicus. Could we -'

'Honoured Decurion,' said Urbanicus, 'do you mind if I speak private family business with my sister-in-law?'

'Not at all.' Anguis walked off into the garden.

'Firstly I must apologise for taking the liberty of borrowing money without asking,' said Urbanicus, once the Decurion was out of earshot. 'I needed the cash in a hurry when I rushed after Marcellus, and I couldn't find you.'

228

'There were some men, Novus and Septimus...'

'Really? I'm sorry if they worried you.' Urbanicus linked Lucretia's arm through his elbow and patted her hand. 'I once did some business with their master, Primus. There was a misunderstanding. But it's all resolved now and here is your money returned threefold.'

'You haven't been gambling have you, my ... my dear.'

'Certainly not, my ... darling. I hope that things have been peaceful in my absence.'

'Well not really,' said Lucretia. 'I need to tell you -'

'We must get Fabio into the army, you know.'

'I agree. And we must get Camilla married to Anguis as soon as possible.'

'Well, maybe.' Urbanicus smiled, his hand now gently stroking Lucretia's.

'Why not?' she argued. 'The marriage would maintain his interest in the spring and his influence is not to be sniffed at.'

'Yes but we needn't marry Camilla off immediately. We could keep her in store, so to speak.'

'For whom do you intend to store her?'

'I'm sure the right person will become available. Eventually.'

'Technically,' Lucretia pointed out, 'she is not ours to marry off. She belongs to my sister's husband's father.'

'Nonsense. This is her family home. She belongs here.'

'Until we have more slaves,' said Lucretia, 'I'm not sure I can cope with Camilla on top of everything else. She is very argumentative. However, hopefully that's the wagon with my new purchases coming up the lane now.' She frowned. 'Oh for the love of Gaia, it's not.

229

It's Tryssa. Why is that woman here again?' said Lucretia. 'Will no-one give me any peace?'

Olivarius helped Tryssa out of the cart and the guard tethered his pony. Poppaea came out of the house and greeted her. Anguis strode back to join them.

'I've come to see the body,' said Tryssa. She looked askance at Lucretia's hair.

'Poppaea and Camilla helped tend him all night and he still died,' said Lucretia. 'It was quite unnecessary since Blod and Lollia could have done it on their own. Everyone is quite exhausted this morning.'

'We did our best,' said Poppaea, ignoring Lucretia. 'There was nothing we could do.'

'Ah,' said Urbanicus, 'another slave has died, I see.'

'No, it is Pomponius.'

Urbanicus started. 'Pomponius?'

'Why are you so startled?' said Tryssa.

'I thought he was already d -' he coughed. 'Sorry, my throat's full of dust. I thought he was already definitely back in Isca.'

'Why would you think that?' asked Tryssa.

'Never mind any of that,' said Lucretia. 'If the fool of a city boy will go hunting and falls on his own knife...'

Tryssa tried to interpose. 'Lucretia...'

'Urbanicus,' said Lucretia, 'Marcellus has still not returned. You said there would be news by now and his note ... it said nothing about Aquae Sulis, it was about chewing.'

'Ah, my dear lady,' said Urbanicus, his face woeful, 'I didn't think to explain the message was in code. You cannot be too careful. But I am afraid I have bad news, nonetheless. Your son was indeed attacked by brigands on the road and his injuries are overwhelming him. I fear Marcellus will never return.'

Lucretia gasped. She stared across at her daughter-in-law, with rosy face and full hair, unquestionably with child. Poppaea's eyes were filling at the news and her lip trembled.

'No,' she whispered, 'no. Marcellus will return. He must.'

Tryssa spoke into the silence. 'Where is Tullia?'

'She's gone daydreaming at the spring,' said Lucretia. 'What does that matter when my son -'

'She went to the spring on her own?'

'The stupid woman dismissed Lollia. But what's more important is -'

A cry came from the kitchen door. Blod shrieked, 'It's a monster!'

They all turned to follow her hand which pointed up the slopes towards a misshapen hulk staggering along the lumpy ground. It was Hastorix, hunched under a burden and pulling something behind him.

Anguis commanded a passing slave. 'Quick, get some more help!'

Budic came running from the orchard and they all converged as Hastorix drew near with a small, slight form over his left shoulder, dragging a man along the ground with his right hand. A belt which had been bound round the captive's wrists.

Olivarius started to move forward, but Tryssa grabbed his arm and whispered in his ear. He placed himself behind Urbanicus. Urbanicus took a step back but Olivarius tripped him up, sending him sprawling.

'What are you doing?' snapped Lucretia.

'I do apologise, said Olivarius, reaching down for Urbanicus. He helped him up, without releasing his arm.

Fabio pushed past, his face white, his breath catching. He threw himself at Hastorix, pulling at the form on his shoulder. He yelled for his sister.

'Oh no!' said Poppaea.

Camilla rushed out of the house. 'It's Mother! It's Mother!'

'Whatever do you mean?' Lucretia frowned, the wig wobbling.

'Hastorix is carrying Mother,' said Fabio. 'I think she's dead.'

Camilla pulled on Tryssa and dragged at Lucretia. Anguis steadied Lucretia with a hand light on her shoulder, the black curls trailing on his knuckles. Urbanicus tried to step away but found his arm still clasped by Olivarius.

'I need to get something from my horse,' he said. 'I, er…, Lucretia needs to, er … Lucretia! Come with me my love, your sister will be fine. Come with me! Someone get this oaf off me.'

Lucretia twisted her head back and forth between Tullia on the gladiator's shoulder, Budic, who had taken over dragging the squirming captive through the grass, and Urbanicus, twisting in Olivarius's grip.

Hastorix, barely breaking a sweat, stopped in front of Tryssa and held out Tullia's sodden form. Fabio and Camilla clung to her. Tullia's dress was pinkened with diluted blood which had trickled down her face and through her hair. Her eyes were closed.

Budic strained to hold the prisoner with one hand and use the other to comfort Camilla. He was unable to reach.

Olivarius, gritting his teeth, held tighter onto Urbanicus's arm.

232

'It's all right,' said Tryssa, putting her arm round Camilla. 'It's all right. It's not like Pomponius. This was a very light blow. Your mother was saved in time.'

'He hit her and left her face down in the pool,' said Hastorix, kicking at the captive. 'So I hit him. I have tracked him for days. Now it is his turn to face death.'

'But who is it?' said Anguis.

'Vulpo!' exclaimed Lucretia. 'It must be. I told you he shouldn't be released.'

Budic pulled at the form on the ground and Hastorix, putting Tullia into Fabio's arms, helped wrench the captive up.

Camilla and Lucretia gasped.

Anguis looked blank. 'I am none the wiser,' he said. 'Who is this person?'

'It's Briccio!' cried Lollia, running forward. 'But you were dead!'

The bound man laughed. 'Like you care.'

Lollia gasped. 'Was it you who killed Lucco?' she whispered.

Briccio shrugged. 'It's not me you should blame.'

'But you killed him!' Lollia grabbed his filthy arm. Her nails dug into his grimy skin. Briccio swore and tried to lash out.

'If the old fool had kept his mouth shut he'd have been all right,' he snarled. 'But he knew that body wasn't me and he kept trying to tell people. I heard. In the end, I had no choice. I sort of regret that. Sort of. But none of it was my idea. And if I get protected like I was promised...'

'Are you responsible for the other murders?' said Anguis, 'You don't look like you have the brains.'

'Oh don't I?'

'Why didn't you just run away rather than wait all that time before killing Mistress Prisca?' sobbed Lollia.

'Why did you do it? She wasn't so bad. And then to kill my Lucco...'

'It didn't start with Prisca,' said Tryssa quietly. 'It started with Enrys, didn't it?'

'Enrys?' said Lucretia.

Briccio, pulling on the belt binding his wrists, sniggered. 'Huh. Soppy Enrys was no challenge...'

'Enrys?' repeated Lucretia.

'Dondras's lad,' said Tryssa.

Briccio spat. 'Not even much of a lad. Crying after the girl I'd softened up, dripping on about that made-up goddess, thought she'd solve all his problems didn't he? Find him a girl who'd be true, make his father more understanding. All I had to do was get him drunk and he poured it all out. I wasn't interested in killing him. But then he sneaked up to the spring, spying, listening in. He said he wasn't, but we'd come so far we weren't going to take any chances, were we? And then we realised Enrys was just the same size as me. All we had to do was mess him up and everyone would think, *that's the runaway Briccio, his face eaten off. Serves him right.* You just saw the clothes. None of you really knew whose body it was, did you? Why would you worry so much about a slave you'd look properly? You're all blind. All but Lucco.'

He glared at Lollia. Budic wrenched on the belt tying Briccio's wrists.

'What harm did he do you?' cried Lollia.

'None. But he knew the body wasn't mine. I heard him. It wasn't as if he didn't drop enough hints. Kept talking about being low, at ground level. He knew what my feet looked like. Any fool could have realised those feet weren't a slave's feet, but none of you did. No-one but Lucco. And after that it was following orders all the way.'

234

'And so you murdered the others?' said Tryssa. 'Porcius, Ritonix, Prisca, Pomponius.'

'Oh as if they're a loss. Drunken Porcius, suspicious Ritonix, prissy Prisca, pathetic Pomponius...'

'And you murdered them?'

Briccio shrugged and spat again.

'And Marcellus?' whispered Poppaea, 'did you murder Marcellus?'

'Hah!' said Briccio. 'It was a fate worse than death for him.' He laughed.

'What do you mean?' begged Poppaea.

'Are you confessing this?' said Tryssa.

'This lump of muscle, whoever he is, says I hit old Tullia and you all seem to believe him. Am I going to get off with just a night in jail after that? I doubt it. Might as well get the glory for all the others. You've no idea how hard it all was, and you think I'm stupid. Took two of us to work it out. And Blod, the snivelling cow, she was next if she didn't keep quiet. She saw me the night I stole old Vulpo's fork.'

There was a loud wail from the shrubbery. Briccio rolled his eyes.

'Women! I wouldn't have done that to old Tullia if I hadn't known what my orders were. She was about to ruin everything. It all comes down to people not keeping their thoughts to themselves, or being in the wrong place seeing the wrong things. If it had all gone to plan, we'd have made a fortune. I might as well get half the glory, since I did most of the hard work.'

'But why?' cried Poppaea. Lollia held her.

'Cos I was promised my cut. I'd have been free and rich. I just had to follow orders same as I always did. Only these orders were fun.' He laughed again and licked his bloodied lips.

'Orders? What orders?' said Anguis. He moved his hand from Lucretia's shoulder and stared at her. The wig, caught in his ornate ring, slipped off, leaving her straight thin greying braids.

'You can't think that I..?.' she said. 'My own daughter, sister...'

'The more people, the less sharesies though, isn't it?' snarled Briccio. 'Once those baths are up and running with that goddess you made up, you'll be raking it in. Why share it with someone who'll drink it all away, or squander it on gladiators, when it could be all yours?'

'Lucretia, I can't -' Anguis took a stride away, appalled.

'Oh but it wasn't her. Was it, missus?' Briccio breathed into Lucretia's face, his filthy body inches from hers. 'She think she knows everything, but she hadn't got the brains to see that someone had been playing her all along. And I'd had enough of orders from her anyway. I wouldn't have murdered a fly for the old -'

'Get away from me, you filthy pig!' cried Lucretia. 'Who were you murdering for? Answer me!'

'And what'll I get if I tell you?'

The guard slapped Briccio's head. 'I might sharpen the spikes and find your heart faster,' he growled.

Briccio spat. 'And what will you do to the gentry, eh? The one whose idea it all was. I wouldn't have wasted my energy on this if he hadn't asked me to. Putting ideas in people's heads, that's what he's good at. Keeping in the shadows, playing the fool and all the while, making promises. Are you going to let him get finished off nice and quick after he played you for a fool, *Lady* Lucretia? After he planned the slaughter of your own daughter and the fate of your son. Do you

236

think you'd have been safe after he'd got what he wanted, when you have a ripe young niece in the offing? He didn't want any of your brood in his nest. He was about to get me to poison your own grandchild in the womb.'

Everyone turned to Poppaea, and then back to Lucretia. She had balled her fists, red-faced under the white paint, her wig more askew than ever, but furious. Everyone recoiled from the iron in her glare. The warriors in her ancestry sparked out of her eyes and in her cold words, spoken slow and deep.

'Who gave you the orders? I will personally see to it that he pays in full. I will not do it because you asked, you pitiful worm, but to avenge my daughter as I said I would.'

'Him!' Briccio glared over Lucretia's head. 'He's the one who planted the whole idea in your head in the first place. The "shy" bridegroom. Him.'

Urbanicus pulled himself free of Olivarius, only to find himself in the arms of the guard.

'It's lies, all lies!' shouted Urbanicus. 'I am a Roman citizen! You can't believe the word of a slave over mine!'

'All change now then is it, you traitor?' snarled Briccio. 'Should've guessed. And there's me holed up in that damp, miserable forest for weeks keeping an eye on things. I sorted out those two henchmen from Londinium for you and I didn't even pocket that bauble. I could have taken it and disappeared, but you said it would work out, you just wanted two more jobs. And this is the thanks I get. Well, it won't be just thugs sold down the river, will it? Once I've turned evidence on you, *Master*, it'll be the same result for both of us in the end. I hope you get the same execution as a slave, but even if your citizenship gets a quicker, cleaner execution, I'll be waiting for you in Hades.' He spat at Urbanicus.

'Take them away,' said Tryssa to the guard.

'And what about him?' The guard nodded at at the gladiator. 'That's Hastorix the runaway, that is.'

'Nonsense,' said Tryssa. 'You're completely mistaken. Hastorix looks entirely different. This hero is a free man.'

The guard shrugged and with the help of Olivarius and Budic, chained Briccio to Urbanicus and bundled them into his cart.

Poppaea stared up at the prisoners. 'What do you mean, "Marcellus met a fate worse than death"?' she said.

Briccio sniggered but did not reply.

'I am a citizen!' cried Urbanicus. 'Anguis Superbus! Lucretia, darling! Save me!'

'Citizen or not,' said the guard. 'I've got a nice bed waiting in the jail. But don't worry. Citizens get less rats.'

He clambered aboard the cart and started to steer it away.

'What did he mean, "a fate worse than death"?' Poppaea begged Urbanicus.

A cry made them all turn. The villa's wagon was rattling up the lane, the horse gasping. Fabio and Ondi clung to the reins and a third man between them, thin and pale, half-rose then fell back. The horse staggered to a stop and sagged in the harness. Everyone stared.

'And on top of everything,' said Lucretia, her voice cracking, 'I can't even send my nephew on a simple errand to get us some more staff. Is that scarecrow the best slave you could find?'

'It's not a slave,' gasped Poppaea, rushing over. 'It's your son! It's Marcellus!'

Marcellus stumbled over Fabio's legs and fell off the wagon at Poppaea's feet.

She dropped into the dust and held him, brushing the hair from his eyes and stroking the beard on his thin cheekbones, her tears mingling with his.

'I knew you'd come back,' she said.

'I forgot who I was,' sobbed Marcellus. 'They hit me so hard that when I woke up, I couldn't remember anything. They said they'd keep me in the market till they could sell me to make a bit of sport with the wild beasts in the arena. And then this morning, someone recited a poem about a quiet beautiful girl and I remembered. I remembered you. They wouldn't believe it when I said who I was, but I had to get back to you. I know you wanted to tell me something and I didn't stop to listen. I've never been sure if you loved me, but I love you so much. Oh my darling, oh my darling, I'm here!'

Chapter Twenty-Nine - A New Month
July 1st (Kalendas Julias)

'So,' said Lucretia, wincing as Blod pulled on her hair, 'of course I knew all it was Briccio all along, but how did you know?'

'I was there when Ritonix died,' said Tryssa. 'He was very troubled. He never regained consciousness, but he mumbled. "The poor lad," he repeated, "his poor father. You must explain.". It seemed an odd thing to say about Briccio. Briccio was hardly a lad and no-one would know who his father was, least of all Briccio. Then I thought he must be thinking that Dondras's son had the same fate as Briccio when they ran off together through the forest, and it was only a matter of time before his body was found. It was only after Lucco mentioned something about viewpoints that I realised he knew what Briccio's feet looked like, and since that was the only recognisable bit of the body found in the woods, he knew the body wasn't Briccio's. Somehow Ritonix must have realised too and tried to tell Marcellus. Marcellus, of course, was in a fever, and unsure what was real and what he'd dreamed. When he worked it out, he headed into town to tell Dondras, but Urbanicus had been waiting for a chance to find out what he'd been working on and got hold of his scribblings. I think he was probably disguised as a slave, and when he saw what Marcellus had written, made sure he never got to town. The rest, of course, is obvious.'

'Of course,' said Lucretia, and waited.

Tryssa smirked. 'Blod was unhappy in an entirely different way the night Prisca died. She had gone from bereaved to terrified.'

'Of course. Anyone could see that.'

'Indeed, and Pomponius's last words made it clear that he had been surprised to see his assailant. I did wonder at that point if it was Urbanicus, but then the workmen had been muttering about a face in the woods for ages and I knew Urbanicus didn't know his way round a forest.'

'It could have been Budic. He's been hanging around trying to rediscover his ancient heritage. Not, as far as I'm aware, that any of his ancestors lived in trees. I swear his father is from the coast.'

'It wasn't Budic. That was all talk. He's been clerking away as he should and sneaking off when he thought he'd see Camilla in the orchard. Neither of them would last five minutes growing turnips, let alone foraging in the forest. No, the face in the woods was not Budic.'

'I told the workmen it was Diffis.'

'And of course Camilla thought Olivarius was after her money or her honour, when what he was actually trying to do was save her from being murdered. He was convinced you were going to be murdered one by one, which was roughly true. He was almost right except that the one person who was safe was Camilla.'

'Why? She's a very annoying and disobedient girl.'

'Because one by one your heirs would be reduced until by the time you were safely married to Urbanicus, Camilla would be the only one left. And no-one would be surprised if the new bride died, considering she was in her middle fifties. Then Urbanicus could marry Camilla, and all the wealth would be his.'

'Diffis would never allow that to happen to her descendant. That is, me.'

'Lucretia, Rhee, don't you think it's time to give up?'

'Whatever do you mean?'

241

'There was never a goddess, there was just a chance to make money. You went for a walk and saw the stream and...'

'I remembered Rhys.'

'Ah.'

'I remembered being at that spot at the edge of the woods waiting for him to come out. I tried to imagine the way he felt, the way Tullia feels about trees and all that.'

'That sounds very unlike you, Rhee.'

'It was just a moment's thought. Could I feel the same as Tullia? No. I felt nothing. I could hear...'

'What?'

'A boar probably. And a voice. Rhys's voice.'

'Rhys's voice? He's been dead for nearly forty years.'

'I know. I remembered when he died and Father turned to me to carry things on. I remembered that I was the important one. I saw my house down the slope and Porcius was bumbling about and I wondered what it would be like if people really appreciated me. And I thought I heard a voice.'

'I can't imagine you ever hearing a voice which wasn't your own, but you mentioned all this to Urbanicus.'

'He was very interested. He knew a great deal about the old legends, you know.'

'And a lot more about losing money.'

'I did not know that.'

Tryssa pursed her lips. 'And Anguis had money and connections and was happy to have a cut.'

'Naturally he held me in high esteem, and I could have sworn I heard a voice.'

'No you couldn't. Unless...' Tryssa frowned and touched the bangle on her wrist. 'Unless it was Rhys's ghost, of course.'

'Nonsense,' said Lucretia. 'I refuse to believe that.'

'Well, it's all over now. Tullia is about to go back to Glevum, I gather.'

'Hmm. Yes, it will soon be quiet. Or at least, it will be until Poppaea has that wretched baby.'

'If it is not a boy, don't be harsh,' said Tryssa. 'After all, you inherited. And you're a girl.'

Lucretia brightened. 'I could bring Julia up to be like me!'

'Please don't.'

'I gather Camilla hasn't quite made her mind up between those two fools Olivarius and Budic.'

'Camilla *has* made up her mind. She's staying with me to train as a wise woman.'

'Oh, really.'

'And she is learning to read, so it will be even better.'

'She'd have been better marrying Olivarius. At least he promised her a life outside a village.'

'She may find just as much adventure within one.'

'Hard to imagine there's any more excitement to be had after this summer. I wish people would think of me. Fabio has made me free Lollia and give her a pension. What am I supposed to do without her? Do you think I could get her to stay for a salary? The only good news is that the sneak Gwil has stopped pretending to be Rhys's son. I can't make my mind up whether to sue him or just pay him to leave.'

'It think he wants to stay and get to know Lollia first,' said Tryssa, rising.

'Lollia?'

'Yes. Lollia. Didn't you know? And I thought you knew everything. I think he's her son.'

'How could he be her son? We sold all her children. None of them would be able to find her.'

'I suspect he isn't one of those you sold. I suspect he is the one you thought had died. She must have found a way of giving the baby away to someone who would bring him up as a free man. Perhaps he has been searching for her for years. Perhaps, once he found her, he just thought he'd make your life a little uncomfortable for a while.'

'Well, if he was born to Lollia and Lucco, technically he's a slave and technically he's my property.'

'Well, it's all hypothetical. No-one is going to prove it. I think you'd best let it lie.'

'Why does no-one think of me? It's very unfair. And here I am, a poor, neglected widow. If Porcius hadn't been a glutton, he'd be here to… Well, anyway, I wouldn't be a widow.'

'Porcius was poisoned by Briccio. Urbanicus arranged it so he could marry you.'

'Well I am very…'

'Rich.'

'Mmm.' Lucretia curled her hair around her finger and pondered. After a while she smiled.

'Of course, Anguis still seems to appreciate me. And he could do with a mature and interesting wife rather than some feather-headed adolescent. I think it's time for another dinner. What do you think?'

If you enjoyed this book why not check out
Murder Durnovaria?

Acknowledgements and Historical Note

I wish to pay tribute to my Latin teachers who, if they read this, are likely to disown or haunt me, depending on their current circumstances. I would like to reassure them that this is no reflection on their teaching skills. While I have retained very little Latin, I never lost my interest in Roman culture and its impact on Britain, or an interest in the development of language.

Glossary:

Atrium: a kind of hall-way with an opening in the roof (impluvium) which allowed rain to fall into a pool (compluvium). Probably more practical in Rome than Britain.

Durotriges, Silures, Iceni: names British tribes respectively (broadly speaking living in modern day Southern England, South Wales and Eastern England respectively).

Hypocaust: Roman underfloor heating.

Manumission: the paperwork for freeing a slave.

Place-names:

Aquae Sulis: modern day Bath Spa. The natural springs were attributed to the local goddess Sulis who was adopted by the Romans and called Sulis Minerva after their own goddess Minerva.

Glevum: modern day Gloucester.

Isca: there were several Iscas, but the one referred to is modern day Caerleon.

Nidum: modern day Neath.

The area in which this story is set is broadly speaking north of Cardiff which is where my husband's family is from. As far as I know there was never a town called Pecunia, nor was there a villa owned by someone called Lucretia, nor was there a sacred spring. But then again, you never know what will turn up at an archaeological dig one day.

I wish to thank Liz Hedgecock for her very thorough proof-reading and suggesting edits for this book through thick and thin of various shared IT issues and while trying to edit other things at the same time. It made a huge difference.

Thanks also to those who read earlier drafts as beta readers: Val Portelli, Paul Saville, Christine Downes and Gary Bonn.

Many thanks to the passengers on South West trains who had to put up with me muttering to myself and pulling faces while writing on the commute to and from Waterloo once a week.

And huge thanks to my family who have had to put up with me being vaguer than normal while writing and editing.

And to my mother-in-law Patricia, fan of murder mysteries - I hope this meets approval and thanks again for being nothing whatsoever like Lucretia!

Books by Paula Harmon

THE MURDER BRITANNICA SERIES
<u>Murder Britannica</u>

AD 190 Britain. Lucretia won't let her get-rich-quick scheme be undermined by minor things like her husband's death. But a gruesome discovery leads wise-woman Tryssa to ask awkward questions.

<u>Murder Durnovaria</u>

It's AD 191. Lucretia last saw Durnovaria as a teenager. Now she's back to claim an inheritance. Who could imagine an old ring from the forum means Tryssa must help local magistrate Amicus discover who would rather kill than reveal long-buried truths.

THE MARGARET DEMERAY SERIES
<u>The Wrong Sort To Die</u>

London 1910. Dr Margaret Demeray is approached by a stranger to help find out what's killed two impoverished men. How can a memory she'd buried possibly be linked to the deaths? And how come the closer she gets to Fox the more danger she faces herself?

THE CASTER AND FLEET SERIES
(six book series with Liz Hedgecock)

When Katherine Demeray opens a letter addressed to her missing father in 1890, little does she imagine that she will find herself in partnership with socialite Connie Swift, racing against time to solve mysteries and right wrongs.

<u>The Case of the Black Tulips</u>
<u>The Case of the Runaway Client</u>
<u>The Case of the Deceased Clerk</u>
<u>The Case of the Masquerade Mob</u>
<u>The Case of the Fateful Legacy</u>
<u>The Case of the Crystal Kisses</u>

OTHER BOOKS BY PAULA HARMON
<u>The Cluttering Discombobulator</u>
Can everything be fixed with duct tape? Dad thinks so. The story of one man's battle against common sense and the family caught up in the chaos around him.

<u>Kindling</u>
Secrets and mysteries, strangers and friends. Stories as varied and changing as British skies.

<u>The Advent Calendar</u>
Christmas without the hype - stories for midwinter.

<u>The Quest</u>
In a parallel universe, Dorissa and Menilly, descendants of the distrusted dragon people, are desperate to find their runaway brother.

<u>The Seaside Dragon</u>
For 7-11 year olds. When Laura and Jane go on holiday to a remote cottage, the last thing they expect is strange creatures with an ancient grudge.

<u>Weird and Peculiar Tales</u> (with Val Portelli)
Short stories from this world and beyond**.**

About Paula Harmon

Paula Harmon was born in North London to parents of English, Scottish and Irish descent. Perhaps feeling the need to add a Welsh connection, her father relocated the family every two years from country town to country town moving slowly westwards until they settled in South Wales when Paula was eight. She later graduated from Chichester University before making her home in Gloucestershire and then Dorset where she has lived since 2005.

She is a civil servant, married with two adult children. Paula has several writing projects underway and wonders where the housework fairies are, because the house is a mess and she can't think why.

https://paulaharmondownes.wordpress.com
https://www.facebook.com/pg/paulaharmonwrites
https://twitter.com/Paula_S_Harmon
viewauthor.at/PHAuthorpage

Made in the USA
Monee, IL
13 December 2021